Praise for
The Complete Short Stories of Marcel Proust

"Proust buffs prick up your ears! This book contains a new translation of his 1896 collection *Pleasures and Days* as well as six recently discovered stories. Joachim Neugroschel, who compiled and translated the stories, has won the PEN Translation Award three times." —*Publishers Weekly*

"Proust is developing into one of the most influential writers of the twentieth century. . . . Both this new collection and *Remembrance of Things Past* share the glitzy backdrop of Parisian high society and tiptoe through the same topics: addressing vanity, investigating the validity of sexual mores, and pondering the impact of sickness on life." —*Booklist*

"Neugroschel's sensitive translation, at once mournful and lyric, vivifies Proust's abstractions, sharpens his fleeting memories, and elegantly transforms French reality into English. In his hands, these stories evoke the sources of Proust's creativity, producing precious insights as the past is recaptured in the present." —**Jeffrey Meyers**, biographer of Fitzgerald, Poe, Conrad, Orwell, and Gary Cooper, and editor of *The Sir Arthur Conan Doyle Reader: From Sherlock Holmes to Spiritualism*

"The resemblance between Proust's earliest and latest works goes beyond their shared worldview. It seems clear that the young Marcel was training to become the mature Proust from the time of his earliest published pieces. . . . At times Proust can be mordant and witty. He reveals a gift for mimicry and a sharp eye for social folly. . . . We should read this book because Proust wrote it, but we should read Proust because he wrote *Remembrance of Things Past*." —**James Gardner**, art critic, *National Review*

Praise for
The Complete Short Stories of Marcel Proust

"The translation is expert and elegant." —**Ned Rorem**, Pulitzer Prize–winning composer and author of *The Paris Diary & The New York Diary*

"A welcome addition to Proust's writings in English, this collection offers a charming snapshot of a genius whose talent is beginning to bloom. These early stories, including the previously untranslated 'Before the Night' and 'The Indifferent Man' provide fascinating sketches of two key Proustian themes: same-sex love and obsessive infatuation." —**William C. Carter**, author of *Marcel Proust*

"Who is now likely to read this new and accomplished translation? The answer must surely be those who have read *Remembrance of Things Past* in part if not in whole (for let us be realists here). In these stories, the reader has access to some of Proust's most enduring and memorable themes in embryo. Among these are the vital and deeply resonant episode of the mother's bedtime kiss with its repercussions; the equation of love as suffering; the theme of obsessive self-destructive love for a person one hardly knows—or even likes; the yielding to sensual pleasure and lust. . . . In these stories, Proust, the incomparable observer with his gift for psychological penetration, is already at work. Already the worm is in the bud of joy: the awareness of the ravages of time and the presence of death." —*New Criterion*

"The flashes of true brilliance make this book a remarkable performance in its own right. This new translation, with Roger Shattuck's succinct and lucid introduction, provides the perfect entrance into Proust's endlessly ornate world." —**Mark Polizzotti**, author of *Revolution of the Mind: The Life of André Breton*

THE COMPLETE SHORT STORIES OF MARCEL PROUST

■ Compiled and Translated
by Joachim Neugroschel

Foreword by Roger Shattuck

 Cooper Square Press

Cooper Square Press paperback edition 2003.

This Cooper Square Press paperback edition of *The Complete Short Stories of Marcel Proust* is an unabridged republication of the edition first published in New York in 2001. It is reprinted by arrangement with the translator.

Published by Cooper Square Press
A Member of the Rowman & Littlefield Publishing Group, Inc.
200 Park Avenue South, Suite 1109
New York, New York 10003-1503
www.coopersquarepress.com

Distributed by National Book Network

The Library of Congress cataloged the hardcover edition of this book as follows:

Proust, Marcel, 1871–1922.
　　[Short stories. English]
　　The complete short stories of Marcel Proust / compiled and translated by
　Joachim Neugroschel ; foreword by Roger Shattuck.
　　　p. cm.
　　　1. Proust, Marcel, 1871–1922—Translations into English. I. Neugroschel,
　Joachim. II. Title.

　　PQ2631.R63 A265　2001
　　843'.912—dc21　　　　　　　　　　　　　　　　　　　　00-065739

　ISBN 0-8154-1136-7 (cloth : alk. paper) — 0-8154-1264-9 (pbk. : alk. paper)

♾™ The paper used in this publication meets the minimum requirements of American National Standard for Information Sciences—Permanence of Paper for Printed Library Materials, ANSI/NISO Z39.48-1992.

Manufactured in the United States of America.

CONTENTS

EARLY STORIES

Foreword

Proust's Own Sound

Homer still suits us just fine. We turn to him for larger-than-life tales of bravery in battle and for the adventures of a resourceful hero finding his way home again after years of war. Odysseus' exploits will stay with us because Homer gave them the sturdy shape of epic. The *Odyssey* has come to look like part of the landscape we live in.

We tend to neglect Homer's principal rival, Hesiod, another great collector of stories. In *Works and Days,* Hesiod wrote both poetically and practically about the seasonal round of work on a farm. In the *Theogony,* he produced the first gathering of divine myths constituting Greek religious beliefs. Compared with Homer, Hesiod aimed either too low or too high to capture the stuff of epic poetry for the ages. Therefore, we are a bit surprised that in a moment of need Marcel Proust turned not to Homer but to Hesiod for help. Proust was just starting out.

Barely twenty and taking courses in law and philosophy at the Sorbonne, Proust began publishing stories and articles in literary reviews. Admired for his wit and his talents as a mime, he was invited to exclusive literary salons. He managed to find a "job" as a librarian—with no salary, few duties, and a year's leave of absence to start off. Still, the best way to establish himself as an author would be to publish a book. He succeeded in doing so, but only after four years of planning and shamelessly using his connections. His salon hostess, Madeleine Lemaire, who was also a flower painter, agreed to illustrate the book. He obtained a preface from a celebrated novelist he had met some years earlier in another literary salon, Anatole France. A gifted young friend and musician, Reynaldo Hahn, provided a musical setting for several poems.

Just a few months before publication, Proust decided he must find a new title for his book. This is the juncture where Hesiod enters the story. Proust had read him in Lamartine's flowing translation. The Greek author's title, *Works and Days,* could suitably be borrowed for a miscellaneous collection dealing with modern experiences. But Proust did not want to emphasize the motif of working for a living to which Hesiod attached great importance. Proust's sly revision, *Pleasures and Days,* gives a reverse, almost a perverse, twist to the classic title. It is true that a yearning for pleasure runs like a colored thread through most of the stories and pieces. Even so, Hesiod's title modified to suggest a garden of delights does not entirely suit the contents. The bulk of writing Proust put into this volume concerns frustration, disappointment, and death. At this early age, Proust did not yet know or could not acknowledge that his true theme was not pleasure but suffering.

Pleasures and Days contains five substantial stories interspersed with fragments, parodies, portraits in the style of the seventeenth-century moralist La Bruyère, nature descriptions, and philosophical meditations. Calmann-Lévy, a leading publishing house of the era, brought it out in a deluxe edition at a high price. Framed by a trophy preface, illustrated by a society painter, and containing music by a young prodigy, Proust's writing was overwhelmed as much as it was enthroned. As William Carter writes in his fine biography, "Friends and reviewers . . . wondered whether *Pleasures and Days* was a book or a social event."

The book was launched by the publication, on the same day and on the front page of two Paris dailies, of Anatole France's preface. It was a splendid publicity coup. With just a hint of detachment, even irony, France referred to Proust's charm and grace and to the sadness of the book's hothouse atmosphere. "The book is young with the youth of the author. Yet it is old with the oldness of the world." The half-dozen reviews ran from outright mocking of "these elegant nothings" to measured judgment of a promising talent to full endorsement of the book's wisdom and originality. Priced out of the range of most readers, the book sold hardly any copies. At the time, Proust himself spoke disparagingly about the whole undertaking. Twenty years later he compared this early writing favorably with his later style. It would be seventeen years before he published another book of his own.

■

The five major stories that provide the armature of *Pleasures and Days* all deal with some form of moral weakness that brings corruption: vainglory, snobbery, emotional caprice, voluptuousness, and jealousy. And all end in death or some equivalent—boredom and the yoke of habit. The most shocking story, "Confessions of a Young Girl," entails a double death. A young woman dying by a half-botched suicide relates how her mother's seeing her with a lover *in flagrante delicto* causes the apoplexy that kills her mother. The theme of matricide remained with Proust to the end of his life. Several times he accuses himself of being guilty of the crime, at least indirectly.

The last and longest story, "The End of Jealousy," comes close to shifting the meaning of death from curse to salvation. The lover whose passion metastasizes into an all-devouring jealousy finds some consolation when an accident first maims him and then takes his life. But there is an irresolute, sentimental gesturing in the closing pages that will disappear when Proust fleshes out this story into *Swann in Love,* the opening volume of *In Search of Lost Time.*

To separate and lighten these gloomy stories, Proust intersperses them with lively literary exercises that display his versatility. "Fragments of Commedia dell'Arte" applies Italian conventions to the chic poses of Parisian society. "Regrets, Reveries the Color of Time," a collection of short fragments, reveals his uncertainty about which way to turn in his writing. Monet began as a caricaturist on the beach at Honfleur. Proust began by doing satirical portraits, Baudelairean prose poems, nature descriptions, sentimental pieces about memory, Poe-like allegories, and psychophilosophical meditations. He flirted with every genre.

■

> Ambition is more intoxicating than fame; desire makes all things blossom, possession wilts them; it is better to dream your life than to live it, even if living it means dreaming it, though both less mysteriously and less vividly in a murky and sluggish dream, like the straggling dream in the feeble awareness of ruminant creatures. (115)

This reflection is followed by an anecdote about a precocious ten-year-old boy in love with an older girl. He cannot live without her. At the same time her physical presence disappoints and frustrates him. He jumps out a window. Thirty pages later Proust comes back to the same dilemma, now furnished with a potential cure or prosthesis:

> No sooner does an approaching hour become the present for us than it sheds all its charms, only to regain them, it is true, on the roads of memory, when we have left that hour behind us, and so long as our soul is vast enough to disclose deep *perspectives.* (142)

The fateful and perverse disappointment of life, which I have called "Proust's complaint," here finds a form of redemption in the operations of memory. But we obtain barely a glimpse of these "deep perspectives." It will take Proust twenty years to explore them and to write his long novelistic report about them. Meanwhile, in the same meditation called "Critique of Hope in the Light of Love," Proust leaves us with an incurable case of metaphysical hunger:

> I unpin your flowers, I lift your hair, I tear off your jewels, I reach your flesh, my kisses sweep over your body and beat it like the tide rising across the sand; but you yourself elude me, and with you happiness. (144)

One consolation remains to help us through our despair: nature. The last three parts in this section describe Proust's response to the Normandy coastline:

> The sea has the magic of things that never fall silent at night, that permit our anxious lives to sleep, promising us that everything will not be obliterated, comforting us like the glow of a night light that makes little children feel less alone. (147)

A reader familiar with Proust's later work can play a revealing recognition game in the pages of *Pleasures and Days*. For, naturally, Proust is already planting and transplanting motifs that will return in different forms. Not only snobbery and jealousy and Proust's complaint about life as a perpetual let-down after great expectations make their appearance. These early pages also give important treatment to weakness of will as the great scourge, to homosexuality ("Violante" and "Before the Night"), and to solitude as superior to the illusions of love and friendship ("The Stranger").

■

Why publish, why read a great author's juvenilia? Is there any reason to spend our time on early work when the later work dramatically surpasses it in quality and has enough bulk to absorb our attentions? I shall use a comparison in order to answer the question.

James Joyce's *Ulysses* appeared in Paris in 1922 and in New York in 1933 after years of excerpts published in literary reviews, fanfares announcing the novel's importance, and a notorious obscenity trial in the United States decided by a landmark First Amendment verdict. *Ulysses* had as effective advance publicity as Goethe's *Faust* in its successive versions. Critics have hailed Joyce's book as the greatest novel of the twentieth century.

Why then do we often turn back to *Dubliners,* stories finished when Joyce was twenty-two? In this still debated instance, I believe we value *Dubliners* because it allows us to discover how directly and delicately Joyce could tell a story before he yielded to the temptations of word play, stylistic innovation, the Homeric template, and constant allusiveness. Many profoundly literary readers admire *Dubliners* more than *Ulysses* and admit they have never finished the latter. But for the purposes of literary history and college curricula, *Ulysses* remains the great literary monument. *Dubliners,* the modest cousin who lives nearby, gives us enough simple evidence of genius to accept the official monument at face value. Nevertheless, some of us believe the most effective of Joyce's writing lies in *Dubliners* and *Portrait of the Artist as a Young Man.*

Pleasures and Days presents a different case but not the opposite. Proust's first tryouts and exercises as a writer do not display his full powers. He has not yet matured enough to detach himself from the spell of aristocracy and of social institutions such as the salon and the elegant dinner party. He has not assimilated his gifts as a comic genius (though the pastiche of Flaubert's *Bouvard and Pécuchet* makes a foray in that direction). He trails behind him the flowing garments of decadent aestheticism that belonged to the fin de siècle. And he has not yet begun to assemble the patient, slow-motion, marathon sense of structure that will make him the greatest long-distance novelist of our era and perhaps of all time. *Pleasures and Days* will never rival *In Search of Lost Time.* It provides the benchmark from which we can measure the accomplishment of that all-encompassing novel. These baby pictures are both endearing and revealing. They point up the steady evolution of a writer rather than, as in the case of Joyce, deflection from immense promise.

Pleasures and Days also brings its own reward that does not arise from comparison with more mature writings. Behind the artificialities of personal posing and social arrangements that propel them, the stories reveal a growing counterforce. The fourteen-year-old boy who observes his uncle's early and anxious death in the opening story has come to rely on frequent rides on his new horse. This physical exertion "aroused in him . . . a sensation accompanying youth as a dim inkling of the depth of its resources and the power of its joyfulness" (17). In the closing story, "The End of Jealousy," it is as if that boy has survived with his inklings into maturity. For here, Proust describes the male protagonist's obsessive jealousy in equally physical terms. "While dressing for dinner, [Honoré] automatically kept his mind focused on the moment when he would see her again, the way an acrobat already touches the still faraway trapeze toward which he is flying" (151). Before the accident that finally takes his life and releases him from jealousy, Honoré has been out for an early morning walk among the galloping horses in the street. In the cool, sweet air he recognizes "the same profound joy that embellished life that morning, the life of the sun, of the shade, of the sky, of the stones, of the east wind, and of the trees" (161). I have elsewhere given the medical term *cœnesthesia* to these moments of heightened awareness in Proust, as in any writer who remains aware of concrete sensuous experiences. The term refers to the direct physical sensation of being alive as oneself in the world, a sensation that arises equally from the dynamic functioning of our inner systems and organs and from our response to the variegated circumstances that surround us. The hovering despair of these early stories is cut through at intervals by an unexpected gush of vitality from a spoiled, asthmatic, highly cultivated young author. Yes, he unerringly chose Mallarmé's famous decadent line as one of his epigraphs: "The flesh is sad, alas! And I've read all the books." But for the following chapter he found in Madame Sévigné's letters the appropriate retort to Mallarmé's aestheticism: "His youth is roaring inside him, he does not hear."

When he assembled *Pleasures and Days* in his early twenties, Proust did not hear as much of himself and of the world as he would a decade later. But in the supple translations of Joachim Neugroschel, we can discern the extent to which the youthful Proust had already found his own sound and his own direction.

ROGER SHATTUCK
Lincoln, Vermont
September 2000

Roger Shattuck's books include *Forbidden Knowledge: From Prometheus to Pornography; The Banquet Years: The Origins of the Avant Garde in France; Candor and Perversion: Literature, Education, and the Arts; The Forbidden Experiment: The Story of the Wild Boy of Aveyron*; and the acclaimed *Proust's Way: A Field Guide to* In Search of Lost Time. A world-renowned Proust scholar, his *Marcel Proust*, commissioned by Frank Kermode for the Modern Masters series, won the National Book Award in 1974. He resides in Vermont and is professor emeritus of comparative literature at Boston University.

Translator's Preface

PROUST AND THE MYTHOLOGY OF PARIS

For Balzac and Zola, the Paris of the nineteenth century was a city of light and dark, and the panoramic cross-sections of their fiction exposed and interwove all facets, classes, and issues of the French capital—indeed of France itself. But for Marcel Proust, fin-de-siècle Paris is a metropolis of rapture and privilege, hierarchy and opulence, eroticism and frustration—all held together by a devout and yet sometimes derided faith in wealth, art, and leisure, in elegance and sensuality.

Other French novelists created a Parisian mythology that was elastic and all-encompassing in its vast array of intertwining experiences and characters. But for Proust, Paris is a world of *Pleasures and Days*, whereby this title of his first book, in parodying Hesiod's title *Works and Days*, blatantly spotlights the chief concerns of Parisian high society. Indeed, Proust intensifies the mythological character of the capital by placing some tales in exotic Never-Never-Lands that serve as flimsy fairy-tale disguises for Paris.

Like James Joyce's *Dubliners*, the various stories that Proust wrote in the 1890s are psychological epiphanies fusing into a mosaic in which the privileged metropolis itself plays the lead role, while each human character presents yet another emotional angle.

A number of Proust's short texts may have rural settings—as do many of the paintings he loves. But whether as a direct or as an artistic experience, these locales form a rustic mythology that never exists in an absolute state. Rather, the forests, the beaches, the ocean, in offering a temporary escape from, a contrast with, the city, throw the latter into relief. The country reminds us of the city, but not vice versa: enhancing the mythology of Paris, the resulting dialectic is one-sided.

In his endless Ciceronian periods and in sprawling paragraphs that stress prosiness and thereby challenge the lyrical rhythms and the sumptuous vocabulary, Proust coalesces a variety of forms: tales, sketches, narrative prose poems, biographical verses. His goal is to produce a subjective collage that binds all those elements together while fostering their individuality.

In providing a new and contemporary translation that tries to render the vital strength, delicacy, and irony of Proust's bewitching psychology and language, I have added a half dozen pieces that were originally published in journals but not included in *Pleasures and Days*. Most of what ultimately imbues the seven huge volumes of *Remembrance of Things Past* (often translated today as *In Search of Lost Time*) is already explored and adumbrated in Proust's first book.

The author probes the precarious nuances of physical and spiritual love, the frail mysteries of time and memory. We find his deft, pungent, and even humorous characterizations, his vivid, sometimes tongue-in-cheek descriptions of Parisian high society, the visual and aural details, the tastes and fragrances, the decadence, the sexual confusion, the amorous adventures and follies, the indifference to politics and to life outside the aristocratic cosmos. In addition to displaying the writer's precise, evocative, and sensual diction, these stories reveal his very fine ear for dialogue, while his monologues hint at the technique of stream of consciousness invented by Édouard Desjardins in the 1880s and then developed mainly by Arthur Schnitzler, James Joyce, and Virginia Woolf.

A social climber who poked fun at other social climbers, yet hoped that his writings would make him more acceptable to high society, Marcel Proust conjured up his ideal of an aristocratic Paris that was all light—despite the agonies of unrequited love, the lurking of old age and death. Proust turned these universal elements into experiences endured purely by the city's bourgeoisie and aristocracy. His mythology, so exclusive in ignoring the outside world, was self-contained. In the minds of his characters and in the consciousness of the people they were based on, this mythology was indisputable and infinite. Nothing else existed. It was their sole reality.

For Proust, however, the reality of art vied with the art of reality. Along with the mythology of Paris, it is art, style, especially language art and style, that hold all these pieces together: the author's personal sensibility fuses with the disposition of French high society and its specific, mythical Paris.

JOACHIM NEUGROSCHEL
Belle Harbor, New York
October 2000

PLEASURES AND DAYS

PREFACE

Why has he asked me to present his book to curious minds? And why did I promise to take on this very agreeable but quite unnecessary task? His book is like a young countenance imbued with rare charm and delicate grace. It recommends itself on its own, speaks for itself, and presents itself, willingly or not.

It is young, I daresay. It is young with the youth of the author. Yet it is old with the oldness of the world. It is the springtime of leaves on ancient boughs in the forest of centuries. One might think that the new sprouts are saddened by the profound past of the woods and that they are mourning so many dead springtimes.

Grave Hesiod spoke to the goatherds of Helicon about *Works and Days*. It is a more melancholy effort to tell our sophisticates, male and female, about *Pleasures and Days* if, as that British statesman says, life would be tolerable but for its amusements. Thus our young friend's book contains weary smiles and jaded attitudes that are not without beauty and nobility.

We will find its very sadness amusing and quite varied, guided and sustained as it is by a marvelous sense of observation, by a limber, piercing, and truly subtle intelligence. This almanac of *Pleasures and Days* indicates nature's hours through harmonious depictions of sky, sea, woods, and it indicates human hours through faithful portraits and genre paintings that are marvelously rendered.

3

Marcel Proust enjoys describing both the desolate splendor of the setting sun and the vanities that agitate a snobbish soul. He excels in portraying the elegant sorrows, the artificial sufferings that are at least as cruel as the ones that nature inflicts on us with motherly extravagance. I admit that these fictitious sufferings, these sorrows discovered by human genius, these artistic sorrows strike me as endlessly interesting and precious, and I am grateful to Marcel Proust for studying and describing a few chosen examples.

He draws us into a hothouse atmosphere, keeping us among intricate orchids that do not nourish their strange and morbid beauty in earth. All at once a luminous arrow whizzes through the heavy and delicious air, a lightning bolt that, like the German doctor's ray, passes through solid bodies. In a flash the poet has penetrated secret thoughts and unavowed desires.

That is his manner and his art. He reveals a self-assurance that surprises us in so young an archer. He is not the least bit innocent. But he is so sincere and so truthful as to become naive and therefore appealing. There is something of a depraved Bernardin de Saint-Pierre and an ingenuous Petronius about him.

This is a fortunate book! It will go into the city, go all decorated by, all fragrant with, the flowers that Madeleine Lemaire has strewn through its pages with her divine hand, which scatters roses glistening with their dew.

ANATOLE FRANCE
Paris
April 21, 1896

PROUST'S DEDICATION

To My Friend Willy Heath
Died in Paris on October 3, 1893

From the bosom of God wherein you rest ... reveal to me those truths that
conquer death, preventing us from fearing it and almost making us love it.

The ancient Greeks brought cakes, milk, and wine to their dead.
Seduced by a more refined if not more sagacious illusion, we
offer them flowers and books. I give you this book because, for
one thing, it is a picture book. Despite the "legends," it will be, if
not read, then at least viewed by all the admirers of the great
artist who has, in all her simplicity, brought me this magnificent
present. One could say that, to quote Alexandre Dumas, the
younger, "it is she who has created the most roses after God."
Monsieur Robert de Montesquiou, in still unpublished verses, has
also sung her praises with that ingenious gravity, that sententious
and subtle eloquence, that rigorous order that sometimes recalls
the seventeenth century. In speaking about flowers he told her:

> To pose for your brushes impels them to blossom.

> You are their Vigée and you are their Flora,
> Who makes them immortal while the other one kills.

Her admirers are an elite, yet they form a throng. I wanted
them to see your name on the very first page, the name of the

person whom they had no time to get to know and whom they would have admired. I myself, dear friend, I knew you very briefly. It was in the Bois de Boulogne that I found you on numerous mornings when you had noticed me and awaited me under the trees, standing, but relaxed, like one of Van Dyck's aristocrats, whose pensive elegance you shared. Indeed, their elegance, like yours, resides less in their clothes than in their bodies, and their bodies themselves appear to have received it and to keep receiving it from their souls: it is a moral elegance. Everything, incidentally, contributed to emphasizing that melancholy resemblance down to the leafy background in whose shade Van Dyck often captured the strolling of a king. Like so many of his sitters, you had to die an early death, and in your eyes as in theirs, one could see the gloom of forebodings alternating with the soft light of resignation. But if Van Dyck's art could properly be credited with the grace of your pride, the mysterious intensity of your spiritual life actually derived from Da Vinci. Frequently, with your finger raised, your impenetrable eyes smiling at the enigma that you concealed, you looked like Leonardo's Saint John the Baptist. We developed a dream, almost a plan, to live together more and more, in a circle of select and magnanimous women and men, far enough from vice, stupidity, and malice to feel safe from their vulgar shafts.

Your life, such as you wished it, was to be one of those works that require a sublime inspiration. We could derive inspiration from love as we could from faith and genius. But it was death that would give it to you. In death and even in its approach there are hidden forces and secret aids, a "grace" that does not exist in life. Akin to lovers when falling in love, akin to poets when singing, ill people feel closer to their souls. Life is a hard thing that presses us too tightly, forever hurting our souls. Upon feeling those restraints loosen for a moment, one can experience clear-sighted pleasures. When I was a little boy, no biblical figure struck me as suffering a more wretched fate than Noah, because of the Deluge that imprisoned him in the ark for forty days. Later on I was often sick and I, too, had to spend long days in the "ark." I now understood that Noah could not have seen the world so clearly as from the ark, even though the ark was shut and the earth was shrouded in night. When my convalescence began, my mother, who had not left my side, remaining with me every night, "opened the door of the ark" and left. Yet like the dove, "she returned that evening." Then I was fully recovered, and like the dove, "she did not return." I had to resume living, to turn away from myself, to hear words harsher than my mother's; furthermore, her words, always gentle until this point, were no longer the same; they were stamped with the severity of life, the severity of the duties that she had to teach me.

Gentle dove of the Deluge, how could I but think that the Patriarch, in seeing you flutter away, felt some sadness mingling with the joy at the rebirth of the world. Gentleness of the abeyance of life, gentleness of the real "Truce of God," which suspends labors, evil desires, "Grace" of the illness that brings us closer to the realities beyond death—and its charms, too, charms of "those vain ornaments and those veils that crush," charms of the hair that an obtrusive hand "took care to arrange"; a mother's and a friend's sweet signs of fidelity, which have so often looked like the very face of our sadness or like the protective gesture begged for by our weakness, signs that will halt at the threshold of convalescence—I have often suffered at feeling you so far away from me, all of you, the exiled descendants of the dove in the ark. And who among us has not had moments, dear Willy, when he has wanted to be where you are. We accept so many commitments in regard to life that a time comes when, despairing of ever managing to fulfill them all, we face the graves, we call upon death, "death, which brings help to destinies that have trouble coming true." But while death may exempt us from commitments we have made in regard to life, it cannot exempt us from our commitments to ourselves, especially the most important one: namely, the commitment to live in order to be worthy and deserving.

More earnest than the rest of us, you were also the most childlike, not only because of your purity of heart, but also because of your unaffected and delightful merriment. Charles de Grancy had a gift for which I envy him: by recalling school days he could abruptly arouse that laughter, which was never dormant for long and which we will never hear again.

While a few of these pages were written when I was twenty-three, many others ("Violante," nearly all the "Fragments of Commedia dell'Arte," etc.) go back to my twentieth year. They are all nothing but the vain foam of an agitated life that is now calming down. May my life someday be so limpid that the Muses will deign to mirror themselves in it and that we can see the reflections of their smiles and their dances skimming across its surface.

I give you this book. You are, alas, my only friend whose criticism it need not fear. I am at least confident that no freedom of tone would have shocked you anywhere. I have never depicted immorality except in people with delicate consciences. Too feeble to want good, too noble to fully enjoy evil, they know nothing but suffering; I therefore could speak about them only with a pity too sincere not to purify these little texts. I hope that the true friend and the illustrious and beloved Master—who gave them, respectively, the poetry of his music and the music of his incomparable poetry—and also Monsieur Darlu, the great philosopher, whose inspired words, more certain to endure than any writings, have stirred my mind and so many other minds— I hope they can forgive me for reserving for you this final token of affection and I hope they realize that a living man, no matter how great or dear, can be honored only after a dead man.

July 1894

THE DEATH OF BALDASSARE SILVANDE, VISCOUNT OF SYLVANIA

1

The poets say that Apollo tended the flocks of Admetus; so too each man is a God in disguise who plays the fool.

—RALPH WALDO EMERSON

"Don't cry like that, Master Alexis. Monsieur the Viscount of Sylvania may be giving you a horse."

"A big horse, Beppo, or a pony?"

"Perhaps a big horse, like Monsieur Cardenio's. But please don't cry like that . . . on your thirteenth birthday of all days!"

The hope of getting a horse and the reminder that he was thirteen made Alexis's eyes light up through his tears. Yet he was not consoled since he had to go and visit his uncle, Baldassare Silvande, Viscount of Sylvania. Granted, ever since he had heard that his uncle's disease was incurable, Alexis had been to see him several times. But meanwhile everything had changed. Baldassare was now aware of the full scope of his disease and he knew he had at most three years to live. Without, incidentally, grasping why the anguish had not killed his uncle, the certainty had not driven him insane, Alexis felt incapable of enduring the pain of seeing him. Convinced that his uncle would be talking to him about his imminent end, Alexis did not think he had the strength not only to console him, but also to choke back his own sobs. He had always adored his uncle, the grandest, handsomest, youngest, liveliest, gentlest of his relatives. He loved his gray eyes, his blond moustache, his lap—a deep and sweet place of delight and refuge when Alexis had been younger, a place that had seemed as unassailable as a citadel, as enjoyable as the wooden horses of a merry-go-round, and more inviolable than a temple.

Alexis, who highly disapproved of his father's severe and somber wardrobe and dreamed about a future in which, always on horseback, he would be as elegant as a lady and as splendid as a king, recognized Baldassare as what he, the nephew, considered the most sublime epitome of a man. He knew that his uncle was handsome, that he, Alexis, resembled him; he also knew that his uncle was intelligent, generous, and as powerful as a bishop or a general. Truth to tell, his parents' criticism had taught Alexis that the viscount had his faults. He even remembered his uncle's violent anger the day his cousin Jean Galeas had made fun of him; his blazing eyes had hinted at the joys of his vanity when the Duke of Parma had offered him his sister's hand (trying to disguise his pleasure, the viscount had clenched his teeth in a habitual grimace that Alexis despised); and the boy recalled his uncle's scornful tone when talking to Lucretia, who had openly stated that she did not care for his music.

Often Alexis's parents would allude to other things that his uncle had done and that the boy did not understand, though he heard them being sharply condemned.

But all of Baldassare's faults, his commonplace grimace, had undoubtedly disappeared. When he had learned he might be dead in two years, how indifferent he must have become to the mockeries of Jean Galeas, to his friendship with the Duke of Parma, and to his own music. Alexis pictured his uncle as still handsome, but solemn and even more perfect than he had been before. Yes, solemn, and already not completely of this world. Hence, a little disquiet and terror mingled with the boy's despair.

The horses had been harnessed long ago, it was time to leave; the boy stepped into the carriage, then climbed down

again in order to ask his tutor for some final advice. When
Alexis spoke, his face turned very crimson: .

"Monsieur Legrand, is it better for my uncle to believe or not
believe that I know that he knows that he's dying?"

"He must not believe it, Alexis!"

"But what if he brings it up?"

"He won't bring it up."

"He won't bring it up?" said Alexis, astonished, for that was
the only alternative he had not foreseen: whenever he imagined
his visit with his uncle, he could hear him talking about death
with the gentleness of a priest.

"But what if he does bring it up after all?"

"You'll tell him he's mistaken."

"And what if I cry?"

"You've cried too much this morning, you won't cry in his
home."

"I won't cry!" Alexis exclaimed in despair. "But he'll think
that I don't care, that I don't love him . . . my dear, sweet uncle!"

And he burst into tears. His mother, losing patience, came
looking for him; they left.

■

After handing his little overcoat to a servant who stood in the
vestibule, wearing a green and white livery with the Sylvanian
arms, Alexis momentarily halted with his mother and listened to
a violin melody coming from an adjacent room. Then the visitors were ushered into a huge, round, glass-enclosed atrium,
where the viscount spent much of his time. Upon entering, you
faced the ocean, and upon turning your head, you saw lawns,
pastures, and woods; at the other end of the room there were
two cats, plus roses, poppies, and numerous musical instru-
ments. The guests waited for an instant.

Alexis flung himself on his mother; she thought he wanted
to kiss her, but, pressing his lips against her ear, he whispered:

"How old is my uncle?"

"He'll be thirty-six this June."

11

Alexis wanted to ask: "Do you think he'll ever reach thirty-six?", but he did not dare.

A door opened, Alexis trembled, a domestic said: "The viscount is coming shortly."

Soon the domestic returned, with two peacocks and a kid, which the viscount took along everywhere. Then, more steps were heard, and the door opened again.

"It's nothing," Alexis thought to himself, his heart beating whenever he heard noise. "It's probably a servant, yes, quite probably a servant."

But at the same time he heard a soft voice: "*Bonjour,* my little Alexis, I wish you a happy birthday."

His uncle, kissing the boy, frightened him. He must have sensed it, for, paying him no further heed in order to give him time to recover, the viscount started brightly chatting with Alexis's mother, his sister-in-law, who, ever since his mother's death, was the person he loved most in the world.

Now, Alexis, reassured, felt nothing but immense tenderness for this still charming young man, who was a wee bit paler and so heroic as to feign gaiety in these tragic minutes. The boy wanted to throw his arms around him but did not dare, afraid he might sap his uncle's strength and make him lose his self-control. More than anything else the viscount's sad, sweet gaze made the boy feel like crying. Alexis knew that those eyes had always been sad and, even in the happiest moments, they seemed to implore a consolation for sufferings that he did not appear to experience. But at this moment Alexis believed that his uncle's sadness, courageously banished from his conversation, had taken refuge in his eyes, which, along with his sunken cheeks, were the only sincere things about his entire person.

"I know you'd like to drive a carriage and pair, my little Alexis," said Baldassare, "you'll get one horse tomorrow. Next year I'll complete the pair and in two years I'll give you the carriage. But this year perhaps you'll learn how to ride a horse; we'll try when I come back. You see, I'm definitely leaving tomorrow," he added, "but not for long. I'll be back in less than a month, and we'll go to the matinee, you know, the comedy I promised I'd take you to."

Alexis knew that his uncle was going to visit a friend for several weeks; he also knew that his uncle was still allowed to go to the theater; but Alexis was thoroughly imbued with the idea of death, which had deeply upset him prior to his coming here, and so his uncle's words gave him a deep and painful shock.

"I won't go," Alexis thought to himself. "He'll suffer awfully when he hears the buffoonery of the actors and the laughter of the audience."

"What was that lovely melody we heard when we came in?" Alexis's mother asked.

"Oh, you found it lovely?" Baldassare exclaimed vividly and joyfully. "It's the love song I told you about."

"Is he play-acting?" Alexis wondered to himself. "How can the success of his music still bring him any pleasure?"

At that moment the viscount's face took on an expression of deep pain; his cheeks paled, he frowned, his lips puckered, his eyes filled with tears.

"My God!" Alexis cried out mentally. "His play-acting's too much for him. My poor uncle! But why is he so scared of hurting us? Why is he forcing himself so hard?"

However, the pains of general paralysis, which at times squeezed Baldassare like an iron corset, the torture often leaving marks on his body and, despite all his efforts, making his face cramp up, had now dissipated.

After wiping his eyes he resumed chatting in a good mood.

"Am I mistaken," Alexis's mother tactlessly asked, "or has the Duke of Parma been less friendly to you for some time now?"

"The Duke of Parma!" Baldassare furiously snapped. "The Duke of Parma less friendly! Are you joking, my dear? He wrote me this very morning, offering to put his Illyrian castle at my disposal if mountain air could do me any good."

He jumped up, re-triggering his dreadful pain, which made him pause for a moment; no sooner was the pain gone than he called to his servant:

"Bring me the letter that's by my bed."

13

And he then read in a lively voice:

"'My dear Baldassare, how bored I am without you, etc., etc.'"

As the prince's amiability unfolded in the letter, Baldassare's features softened and they shone with happy confidence. All at once, probably to cloak a joy that did not strike him as very sublime, he clenched his teeth and made the pretty little grimace that Alexis had thought forever banished from that face bearing the çalm of death.

With this little grimace 'crinkling Baldassare's lips as it normally did, the scales dropped from Alexis's eyes; ever since he had been with his uncle, he had believed, had wished he were viewing a dying man's face forever detached from humdrum realities and containing only a flickering smile that was heroically constrained, sadly tender, celestial and wistful. Now the boy no longer doubted that when teasing Baldassare, Jean Galeas would have infuriated him as before, nor did Alexis doubt that the sick man's gaiety, his desire to go to the theater were neither deceitful nor courageous, and that, arriving so close to death, Baldassare would keep thinking only of life.

Upon their coming home, it vividly dawned on Alexis that he too would die someday and that while he had far more time than his uncle, still Baldassare's old gardener, Rocco, and the viscount's cousin, the Duchess of Alériouvres, would certainly not outlive him by much. Yet, though rich enough to retire, Rocco continued working nonstop in order to earn more money and to obtain a prize for his roses. The duchess, albeit seventy, carefully dyed her hair and paid for newspaper articles that celebrated her youthful gait, her elegant receptions, and the refinements of her table and her mind.

These examples, which did not diminish Alexis's amazement at his uncle's attitude, inspired a similar astonishment that, growing by degrees, expanded into an immense stupefaction at the universal odiousness of those existences—not excluding his—that move backward toward death while staring at life.

Determined not to imitate so shocking an aberration, Alexis, emulating the ancient prophets whose glory he had been taught about, decided to withdraw into the desert with some of his little friends, and he informed his parents of his plans.

Fortunately, life, which was more powerful than their mockery and whose sweet and strengthening milk he had not fully drained, held out its breast to dissuade him. And he resumed drinking with a joyous voracity, his rich and credulous imagination listening naïvely to the grievances of that ravenousness and making wonderful amends for its blighted hopes.

2

My flesh is sad, alas! . . .

—STÉPHANE MALLARMÉ

The day after Alexis's visit, the Viscount of Sylvania left to spend three or four weeks at the nearby castle, where the presence of numerous guests could take his mind off the sorrow that followed many of his attacks.

Soon all his pleasures there were concentrated in the company of a young woman who doubled his pleasures by sharing them. While believing that he could sense she loved him, he was somewhat reserved toward her: he knew that she was absolutely pure and that, moreover, she was looking forward to her husband's arrival; besides, Baldassare was not sure he really loved her and he vaguely felt how sinful it would be to lead her astray. Subsequently he could never recall at what point the nature of their relationship had changed. But now, as if by some tacit agreement that he could no longer pinpoint, he kissed her wrists and put his arm around her neck. They seemed so happy that one evening he went further: he began by kissing her; next he caressed her on and on and then he kissed her eyes, her cheek, her lip, her throat, the sides of her nose. The young woman's smiling lips met his caresses halfway, and her eyes shone in their depths like pools warmed by the sun. Meanwhile Baldassare's caresses had gotten bolder; at a certain moment he looked at her: he was struck by her pallor, by the infinite despair emanating from her lifeless forehead, from her weary, grieving eyes, which wept with gazes sadder than tears, like the torture suffered during a crucifixion or after the irrevocable loss of an adored person. Baldassare peered at her for an instant; and then, with a supreme effort, she looked at him, raising her entreating eyes which begged for mercy at the same time that her avid mouth, with an unconscious and convulsive movement, asked for more kisses.

Overpowered again by the pleasure that hovered around them in the fragrance of their kisses and the memory of their caresses, the two of them pounced on each other, closing their eyes, those cruel eyes that showed them the distress of their souls; they did not want to see that distress, and he, especially, closed his eyes with all his strength, like a remorseful executioner who senses that his arm would tremble the instant it struck if, rather than imagine his victim provoking his rage and forcing him to satisfy it, he could look him in the face and feel his pain for a moment.

The night had come, and she was still in his room, her eyes blank and tearless. Without saying a word, she left, kissing his hand with passionate sadness.

He, however, could not sleep, and if he dozed off for a moment, he shuddered when feeling upon himself the desperate and entreating eyes of the gentle victim. Suddenly he pictured her as she must be now: sleepless, too, and feeling so alone. He dressed and walked softly to her room, not daring to make a sound for fear of awakening her if she slept, yet not daring to return to his room, where the sky and the earth and his soul were suffocating him under their weight. He stayed there, at her threshold, believing at every moment that he could not hold back for another instant and that he was about to go in. But then he was terrified at the thought of disturbing her sweet oblivion, the sweet and even breathing that he could perceive; he was terrified at the thought of cruelly delivering her to remorse and despair instead of letting her find a moment's peace beyond their clutches; he stayed there at the threshold, either sitting or kneeling or lying. In the morning, Baldassare, chilled but calm, went back to his room, slept for a long time, and woke up with a deep sense of well-being.

They strained their ingenuity to ease one another's consciences; they grew accustomed to remorse, which diminished, to pleasure, which also grew less intense; and when he returned to Sylvania, he, like her, had only a pleasant and slightly cool memory of those cruel and blazing minutes.

3

His youth is roaring inside him, he does not hear.

—MADAME DE SÉVIGNÉ

When Alexis, on his fourteenth birthday, went to see his uncle Baldassare, he did not, although anticipating them, fall prey to the violent emotions of the previous year. In developing his strength, the incessant rides on the horse his uncle had given him had lulled the boy's jangled nerves and aroused in him that constant spirit of good health, a sensation accompanying youth as a dim inkling of the depth of its resources and the power of its joyfulness. Under the breeze stirred up by his gallop, he felt his chest swelling like a sail, his body burning like a winter fire, and his forehead as cool as the fleeing foliage that wreathed him when he charged by; and then, upon returning home, he tautened his body under cold water or relaxed it for long periods of savory digestion; whereby all these experiences augmented his life forces, which, after being the tumultuous pride of Baldassare, had abandoned him forever, to gladden younger souls that they would someday desert in turn.

Nothing in Alexis could now falter because of his uncle's feebleness, could die because of his uncle's imminent death. The joyful humming of the nephew's blood in his veins and of his desires in his mind drowned out the sick man's exhausted complaints. Alexis had entered that ardent period in which the body labors so robustly at raising its palaces between the flesh and the soul that the soul quickly seems to have vanished, until the day when illness or sorrow has slowly undermined the barriers and transcended the painful fissure, allowing the soul to reappear. Alexis was now accustomed to his uncle's fatal disease as we are to all things that last around us; and because he had once made his nephew cry as the dead make us cry, the boy, even though his uncle was still alive, treated him like a dead man: he had begun to forget him.

When his uncle said to him that day, "My little Alexis, I'm giving you the carriage along with the second horse," the boy grasped what his uncle was thinking: "Otherwise you may never get the carriage"; and Alexis knew that it was an extremely sad thought. But he did not feel it was sad, for he no longer had room for profound sadness.

Several days later, the boy, while reading, was struck by the description of a villain who was unmoved by the most poignant affection of a dying man who adored him.

That night, the fear of being the villain, in whom he thought he saw his own portrait, kept him from falling asleep. The next day, however, he had such a wonderful horseback ride, worked so well, and felt, incidentally, so much affection for his living relatives that he went back to enjoying himself without scruples and sleeping without remorse.

Meanwhile the Viscount of Sylvania, who could no longer walk, now seldom left his castle. His friends and his family were with him all day, and he could own up to the most blameworthy folly, the most absurd extravagance, state the most flagrant paradox, or imply the most shocking fault without his kinsmen reproaching him or his friends joking or disagreeing with him. It was as if they had tacitly absolved him of any responsibility for his deeds and words. Above all they seemed to be trying to keep him from hearing the last sounds, to muffle with sweetness, if not drown out with tenderness, the final creakings of his body, from which life was ebbing.

He spent long and charming hours reclining and having a tête-à-tête with himself, the only guest he had neglected to ask to supper in his lifetime. He tried to adorn his suffering body, to lean in resignation on the windowsill, gazing at the sea, a melancholy joy. With ardent sadness he contemplated the scene of his death for a long time, endlessly revising it like a work of art and surrounding it with images of this world, images that still imbued his thoughts, but that, already slipping away from him in his gradual departure, became vague and beautiful. His imagination already sketched his farewell to Duchess Oliviane, his great platonic friend, whose salon he had ruled even though it brought together all the grandest noblemen, the most glorious artists, and the finest minds in Europe. He felt he could already read the account of his final conversation with the duchess:

". . . The sun was down, and the sea, glimpsed through the apple trees, was mauve. As airy as pale, faded wreaths and as persistent as regrets, blue and rosy cloudlets drifted along the horizon. A melancholy row of poplars sank into the shadows, their resigned tops remaining in a churchly rose; the final rays, tinting the branches without touching the trunks, attached garlands of light to these balustrades of darkness. The breeze blended the three scents of ocean, wet leaves, and milk. Never had the Sylvanian countryside softened the evening melancholy more voluptuously.

"'I loved you very much, but I gave you so little, my poor friend,' she said.

"'What are you talking about, Oliviane? What do you mean you gave me so little? You gave all the more the less I asked of you, and actually a lot more than if our senses had played any part in our affection. I worshiped you and, as supernatural as a madonna and as gentle as a wet nurse, you cradled me. I loved you with an affection whose keen sagacity was never marred by any hope for carnal pleasure. What an incomparable friendship you gave me in exchange, what an exquisite tea, a conversation that was adorned in a natural way, and how many bunches of fresh roses! You alone, with your

19

maternal and expressive hands, knew how to cool my feverish forehead, drip honey between my parched lips, and place
noble images in my life.

"'My dear friend, give me your hands and let me kiss them.'"

With all his senses and all his heart he still loved Pia, the
little Syracusian princess, who was smitten with a furious and
invincible love for Castruccio, and it was her indifference to
Baldassare that occasionally reminded him of a crueler reality
which, however, he struggled to forget. Until the last few
days, he had attended some festivities, where, sauntering
with her on his arm, he thought he could humiliate his rival;
but even when strolling at her side, the viscount sensed that
her deep eyes were distracted by another love, which she
tried to conceal only out of pity for the sick man. And now
even that was beyond him. The movements of his legs had
become so unhinged that he could no longer go out. However, she came by frequently and, as if joining the others in
their vast conspiracy of gentleness, she spoke to him incessantly with an ingenious tenderness that was never again be-
lied, as it had been in the past, by the cry of her indifference
or the avowal of her anger. And from her more than from
anyone else, he felt the appeasement created by that gentleness spreading over him and delighting him.

But then one day, as Baldassare was rising from his chair
to go to the dining table, his astonished domestic saw him
walking much better. He sent for the physician, who put off
his diagnosis. The next day Baldassare walked normally. A
week later, he was allowed to go out. His friends and his relatives felt an immense hope. The doctor believed that a simple and curable nervous disease might have at first shown
the symptoms of general paralysis, which were now indeed
starting to disappear. He presented his speculations to Baldassare as a certainty:

"You are saved!"

The condemned man expressed a deep-felt joy upon
learning of his reprieve. But after an interval of great im-
provement, a sharp anxiety began to pierce his joy, which

had already been weakened by the brief habituation. He was sheltered from the inclemencies of life in that propitious atmosphere of encompassing gentleness, of forced rest and free meditation, and the desire for death began obscurely germinating inside him. He was far from suspecting it, and he felt only a dim anxiety at the thought of starting all over, enduring the blows to which he was no longer accustomed, and losing the affection that surrounded him. He also confusedly felt that it was wrong to seek forgetfulness in pleasure or action now that he had gotten to know himself, the brotherly stranger who, while watching the boats plowing the sea, had conversed with him for hours on end, so far and so near: in himself. As if now feeling the awakening of a new and unfamiliar love of native soil, like a young man who is ignorant of the location of his original homeland, he yearned for death, whereas he had initially felt he was going into eternal exile.

He voiced an idea, and Jean Galeas, who knew that Baldassare was cured, disagreed violently and poked fun at him. His sister-in-law, who had been visiting him every morning and every evening for two months, had not shown up in two days. This was too much! He had long since grown unused to the burden of life and he did not want to shoulder it again. For life had not recaptured him with its charms. His strength was restored and, with it, all his desires to live; he went out, began living again, and died a second time for himself. At the end of a month the symptoms of general paralysis recurred. Little by little, as in the past, walking became difficult, impossible, gradually enough for him to adjust to his return to death and to have time to look the other way. His relapse did not even have the quality of the first attack, at the end of which he had started to withdraw from life, not in order to see it in its reality but to view it like a painting. Now, on the contrary, he grew more and more egotistical, irascible, desperately missing the pleasures he could no longer enjoy.

His sister-in-law, whom he loved tenderly, was the only person to sweeten his approaching end, for she came by several times a day with Alexis.

One afternoon, when she was en route to see the viscount, and her carriage had almost arrived, the horses bolted; she was violently flung to the ground, then trampled by a horseman who was galloping past; unconscious, with a fractured skull, she was carried into Baldassare's home.

The coachman, who was unscathed, promptly announced the accident to the viscount, who turned livid. He clenched his teeth, his blazing eyes bulged out of their sockets, and in a dreadful fit of anger he railed and ranted against the coachman, on and on; but apparently his violent outburst was meant to smother a painful cry for help, which could be softly heard during the pauses. It was as if an invalid were moaning next to the furious viscount. Soon, these moans, initially faint, drowned out his shrieks of rage, and the sobbing man collapsed into a chair.

Next he wanted to wash his face so that his sister-in-law would not be upset by the traces of his grief. The domestic sadly shook his head; the injured woman had not regained consciousness. The viscount spent two desperate days and nights at his sister-in-law's bedside. She might die at any moment. The second night, the doctor attempted a hazardous operation. By the third morning her fever had abated, and the patient smiled at Baldassare, who, unable to restrain his tears, wept and wept for joy. When death had inched toward him bit by bit, he had refused to face it; now he suddenly found himself in its presence. Death had terrified him by threatening his most prized possession; the viscount had pleaded with death, had moved it to mercy.

He felt strong and free, proud to see that his own life was not as precious to him as his sister-in-law's, and that he felt as much scorn for his own life as pity for hers. He now looked death in the face and no longer beheld the scenes that would surround his death. He wanted to remain like that until the end, no longer prey to his lies, which, by trying to bring him a beautiful and wonderful agony, would have added the last straw to his profanations by soiling the mysteries of his death just as it had concealed from him the mysteries of his life.

4

Tomorrow, and tomorrow, and tomorrow
Creeps in this petty pace from day to day,
To the last syllable of recorded time;
And all our yesterdays have lighted fools
The way to dusty death. Out, out, brief candle!
Life's but a walking shadow, a poor player
That struts and frets his hour upon the stage
And then is heard no more; it is a tale
Told by an idiot, full of sound and fury,
Signifying nothing.

—SHAKESPEARE: *MACBETH*

Baldassare's emotions and fatigue during his sister-in-law's illness had stepped up the advance of his own disease. He had
just been told by his confessor that he had only one month
left; it was ten A.M., the rain was coming down in <u>torrents</u>. A
carriage halted in front of the castle. It was Duchess Oliviane.
Earlier, when harmoniously adorning the scenes of his death,
he had told himself:

"It will be on a clear evening. The sun will be down, and the
sea, glimpsed through the apple trees, will be mauve. As airy as
pale and faded wreaths and as persistent as regrets, blue and
rosy cloudlets will drift along the horizon. . . ."

It was at ten A.M., in a downpour, under a foul and low-
lying sky, that Duchess Oliviane arrived; exhausted by his illness, fully absorbed in higher interests, and no longer feeling
the grace of things that he had once prized as the charm, the
value, and the refined glory of life, Baldassare had his servant
tell the duchess that he was too weak. She insisted, but he
would not receive her. He was not even acting out of necessity: she meant nothing to him anymore. Death had rapidly
broken the bonds whose enslavement he had been dreading
for several weeks. When he tried to think of Oliviane, nothing

presented itself to his mind's eye: the eyes of his imagination and of his vanity had closed.

Yet roughly a week before his death, his furious jealousy was aroused by the announcement that the Duchess of Bohemia was giving a ball, at which Pia was to lead the cotillion with Castruccio, who was leaving for Denmark the next day. The viscount demanded to see Pia; his sister-in-law was reluctant to summon her; he believed that they were preventing him from seeing her, that they were persecuting him; he lost his temper, so, to avoid tormenting him, they sent for her immediately.

By the time she arrived, he was perfectly calm, but profoundly sad. He drew her close to his bed and instantly spoke about the ball being hosted by the Duchess of Bohemia. He said:

"We're not related, so you won't wear mourning for me, but I have to ask you one favor: Do not go to the ball, promise me you won't."

They locked gazes, showing their souls on the edge of their pupils, their melancholy and passionate souls, which death was unable to unite.

He understood her hesitation; his lips twisting in pain, he gently murmured:

"Oh, don't promise me, after all! Don't break a promise made to a dying man. If you're not certain of yourself, don't promise me anything."

"I can't promise you that; I haven't seen him in two months and I may never see him again; if I miss the ball, I'll be inconsolable for all eternity."

"You're right, since you love him, and since death may come. . . . And since you're still alive with all your strength. . . . But you can do a small something for me; to throw people off the scent, you'd be obliged to spend a bit of time with me at the ball; subtract that time from your evening. Invite my soul to remember a few moments with you, think of me a little."

"I can scarcely promise you even that much, the ball will be so brief. Even if I don't leave, I'll barely have time to see him. But I'll give you a moment every day after that."

"You won't manage, you'll forget me; but if after a year, alas, more perhaps, a sad text, a death, or a rainy evening reminds you of me, you can offer me some altruism! I will never, never be able see you again . . . except in my soul, and this would require that we think about each other simultaneously. I'll think about you forever so that my soul remains open to you endlessly in case you feel like entering it. But the visitor will keep me waiting for a long time! The November rains will have rotted the flowers on my grave, June will have burned them, and my soul will always be weeping impatiently. Ah! I hope that someday the sight of a keepsake, the recurrence of a birthday, the bent of your thoughts will guide your memory within the circle of my tenderness. It will then be as if I've heard you, perceived you, a magic spell will cover everything with flowers for your arrival. Think about the dead man. But, alas! Can I hope that death and your gravity will accomplish what life with its ardors, and our tears, and our merry times, and our lips were unable to achieve?"

5

Now cracks a noble heart. Good night, sweet prince;
And flights of angels sing thee to thy rest!
—SHAKESPEARE: *HAMLET*

Meanwhile a violent fever accompanied by delirium never left the viscount; his bed had been moved to the vast rotunda where Alexis had seen him on his thirteenth birthday, seen him still so joyful: here the sick man could watch the sea, the pier, and, on the other side, the pastures and the woods. Now and then, he began to speak; but his words showed no traces of the thoughts from on high which, during the past few weeks, had purified him with their visits. Savagely cursing an invisible person who was teasing him, he kept repeating that

he was the premier musician of the century and the most illustrious aristocrat in the universe. Then, suddenly calm, he
told his coachmen to drive him to some low den, to have the
horses saddled for the hunt. He asked for stationery in order
to invite all the European sovereigns to a dinner celebrating
his marriage to the sister of the Duke of Parma; horrified at
being unable to pay a gambling debt, he picked up the paper
knife next to his bed and aimed it like a gun. He dispatched
messengers to find out whether the policeman he had
thrashed last night was dead, and he laughingly muttered ob-
scenities to someone whose hand he thought he was holding. Those exterminating angels known as Will and Thought
were no longer present to drive the evil spirits of his senses
and the vile emanations of his memory back into the darkness.

Three days later, around five o'clock, he woke up as if from
a bad dream for which the dreamer is responsible yet which he
barely remembers. He asked whether any friends or relatives
had been here during the hours when he had presented an
image of only his lowliest, most archaic, and most extinct part;
and he told his servants that if he became delirious, they should
have his visitors leave instantly and they should not readmit
them until he regained consciousness.

He raised his eyes, surveyed the room, and smiled at his
black cat, who, perched on a Chinese vase, was playing with
a chrysanthemum and inhaling its fragrance with a mime-like
gesture. He sent everyone away and conversed at length with
the priest who was keeping watch over him. Yet he refused
to take communion and asked the physician to say that the
patient's stomach was in no condition to tolerate a host. An
hour later he had the servant bring in his sister-in-law and
Jean Galeas. He said:

"I'm resigned, I'm happy to die and to come before God."

The air was so mild that they opened the windows facing
the ocean but not seeing it, and because the wind blowing from
the opposite direction was too brisk, they did not open the windows giving upon the pastures and the woods.

Baldassare had them drag his bed near the open windows. A boat was just nosing out to sea, guided by sailors towing the lines on the pier. A handsome cabin boy of about fifteen was leaning over the bow; each <u>billow</u> seemed about to knock him into the water, but he stood firm on his solid legs. With a burning pipe between his wind-salted lips, he spread his net to haul in fish. And the same wind that bellied the sail blew into the rotunda, cooling Baldassare's cheeks and making a piece of paper flutter through the room. He turned his head to avoid seeing the happy tableau of pleasures that he had passionately loved and that he would never enjoy again. He eyed the harbor: a three-master was setting sail.

"It's the ship that's bound for the Indies," said Jean Galeas.

Baldassare was unable to distinguish the people waving their handkerchiefs on the pier, but he sensed their thirst for the unknown, a thirst that was <u>parching</u> their eyes; those people still had a great deal to experience, to get to know, to feel. The anchor was weighed, shouts arose, the ship cut across the dark sea, toward the west, where, in a golden mist, the light blended the skiffs with the clouds, murmuring hazy and irresistible promises to the voyagers.

Baldassare had the servants shut the windows on this side of the rotunda and open the ones facing the pastures and the woods. He gazed at the fields, but he could still hear the farewells shouted from the three-master and he could see the cabin boy holding his pipe between his teeth and spreading his nets.

Baldassare's hand stirred feverishly. All at once he heard a faint, silvery tinkle as deep and indistinct as the beating of a heart. It was the bells pealing in an extremely distant village, a sound that, thanks to the limpid evening air and the favorable breeze, had traveled across many miles of plains and rivers to be picked up by his infallible ear. It was both a current and ancient voice; now he heard his heart beating to the harmonious flight of the bells, the sound pausing the moment they seemed to inhale it, then exhaling with them in a long and feeble breath. Throughout his life, upon hearing faraway bells, he had spontaneously remembered their sweetness in the evening air when, as a little boy, he had crossed the fields on his way home to the castle.

At that instant the physician beckoned everyone over, saying: "It's the end!"

Baldassare was resting, his eyes closed, and his heart was listening to the bells, which his ear, paralyzed by imminent death, could not catch. He saw his mother kissing him upon his return, then putting him to bed at night, rubbing his feet to warm them, remaining with him if he could not fall asleep; he recalled his *Robinson Crusoe* and the evenings in the garden when his sister would sing; he recalled the words of his tutor, who predicted that someday he would be a great musician, and he recalled his mother's thrilled reaction, which she tried but failed to conceal. Now there was no time left to realize the passionate expectations of his mother and his sister, whom he had so cruelly disappointed. He saw the large linden tree under which he had gotten engaged and he saw the day on which his engagement had been broken, and only his mother had managed to console him. He believed he was kissing his old nanny and holding his first violin. He saw all these things in a luminous remoteness as sweet and sad as the one that the windows facing the fields were watching but not seeing.

He saw all these things, and yet not even two seconds had passed since the physician had listened to his heart and said:

"It's the end!"

The physician stood up, saying:

"It's over!"

Alexis, his mother, and Jean Galeas knelt down together with the Duke of Parma, who had just arrived. The servants were weeping in the open doorway.

VIOLANTE OR HIGH SOCIETY

Have few dealings with young men and persons of the upper classes.... Do not desire to appear before the powerful.
                    —THOMAS À KEMPIS: *IMITATION OF CHRIST*, BOOK I, CHAPTER 8

1   Violante's Meditative Childhood

The Viscountess of Styria was generous and affectionate and thoroughly imbued with an enchanting grace. Her husband the viscount had an extremely nimble mind, and his facial features were of an admirable regularity. But any grenadier was more sensitive than he and less vulgar. Far from society, they reared their daughter Violante at their rustic estate in Styria, and she, as lively and attractive as her father and as benevolent and mysteriously seductive as her mother, seemed to unite her parents' qualities in a perfectly harmonious proportion. However, the fickle strivings of her heart and her mind did not encounter a will in her that, without limiting them, could guide them and keep her from becoming their charming and fragile plaything. For her mother this lack of willpower inspired anxieties that might eventually have borne fruit if the viscountess and her husband had not been violently killed in a hunting accident, leaving Violante an orphan at fifteen. Residing nearly alone, under the watchful but awkward supervision of old Augustin, her tutor and the steward of the Styrian castle, Violante, for lack of friends, dreamed up enchanting companions, promising to be faithful to them for the rest of her life. She took them strolling along the paths in the park and through the countryside, and she leaned with them on the balustrade of the terrace that, marking the boundary of the Styrian estate, faced the sea. Raised by her dream friends virtually above herself and initiated by them, Violante was sensitive to the visible world and had a slight inkling of the invisible world. Her joy was infinite, though broken by periods of sadness that were sweeter than her joy.

2 Sensuality

Do not lean on a wind-shaken reed and do not place your faith upon it, for all flesh is like grass, and its glory fades like the flower of the fields.

—THOMAS À KEMPIS: *IMITATION OF CHRIST*

Aside from Augustin and a few local children, Violante saw no one. Her sole guest from time to time was her mother's younger sister, who lived in Julianges, a castle located several miles away. One day, when the aunt came to see her niece, she was accompanied by a friend. His name was Honoré, and he was sixteen years old. Violante did not care for him, but he visited her again. Roaming along a path in the park, he taught her highly inappropriate things, whose existence she had never suspected. She experienced a very sweet pleasure, of which she was instantly ashamed. Then, since the sun was down, and they had walked and walked, they sat down on a bench, no doubt to gaze at the reflections with which the rosy sky was mellowing the sea. Honoré drew closer to Violante so she would not feel cold; he fastened her fur coat around her throat, ingeniously drawing out his action, and he offered to help her try to practice the theories he had just been teaching her in the park. He wanted to whisper, his lips approached her ear, which she did not withdraw; but then they heard a rustling in the foliage.

"It's nothing," Honoré murmured tenderly.

"It's my aunt," said Violante.

It was the wind. But Violante, cooled just in time by the wind and now standing, refused to sit down again; she said goodbye to Honoré despite his pleading. She felt remorse, suffered a hysterical fit, and had a very hard time falling asleep during the next two nights. Her memory was a burning pillow which she kept turning and turning. Two days later Honoré asked to see her. She had her butler reply that she had gone for a walk. Honoré did not believe a word of it and did not dare come back.

The following summer she again thought about Honoré, with tenderness, but also with distress, for she knew that he was a sailor on some ship. After the sun had glided into the sea, Violante would sit on the bench to which he had brought her a year ago, and she would struggle to remember Honoré's lips held out to her, his green eyes half-closed, his gazes sweeping like rays and focusing a little warm and vivid light upon her. And on tender nights, on vast and secretive nights, when the certainty that no one could see her intensified her desire, she heard Honoré's voice whispering the forbidden things into her ear. She conjured him up fully, and he obsessively offered himself to her like a temptation.

One evening at dinner, she sighed as she looked at the steward, who sat across from her.

"I feel very sad, dear Augustin," said Violante. "No one loves me," she added.

"And yet," he countered, "a week ago, when I was straightening out the library at Julianges, I heard someone say about you: 'How beautiful she is!'"

"Who said that?" Violante asked sadly.

A vague smile barely and very softly raised a corner of her mouth the way we try to lift a window curtain in order to admit the gaiety of daylight.

"It was that young man from last year, Monsieur Honoré. . . ."

"I thought he was at sea," said Violante.

"He's back," said Augustin.

Violante promptly stood up and almost staggered into her bedroom in order to write Honoré, asking him to come and see her. Picking up her pen, she had a hitherto unknown feeling of happiness, of power: the feeling that she was arranging her life a bit according to her own whim and pleasure; the feeling that she could nudge along their two destinies, spur the intricate machinery that imprisoned them far apart; the feeling that he would appear at night, on the terrace, rather than in the cruel ecstasy of her unfulfilled desire; the feeling that, between her unheard expressions of tenderness (her perpetual inner romance) and real things, there were truly avenues of communication, along which she would hurry toward the impossible, making it viable by creating it.

The next day she received Honoré's response, which she read, trembling, on the bench where he had kissed her.

Mademoiselle,
    Your letter has reached me an hour before my ship is to sail. We have put into port for only a week, and I will not return for another four years. Be so kind as to keep the memory of
    Your respectful and affectionate
                                                                Honoré.

Gazing now at that terrace to which he would no longer come, where no one could fulfill her desire, gazing also at that sea, which was tearing him away from her, exchanging him, in the girl's imagination, for a bit of its grand, sad, and mysterious charm, the charm of things that do not belong to us, that reflect too many skies and wash too many shores; gazing and gazing, Violante burst into tears.

"My poor Augustin," she said that evening. "Something awful has happened to me."

Her initial need to confide in someone arose from the first disappointments of her sensuality, emerging as naturally as the first satisfactions of love normally emerge. She had not as yet known love. A short time later she suffered from it, which is the only manner in which we get to know it.

3 Pangs of Love

Violante was in love; that is, for several months a young Eng-lishman named Laurence had been the object of her most trivial thoughts, the goal of her most important actions. She had gone hunting with him once and she failed to understand why the de-sire to see him again dominated her thoughts, drove her to roads where she would run into him, deprived her of sleep, and destroyed her peace of mind and her happiness. Violante was smitten; she was spurned. Laurence loved high society; she loved it in order to follow him. But Laurence had no eyes for this twenty-year-old country girl. She fell ill with chagrin and jeal-ousy and, to forget him, she went to take the waters at X.; but her pride was wounded because she had lost out to so many women who could not hold a candle to her; so, in order to tri-umph over them, she decided to beat them at their own game.

"I'm leaving you, my good Augustin," she said, "I'm going to the Austrian court."

"Heaven help us," said Augustin. "The poor in our country will no longer be consoled by your charity once you're in the midst of so many wicked people. You'll no longer play with our children in the forest. Who'll preside at the organ in church? We'll no longer see you painting in the countryside, you'll no longer compose any songs for us."

"Don't worry, Augustin," said Violante, "just keep my castle and my Styrian peasants lovely and faithful. For me high society is only a means to an end. It offers vulgar but invincible weapons, and if I want to be loved someday, I have to possess them. I'm also prodded by curiosity and by a need to live a slightly more material and less meditative life than here. I want both a holiday and an education. Once I gain my status, and my vacation ends, I'll trade the sophisticated world for the country, for our good and simple people, and, what I prefer above everything else, my songs. On a certain and not all too distant day, I'll stop on this slope, I'll return to our Styria and live with you, dear Augustin."

"Will you be able to?" said Augustin.

"One can if one wants to," said Violante.

"But perhaps you won't want the same thing as now," said Augustin.

"Why won't I?" asked Violante.

"Because you'll have changed," said Augustin.

4   The Sophisticated World

The members of high society are so mediocre that Violante merely had to <u>deign</u> to mingle with them in order to eclipse nearly all of them. The most unapproachable lords, the most uncivil artists sought her out and wooed her. She alone had a mind, had taste, and a bearing that was the <u>epitome</u> of all perfection. She launched plays, perfumes, and gowns. Writers, hairdressers, fashion designers begged for her patronage. The most celebrated milliner in Austria requested her permission to call herself Violante's personal modiste; the most illustrious prince in Europe requested her permission to call himself her lover. But she felt obliged to hold back these marks of esteem, which would have definitively consecrated their lofty standing in the fashionable world. Among the young men who asked to be received by Violante, Laurence stood out because of his persistence. After causing her so much grief, he now aroused her disgust. And his base conduct alienated her more than all his earlier scorn.

"I have no right to be <u>indignant</u>," she thought to herself. "I didn't love him for his spiritual grandeur and I sensed very keenly, without daring to admit it to myself, that he was <u>vile</u>. This didn't prevent me from loving him; it only kept me from loving spiritual grandeur to the same degree. I believed that a person could be both vile and lovable. But once you stop loving somebody, you prefer people with a heart. What a strange passion I had for that nasty man: it was all in my head; I had no excuse, I wasn't swept away by sensual feelings. Platonic love is so meaningless."

A bit later, as we shall see, Violante was to regard sensual love as even more meaningless.

Augustin came for a visit and tried to lure her back to Styria.

"You've conquered a veritable kingdom," he said. "Isn't that enough for you? Why not become the old Violante again?"

"I've only just conquered it, Augustin," she retorted. "Let me at least exercise my power for a few months."

An event, unforeseen by Augustin, temporarily exempted Violante from thinking about retirement. After rejecting marriage proposals from twenty most serene highnesses, as many sovereign princes, and one genius, she married the Duke of Bohemia, who had immense charm and five million ducats. The announcement of Honoré's return nearly broke up the marriage on the eve of the nuptials. But disfigured as he was by an illness, his attempts at familiarity were odious to Violante. She wept over the vanity of her desires, which had so ardently flown to the blossoming flesh that now had already withered forever.

The Duchess of Bohemia was as charming as Violante of Styria had been, and the duke's immeasurable fortune served merely to provide a worthy frame for the artwork that she was. From an artwork she became a luxury article through that natural inclination of earthly things to slip lower if a noble effort does not maintain their center of gravity above them. Augustin was amazed at everything he heard from her.

"Why does the duchess," he wrote her, "speak endlessly about things that Violante so thoroughly despised?"

"Because people who live in high society would not like me as much if I were preoccupied," Violante answered, "with things that, being over their heads, are antipathetic to them and incomprehensible. But I'm so bored, my good Augustin."

He came to see her and explained why she was bored:

"You no longer act on your taste in music, in reflection, in charity, in solitude, in rustic life. You're absorbed in success, you're held back by pleasure. But we can find happiness only in doing something we love with the deepest inclinations of the soul."

"How can you know that?—you've never lived," said Violante.

"I've thought, and thinking is living," said Augustin. "I hope that you'll soon be disgusted by this insipid life."

Violante grew more and more bored; she was never cheerful now. Then, high society's immorality, to which she had been indifferent, pounced on her, wounding her deeply, the way the harshness of the seasons beats down the bodies that illness renders incapable of struggling. One day, when she was strolling by herself along a nearly deserted avenue, a woman headed straight toward her after stepping down from a carriage that Violante had failed to notice. The woman approached her and asked if she was Violante of Bohemia; she said that she had been her mother's friend and that she desired to see little Violante, whom she had held in her lap. The woman kissed her with intense emotion, put her arms around Violante's waist, and kissed her so often that Violante dashed away without saying goodbye. The next evening, Violante attended a party in honor of the Princess of Miseno, whom she did not know. Violante recognized her: she was the abominable lady from yesterday. And a dowager, whom Violante had esteemed until now, asked her:

"Would you like me to introduce you to the Princess of Miseno?"

"No!" said Violante.

"Don't be shy," said the dowager. "I'm sure she'll like you. She's very fond of pretty women."

From then on Violante had two mortal enemies, the Princess of Miseno and the dowager, both of whom depicted Violante everywhere as a monster of arrogance and perversity. Violante heard about it and wept for herself and for the wickedness of women. She had long since made up her mind about the wickedness of men. Soon she kept telling her husband every evening:

"The day after tomorrow we're going back to my Styria and we will never leave it again."

But then came a festivity that she might enjoy more than the others, a lovelier gown to show off. The profound need to imagine, to create, to live alone and through the mind, and also to sacrifice herself—those needs had lost too much strength, torturing her because they were not fulfilled, preventing her from finding even a particle of delight in high society; those needs were no longer urgent enough to make her change her way of life, to force her to renounce society and realize her true destiny.

She continued to present the sumptuous and woebegone image of a life made for infinity but gradually reduced to almost nothing and left with only the melancholy shadows of the noble destiny that she could have achieved but from which she was retreating more and more each day. A great surge of far-reaching philanthropy that could have scoured her heart like a tide, leveling all the human inequalities that obstruct an aristocratic heart, was stemmed by the thousand dams of selfishness, coquetry, and ambition. She liked kindness now purely as an elegant gesture. She was still charitable with her money, with even her time and trouble; but a whole part of her had been put aside and was no longer hers.

She still spent each morning in bed, reading or dreaming, but with a distorted mind that now halted on the surface of things and contemplated itself, not to go deeper but to admire itself voluptuously and coquettishly as in a mirror. And if visitors were announced, she did not have the willpower to send them away in order to continue dreaming or reading. She had reached the point at which she could enjoy nature solely with perverted senses, and the enchantment of the seasons existed for her merely to perfume her fashionable status and provide its tonality. The charms of winter became the pleasure of being cold, and the gaiety of hunting closed her heart to the sorrows of autumn. Sometimes, by walking alone in the forest, she tried to rediscover the natural source of true joy. But she wore dazzling gowns under the shadowy foliage. And the delight of being fashionable corrupted her joy of being alone and dreaming.

"Are we leaving tomorrow?" the duke asked.

"The day after," Violante replied.

Then the duke stopped asking her. In response to Augustin's laments, she wrote him: "I'll go back when I'm a bit older."

"Ah!" Augustin answered. "You're deliberately giving them your youth; you will never return to your Styria."

She never returned. While young, she remained in high society to reign over the kingdom of elegance, which she had conquered while still practically a child. Growing old, she remained there to defend her power. It was useless. She lost it. And when she died, she was still in the midst of trying to reconquer it. Augustin had counted on disgust. But he had reckoned without a force that, while nourished at first by vanity, overcomes disgust, contempt, even boredom: it is habit.

Fragments of Commedia dell'Arte

As crabs, goats, scorpions, the balance and the water-pot lose their mean-
ness when hung as signs in the zodiac, so I can see my own vices without
heat in . . . distant persons.

—Ralph Waldo Emerson

1 Fabrizio's Mistresses

Fabrizio's mistress was intelligent and beautiful; he could not
get over it. "She shouldn't understand herself!" he groaned. "Her
beauty is spoiled by her intelligence. Could I still be smitten
with the Mona Lisa whenever I looked at her if I also had to hear
a discourse by even a remarkable critic?"

He left her and took another mistress, who was beautiful
and mindless. But her inexorable want of tact constantly prevented him from enjoying her charm. Moreover she aspired to
intelligence, read a great deal, became a bluestocking, and was
as intellectual as his first mistress, but with less ease and with
ridiculous clumsiness. He asked her to keep silent; but even
when she held her tongue, her beauty cruelly reflected her stupidity. Finally he met a woman who revealed her intelligence
purely in a more subtle grace, who was content with just living
and never dissipated the enchanting mystery of her nature in

overly specific conversations. She was gentle, like graceful and agile animals with deep eyes, and she disturbed you like the morning's vague and agonizing memory of your dreams. But she did not bother to do for him what his other two mistresses had done: she did not love him.

2 Countess Myrto's Female Friends

Of all her friends, Myrto, witty, kind-hearted, and attractive, but with a taste for high society, prefers Parthénis, who is a duchess and more regal than Myrto; yet Myrto enjoys herself with Lalagé, who is exactly as fashionable as she herself; nor is Myrto indifferent to the charms of Cléanthis, who is obscure and does not aspire to a dazzling rank. But the person Myrto cannot endure is Doris: her social position is slightly below Myrto's, and she seeks Myrto out, as Myrto does Parthénis, for being more fashionable.

We point out these preferences and this antipathy because not only does Duchess Parthénis have an advantage over Myrto, but she can love Myrto purely for herself; Lalagé can love her for herself, and in any case, being colleagues and on the same level, they need each other; finally, in cherishing Cléanthis, Myrto proudly feels that she herself is capable of being unselfish, of having a sincere preference, of understanding and loving, and that she is fashionable enough to overlook fashionableness if necessary.

Doris, on the other hand, merely acts on her snobbish desires, which she is unable to fulfill; she visits Myrto like a pug approaching a mastiff that keeps track of its bones: Doris hopes thereby to have a go at Myrto's duchesses and, if possible, shanghai one of them; disagreeable, like Myrto, because of the irksome disproportion between her actual rank and the one she strives for, she ultimately offers Myrto the image of her vice. To her chagrin, Myrto recognizes her friendship with Parthénis in Doris's attentiveness to her, Myrto.

Lalagé and even Cléanthis remind Myrto of her ambitious dreams, and Parthénis at least has begun to make them come true: Doris talks to Myrto only about her paltriness. Thus, being too irritated to play the amusing role of patroness, Myrto feels in regard to Doris the emotions that she, Myrto, would inspire precisely in Parthénis if Parthénis were not above snobbery: Myrto hates Doris.

3 Heldémone, Adelgise, Ercole

After witnessing a slightly indelicate scene, Ercole is reluctant to describe it to Duchess Adelgise, but has no such qualms with Heldémone the courtesan.

"Ercole," Adelgise exclaims, "you don't think I can listen to that story? Ah, I'm quite sure you'd behave differently with the courtesan Heldémone. You respect me: you don't love me."

"Ercole," Heldémone exclaims, "you don't have the decency to conceal that story from me? You be the judge: would you act this way with Duchess Adelgise? You don't respect me: therefore you cannot love me."

4 The Fickle Man

Fabrizio, who wants to, who believes he will, love Béatrice forever, remembers that he wanted the same thing, believed the same thing when he loved Hippolyta, Barbara, and Clélie for six months. So, reviewing Béatrice's actual qualities, he tries to find a reason to believe that after the waning of his passion he will keep visiting her; for he finds the thought of someday living without her incompatible with a sentiment that contains the illusion of its own eternalness. Besides, as a prudent egoist, he would not care to commit himself fully—with his thoughts, his actions, his intentions of the moment and all his future plans—to the companion of only some of his hours. Béatrice has a sharp mind and a good judgment: "Once I stop loving her, what pleasure I'll feel chatting with her about others, about herself, about my vanished love for her . . ." (which will thereby be revived but converted, he hopes, into a more lasting friendship).

But, with his passion for Béatrice gone, he lets two years pass without visiting her, without wanting to see her, without suffering from not wanting to see her. One day, when forced to visit her, he sits there fuming and stays for only ten minutes. For he dreams night and day about Giulia, who is unusually mindless but whose fair hair smells as good as a fine herb and whose eyes are as innocent as two flowers.

5

Life is strangely easy and pleasant with certain people of great natural distinction, people who are witty, loving, but who are capable of all vices although they do not indulge in any vice publicly, so no one can state that they have any vice at all. There is something supple and secretive about them. Then too, their perversity adds a piquant touch to their most innocent actions such as strolling in gardens at night.

 6 Lost Waxes

ONE

I first saw you a little while ago, Cydalise, and right off I admired your blond hair, like a small gold helmet on your pure and melancholy childlike head. A slightly pale red velvet gown softened your unusual head even further, and the lowered eyelids appeared to seal its mystery forever. But then you raised your eyes; they halted on me, Cydalise, and they seemed imbued with the fresh purity of morning, of water running on the first lovely days in spring. Those eyes were like eyes that have never looked at the things that all human eyes are accustomed to reflecting—yours were virginal eyes without earthly experience.

But upon my closer scrutiny, you expressed, above all, an air of loving and suffering, like a person whose wishes were already denied by the fairies before his birth. Even fabrics assumed a sorrowful grace on you, casting a gloom especially on your arms, which were discouraged just enough to remain simple and charming. Then I pictured you as a princess coming from very far away, down through the centuries, bored forever here and with a resigned languor: a princess wearing garments of a rare and ancient harmony, the contemplation of which would have quickly turned into a sweet and intoxicating habit for the eyes. I would have wanted you to tell me your dreams, your cares. I would have wanted to see you hold some goblet or rather one of those ewers with such proud and joyless forms, ewers that, empty in our museums today, raise their drained cups with a useless grace; and yet once, like you, they constituted the fresh sensual pleasures of Venetian banquets, whose final violets and final roses seem to be still floating in the limpid current of the foamy and cloudy glass.

TWO

"How can you prefer Hippolyta to the five others I've just named: why, they're the most undeniably beautiful women in Verona. First of all, her nose is too long and too aquiline."

You can add that her complexion is too fine, that her upper lip is too narrow, and that, by pulling her mouth up too high when she laughs, it creates a very acute angle. Yet I am infinitely affected by her laughter, and the purest profiles leave me cold next to the line of her nose, which you feel is too aquiline, but which I find so exciting and so reminiscent of a bird. Her head, long as it is from her brow to her blond nape, is also slightly birdlike, as are, even more so, her gentle, piercing eyes.

At the theater she often rests her elbows on the railing of her box: her hand, in a white glove, shoots straight up to her chin, which leans on her finger joints. Her perfect body makes her customary white gauzes swell like folded wings. She reminds you of a bird dreaming on a slender and elegant leg. It is also delightful to see her feathery fan throbbing next to her and beating its white wing. Her sons and her nephews all have, like her, aquiline noses, narrow lips, piercing eyes, and overly fine complexions, and I have never managed to meet them without being distressed when recognizing her breed, which probably descends from a goddess and a bird. Through the metamorphosis that now fetters some winged desire to this female shape, I can discern the small royal head of the peacock without the froth or the ocean-blue, ocean-green wave of the peacock's mythological plumage glittering behind the head. She is the epitome of fable blended with the thrill of beauty.

 ## Snobs

ONE

A woman does not mask her love of balls, horse races, even gambling. She states it or simply admits it or boasts about it. But never try to make her say that she loves high society: she would vehemently deny it and blow up properly. It is the only weakness that she carefully conceals, no doubt because it is the only weakness that humbles her vanity. She is willing to depend on playing-cards but not on dukes. She does not feel inferior to anyone simply because she commits a folly; her snobbery, quite the opposite, implies that there are people to whom she is inferior or could become inferior by letting herself relax. Thus we can find a woman who proclaims the utter foolishness of high society yet devotes her mind to it, her finesse, her intelligence, whereas she could instead have written a lovely tale or ingeniously varied her lover's pains and pleasures.

TWO

Clever women are so afraid they will be accused of loving high society that they never mention it by name; when pressed during a conversation, they shift into some paraphrase to avoid uttering the name of this compromising lover. They pounce, if need be, on "Elegance," a name that diverts suspicion and seems at least to pinpoint art rather than vanity as the basis for arranging their lives. Only women who are not yet part of high society or have lost their social standing refer to it by name with the ardor of unsatisfied or abandoned mistresses. Thus, certain young women who are just beginning to ascend and certain old women who are now sliding back enjoy talking about the social standing that others have or, even better, do not have. In fact, while those women derive more pleasure from talking about the standing that others do not have, their talking about the standing that others do have nourishes them more effectively, providing their famished imaginations with more substantial fare. I have known people to thrill, more with delight than envy, at the very thought of a duchess's family connections. In the provinces, it seems, there are female shopkeepers whose brains, like narrow cages, confine desires for social standing that are as ferocious as savage beasts. The mailman brings them *Le Gaulois*. The society page is devoured in the twinkling of an eye. The fidgety provincial women are sated. And for an hour their eyes glow with peace of mind, their pupils dilating with enjoyment and admiration.

THREE: AGAINST A FEMALE SNOB

If you were not part of high society and were told that Élianthe, young, beautiful, rich, loved as she is by friends and suitors, had suddenly broken with them all and was endlessly courting old, ugly, stupid men whom she barely knew, begging for their favors and patiently swallowing their snubs, toiling like a slave to please them, losing her mind over them, regaining it over them, becoming their friend through her attentiveness, their support in case they are poor, their mistress in case they are sensual—if you were told all that, you would wonder: Just what crime has

Élianthe committed, and who are those formidable magistrates whose indulgence she must buy at any price, to whom she sacrifices her friendships, her loves, her freedom of thought, the dignity of her life, her fortune, her time, her most private female aversions? Yet Élianthe has committed no crime. The judges whom she obstinately tries to corrupt barely give her a second thought, and they would let her pure and cheerful life keep flowing tranquilly. But a terrible curse lies upon her: she is a snob.

FOUR: TO A FEMALE SNOB

Your soul is certainly, as Tolstoy says, a dark forest. But its trees are of a particular species; they are family trees. People call you vain? But the universe is not empty for you; it is filled with coats of arms. It is quite a dazzling and symbolic conception of the world. Yet do you not also have your chimeras in the shape and color of the ones we see painted on blazons? Are you not educated? *Le Tout-Paris,* the *Almanach de Gotha, La Société et le High-Life* have taught you the *Bouillet.* In reading the chronicles of the battles won by ancestors, you have found the names of the descendants whom you invite to dinner, and this mnemonic technique has taught you the entire history of France. This lends a certain grandeur to your ambitious dream, to which you have sacrificed your freedom, your hours of pleasure or reflection, your duties, your friendships, and even love. For the faces of your new friends are linked in your imagination to a long series of ancestral portraits. The family trees that you cultivate so meticulously, whose fruit you pick so joyously every year, are deeply rooted in the most ancient French soil. Your dream interlocks the present and the past. The soul of the crusades enlivens some trivial contemporary figures for you, and if you read your guest book so fervently, does not each name allow you to feel an ancient and splendid France awakening, quavering, and almost singing, like a corpse arisen from a slab decorated with armorial bearings?

8 Oranthe

You did not go to bed last night and you still have not washed this morning?

Why proclaim it, Oranthe?

Brilliantly gifted as you are, do you not believe that this sufficiently distinguishes you from the rest of the world, so that you need not cut such a wretched figure?

Your creditors are harassing you, your infidelities are driving your wife to despair, putting on a tuxedo is for you like donning livery, and no one could prevent you from appearing anything but disheveled in society. At dinner you never remove your gloves to show you are not eating, and if you feel jittery at night you have your victoria hitched up and you go for a drive in the Bois de Boulogne.

You can read Lamartine only on a snowy night and listen to Wagner only when burning Chinese cinnamon.

Yet you are an honorable man, rich enough not to incur debts if you do not regard them as crucial to your genius; you are vulnerable enough to suffer from causing your wife a grief that you would consider it bourgeois to spare her; you do not flee social gatherings; you know how to get people to like you; and your wit, for which your long curls are not necessary, would suffice to draw attention. You have a good appetite; you eat well before attending a dinner, where you nevertheless fret and fume about going hungry. It is during your nocturnal drives, an obligation of your eccentricity, that you acquire the only illnesses from which you suffer. You have enough imagination to make snow fall or to burn Chinese cinnamon without the help of winter or an incense burner, and you are literary enough and musical enough to love Lamartine and Wagner in spirit and in reality.

Well then! You have decked out an artist's soul with all the bourgeois prejudices, showing us only their reverse sides without managing to put us off the scent.

9 Against Frankness

It is wise to fear Percy, Laurence, and Augustin equally. Laurence recites poems, Percy gives lectures, Augustin tells the truth. Frank Person: that is Augustin's title, and his profession is True Friend.

Augustin enters a drawing room; I urge you truly: be on your guard and simply do not forget that he is your true friend. Remember that he is never, any more than is Percy or Laurence, received with impunity, and that Augustin will not wait to be asked to tell you some of his truths any more than Laurence will to deliver a monologue or Percy to express his opinion of Verlaine. Augustin lets you neither wait nor interrupt because he is frank for the same reason that Laurence lectures: not for your sake, but for his own pleasure. Granted, your displeasure quickens his pleasure, just as your attention excites Laurence's pleasure. But they could, if necessary, proceed without one or the other. Here we have three shameless rascals, who ought to be refused any encouragement—the feast if not the food of their vice.

Still and all, they have their special audience, which keeps them alive. Indeed, Augustin the truth-teller has a very large following. His audience, led astray by conventional theater psychology and by the absurd maxim, "Spare the rod and spoil the child," refuses to recognize that flattery is sometimes merely an outpouring of affection, and frankness the mud-slinging of a bad mood. Does Augustin practice his wickedness on a friend? In his mind this spectator vaguely compares Roman crudeness with Byzantine hypocrisy, and, his eyes all aglow with the joy of feeling better, rougher, coarser, he proudly exclaims: "He's not the kind who'd treat you with kid gloves. . . . We have to honor him: what a true friend! . . ."

10

A fashionable milieu is one in which each person's opinion is made up of everyone else's opinions. Does each opinion run counter to everyone else's? Then it is a literary milieu.

■

The libertine's demand for virginity is just another form of the eternal tribute that love pays to innocence.

■

After leaving the Xs you call on the Ys, and here the stupidity, the nastiness, the wretched situation of the Xs are laid bare. Filled with admiration for the acumen of the Ys, you blush to think that you originally felt any esteem for the Xs. But when you return to the Xs, they tear the Ys to pieces and more or less in the same way. Going from either home to the other means frequenting both enemy camps. But since neither foe ever hears the other's fusillade, he believes that he alone is armed. Upon realizing that the weaponry is the same and that their strengths or rather their weaknesses are roughly equal, you stop admiring the side that shoots and you despise the side that is shot at. This is the beginning of wisdom. True wisdom would be to break with both sides.

11 Scenario

Honoré is sitting in his room. He stands up and looks at himself in the mirror:

His Tie: You have so often loaded my knot with languor and loosened it dreamily—my expressive and slightly undone knot. You must be in love, my friend, but why are you sad? . . .

His Pen: Yes, why are you sad? For a week now, my master, you have been overworking me, and yet I have thoroughly altered my lifestyle! I, who seemed destined for more glorious tasks, I believe that henceforth I will write only love letters, to judge by this stationery that you have just had made. However, these love letters will be sad, as presaged by the high-strung despair with which you seize me and suddenly put me down. You are in love, my friend, but why are you sad?

Roses, Orchids, Hydrangeas, Maidenhair Ferns, Columbines (all of which fill the room): You have always loved us, but never have you rallied so many of us at once to enchant you with our proud and delicate poses, our eloquent gestures, and the poignant voices of our fragrances. For you we are certainly the very image of the fresh charms of your beloved. You are in love, my friend, but why are you sad? . . .

Books: We were always your prudent advisors, forever questioned, forever unheeded. But while we never caused you to act, we did make you understand; nevertheless you dashed to your doom, but at least you did not struggle in the dark and as if in a nightmare: do not thrust us aside like old and now unwanted tutors. You held us in your childhood hands. Your still pure eyes gaped at us in amazement. If you do not love us for ourselves, then love us for everything we remind you of about yourself, for everything you have been, for everything you could have been, and is not "could have been" almost "have been" while you dreamed about it?

Come listen to our familiar and admonishing voices; we will not tell you why you are in love, but we will tell you why you are sad, and if our child despairs and cries, we will tell him stories, we will lull him as we once did when his mother's voice lent our words its gentle authority before the fire that blazed with all its sparks, with all your hopes and dreams.

Honoré: I am in love with her and I believe I am going to be loved. But my heart tells me that I, who used to be so fickle, I will love her forever, and my good fairy knows that I will be loved for only one month. That is why before entering the paradise of these fleeting joys I have paused at the threshold to dry my eyes.

His Good Fairy: Dear friend, I have come from the heavens to bring you your dispensation; your happiness will depend on you. If, during one month, you play any tricks, thereby running the risk of spoiling the joys you looked forward to at the start of this love, if you disdain the woman you love, if you flirt with other women and pretend indifference, if you miss appointments with her and turn your lips away from the bosom she holds out to you like a sheaf of roses, then your shared and faithful love will be constructed for all eternity on the incorruptible foundation of your patience.

Honoré (jumping for joy): My good fairy, I adore you and I will obey you.

The Small Dresden Clock: Your beloved is late, my hand has already advanced beyond the minute that you have been dreaming about for so long, the minute at which your beloved was due. I fear that my monotonous tick-tock will scan your sensual and melancholy wait for a long time; though I tell time, I understand nothing about life; the sad hours follow the joyous minutes, as indistinguishable for me as bees in a hive. . . .

(The bell rings; a servant goes to open the door.)

The Good Fairy: Remember to obey me and remember that the eternity of your love depends on it.

(The clock ticks feverishly, the fragrances of the roses waft uneasily, and the tormented orchids lean anxiously toward Honoré; one orchid looks wicked. Honoré's inert pen gazes at him, sad that it cannot move. The books do not interrupt their grave murmuring. Everything tells Honoré: Obey the fairy and remember that the eternity of your love depends on that. . . .)

Honoré (without hesitating): Of course I will obey, how can you doubt me?

(The beloved enters; the roses, the orchids, the maidenhair ferns, the pen and the paper, the Dresden clock, and a breathless Honoré all quiver as if in harmony with her.)

Honoré flings himself upon her lips, shouting: "I love you! . . ."

Epilogue: It was as if he had blown out the flame of his beloved's desire. Pretending to be shocked by the impropriety of his action, she fled, and if ever he saw her after that, she would torture him with a severe and indifferent glance. . . .

12 The Fan

Madame, I have painted this fan for you.

May it, as you wish in your retirement, evoke the vain and enchanting figures that peopled your salon, which was so rich with graceful life and is now closed forever.

The chandeliers, whose branches all bear large, pallid flowers, illuminate objets d'art of all eras and all countries. I was thinking about the spirit of our time as my brush led the curious gazes of those chandeliers across the diversity of your knick-knacks. Like them the spirit of our time has contemplated samples of thought or life from all centuries all over the world. It has inordinately widened the circle of its excursions. Out of pleasure, out of boredom, it has varied them as we vary our strolls; and now, deterred from finding not even the destination but just the right path, feeling its strength dwindling and its courage deserting it, the spirit of our time has lain down with its face on the earth to avoid seeing anything, like a brutish beast.

Nevertheless I have painted the rays of your chandeliers delicately; with amorous melancholy these rays have caressed so many things and so many people, and now they are snuffed forever. Despite the small format of this picture, you may recognize the foreground figures, all of whom the impartial artist has highlighted identically, just like your equal sympathies: great lords, beautiful women, and talented men. A bold reconciliation in the eyes of the world, though inadequate and unjust according to reason; yet it turned your society into a small universe that was less divided and more harmonious than that other world, a small world that was full of life and that we will never see again.

I therefore would not want my fan to be viewed by an indifferent person, who has never frequented salons like yours and who would be astonished to see "politesse" unite dukes without arrogance and novelists without pretentiousness. Nor might he, that stranger, comprehend the vices of this rapprochement, which, if excessive, will soon facilitate only one exchange: that of ridiculous things. He would, no doubt, find a pessimistic realism in the spectacle of the bergère on the right, where a great author, to all appearances a snob, is listening to a great lord, who, dipping into a book, seems to be holding forth about a poem, and whose expression, if I have managed to make it foolish enough, shows quite well that he understands nothing.

Near the fireplace you will recognize C.

He is uncorking a scent bottle and explaining to the woman next to him that he has concentrated the most pungent and most exotic perfumes in this blend.

B., despairing of outdoing him, and thinking that the surest way to be ahead of fashion is to be hopelessly out of fashion, is sniffing some cheap violets and glaring scornfully at C.

As for you yourself, have you not gone on one of those artificial returns to nature? Had those details not been too minuscule to remain distinct, I would have depicted, in some obscure nook of your music library at that time, your now abandoned Wagner operas, your now discarded symphonies by Franck and d'Indy and, on your piano, several open scores by Haydn, Handel, or Palestrina.

I did not shy away from depicting you on the pink sofa. T. is seated next to you. He is describing his new bedroom, which he artfully smeared with tar in order to suggest the sensations of an ocean voyage, and he is disclosing all the quintessences of his wardrobe and his furnishings.

Your disdainful smile reveals that you set no store by this feeble imagination, for which a bare chamber does not suffice for conjuring up all the visions of the universe and which conceives of art and beauty in such pitifully material terms.

Your most delightful friends are present. Would they ever forgive me if you showed them the fan? I cannot say. The most unusually beautiful woman, standing out like a living Whistler before our enchanted eyes, would recognize and admire herself only in a portrait by Bouguereau. Women incarnate beauty without understanding it.

Your friends may say: "We simply love a beauty that is not yours. Why should it be beauty any less than yours?"

Let them at least allow me to say: "So few women comprehend their own aesthetics. There are Botticelli madonnas who, but for fashion, would find this painter clumsy and untalented."

Please accept this fan with indulgence. If one of the ghosts that have alighted here after flitting through my memory made you weep long ago, while it was still partaking of life, then recognize that ghost without bitterness and remember that it is a mere shadow and that it will never make you suffer again. I could quite innocently capture these ghosts on the frail paper to which your hand will lend wings, for those ghosts are too unreal and too flimsy to cause any harm. . . .

No more so, perhaps, than in the days when you invited them to stave off death for a few hours and live the vain life of phantoms, in the factitious joy of your salon, under the chandeliers, whose branches were covered with large, pallid flowers.

13 Olivian

Why do people see you, Olivian, heading to the Commedia every evening? Don't your friends have more acumen than Pantalone, Scaramuccio, or Pasquarello? And would it not be more agreeable to have supper with your friends? But you could do even better. If the theater is the refuge of the conversationalist whose friend is mute and whose mistress is insipid, then conversation, even the most exquisite, is the pleasure of men without imagination. It is a waste of time, Olivian, trying to tell you that which need not be shown an intelligent man by candlelight, for he sees it while chatting. The voice of the soul and of the imagination is the only voice that makes the soul and the imagination resonate thoroughly and happily; and had you spent a bit of the time you have killed to please others and had you made that bit come alive, had you nourished it by reading and reflecting at your hearth during winter and in your park during summer, you would be nurturing the rich memory of deeper and fuller hours. Have the courage to take up the rake and the pickax. Someday you will delight in smelling a sweet fragrance drifting up from your memory as if from a gardener's brimming wheelbarrow.

Why do you travel so much? The stagecoaches transport you very slowly to where your dreams would carry you so swiftly. To reach the seashore all you need do is close your eyes. Let people who have only physical eyes move their entire households and settle in Puzzuoli or Naples. You say you want to complete a book there? Where could you work better than in the city? Inside its walls you can have the grandest sceneries that you like roll by; here you will more easily avoid the Princess di Bergamo's luncheons than in Puzzuoli and you will be less tempted to go on idle strolls. Why, above all, are you so bent on enjoying the present and weeping because you fail to do so? As a man with imagination you can enjoy only in regret or in anticipation—that is, in the past or in the future.

That is why, Olivian, you are dissatisfied with your mistress, your summer holidays, and yourself. As for the cause of these ills, you may have already pinpointed it; but then why relish them instead of trying to cure them? The fact is: you are truly miserable, Olivian. You are not yet a man, and you are already a man of letters.

14 Characters in the Commedia of High Society

Just as Scaramuccio is always a braggart in the commedia dell'arte, Arlecchino always a bumpkin, Pasquino's conduct is sheer intrigue and Pantalone's sheer avarice and credulity, so too society has decreed that Guido is witty but perfidious and would not hesitate to sacrifice a friend to a bon mot; that Girolamo hoards a treasure trove of sensitivity behind a gruff frankness; that Castruccio, whose vices should be stigmatized, is the most loyal of friends and the most thoughtful of sons; that Iago, despite the ten fine books he has published, remains an amateur, whereas a few bad newspaper articles have anointed Ercole a writer; that Cesare must have ties with the police as a reporter or a spy. Cardenio is a snob, and Pippo is nothing but a fraud despite his protestations of friendship. As for Fortunata, it has been settled definitively: she is a good person. The rotundity of her embonpoint is enough of a warranty for her benevolence: how could such a fat lady be a wicked person?

Furthermore, each of these individuals, so different by nature from the definitive character picked out for him by society from its storehouse of costumes and characters, deviates from that character all the more as the *a priori* conception of his qualities creates a sort of impunity for him by opening a large credit line for his opposite defects. His immutable persona as a loyal friend in general allows Castruccio to betray each of his friends in particular. The friend alone suffers for it: "What a scoundrel he must be if he was dropped by Castruccio, that loyal friend!"

Fortunata can disgorge torrents of backbiting. Who would be so demented as to look for their source in the folds of her bodice, whose hazy amplitude can hide anything? Girolamo can fearlessly practice flattery, to which his habitual frankness lends the charm of surprise. His gruffness to a friend can be ferocious, for it is understood that Girolamo is brutalizing him for his friend's own good. If Cesare asks me about my health, it is because he plans to report on it to the doge. He has not asked me: how cleverly he hides his cards! Guido comes up to me; he compliments me on how fine I look. "No one is as witty as Guido," those present exclaim in chorus, "but he is really too malicious!"

In their true character, Castruccio, Guido, Cardenio, Ercole, Pippo, Cesare, and Fortunata may differ from the types that they irrevocably embody in the sagacious eyes of society; but this divergence holds no danger for them, because society refuses to see it. Still, it does not last forever. Whatever Girolamo may do, he is a benevolent curmudgeon. Whatever Fortunata may say, she is a good person. The absurd, crushing, and immutable persistence of their types, from which they can endlessly depart without disrupting their serene entrenchment, eventually imposes itself, with an increasing gravitational pull, on these unoriginal people with their incoherent conduct; and ultimately they are fascinated by this sole identity, which remains inflexible amid all their universal variations.

Girolamo, by telling his friend "a few home truths," is thankful to him for serving as his stooge, enabling Girolamo "to rake him over the coals for his own good" and thereby play an honorable, almost glamorous, and now quasi-sincere role. He seasons the vehemence of his diatribes with a quite indulgent pity that is natural toward an inferior who accentuates Girolamo's glory; Girolamo feels genuine gratitude toward him and, in the end, the cordiality which high society has attributed to him for such a long time that he finally holds on to it.

While expanding the sphere of her own personality, Fortunata's embonpoint, growing without blighting her mind or altering her beauty, slightly diminishes her interest in others, and she feels a softening of her acrimony, which was all that prevented her from worthily carrying out the venerable and charming functions that the world had delegated to her. The spirit of the words "benevolence," "goodness," and "rotundity," endlessly uttered in front of her and behind her back, has gradually saturated her speech, which is now habitually laudatory and on which her vast shape confers something like a more pleasing authority. She has the vague and deep sensation of exercising an immense and peaceable magistrature. At times, she seems to overflow her own individuality, as if she were the stormy yet docile plenary council of benevolent judges, an assembly over which she presides and whose approval stirs her in the distance. . . .

During conversations at soirées, each person, untroubled by the contradictory behavior of these figures and heedless of their gradual adaptation to the imposed types, neatly files every figure away with his actions in the quite suitable and carefully defined pigeonhole of his ideal character; and at these moments each person feels with deeply emotional satisfaction that the level of conversation is incontestably rising. Granted, we soon interrupt this labor and avoid dwelling on it, so that people unaccustomed to abstract thinking will not doze off (we are men of the world, after all). Then, after stigmatizing one person's snobbery, another's malevolence, and a third man's libertinism or abusiveness, the guests disperse, convinced that they have paid their generous tribute to modesty, charity, and benevolence; and so, with no remorse, with a clear conscience that has just shown its mettle, each person goes off to indulge in his elegant and multiple vices.

■

If these reflections, inspired by Bergamo's high society, were applied to any other, they would lose their validity. When Arlecchino left the Bergamo stage for the French stage, the bumpkin became a wit. That is why a few societies regard Liduvina as outstanding and Girolamo as clever. We must also add that at times a man may appear for whom society has no ready-made character, or at least no available character, because it is being used by someone else. At first society gives him characters that do not suit him. If he is truly original, and no character is the right size, then society, unable to try to understand him and lacking a character with a proper fit, will simply ostracize him; unless he can gracefully play juvenile leads, who are always in short supply.

SOCIAL AMBITIONS AND MUSICAL TASTES OF BOUVARD AND PÉCUCHET*

1 Social Ambitions

"Now that we have positions," said Bouvard, "why shouldn't we live a life of high society?"

Pécuchet could not have agreed with him more; but they would have to shine, and to do so they would have to study the subjects dealt with in society.

Contemporary literature is of prime importance.

They subscribed to the various journals that disseminate it; they read them aloud and attempted to write reviews, whereby, mindful of their goal, they aimed chiefly at an ease and lightness of style.

Bouvard objected that the style of reviews, even if playful, is not suitable in high society. And they began conversing about their readings in the manner of men of the world.

Bouvard would lean against the mantelpiece and, handling them cautiously to avoid soiling them, he would toy with a pair of light-colored gloves that were brought out specifically for the occasion, and he would address Pécuchet as "Madame" or "General" to complete the illusion.

---

*Needless to say, the opinions ascribed here to Flaubert's two famous characters are by no means those of the author.

Often, however, they would get no further; or else, if one of them would gush on about an author, the other would try in vain to stop him. Beyond that, they pooh-poohed everything. Leconte de Lisle was too impassive, Verlaine too sensitive. They dreamed about a happy medium but never found one.

"Why does Loti keep striking the same note?"

"His novels are all written in the same key."

"His lyre has only one string," Bouvard concluded.

"But André Laurie is no more satisfying; he takes us somewhere else every year, confusing literature with geography. Only his style is worth something. As for Henri de Regné, he's either a fraud or a lunatic; there's no other alternative."

"Get around that, my good man," said Bouvard, "and you'll help contemporary literature out of an awful bottleneck."

"Why rein them in?" said Pécuchet, an indulgent king. "Those colts may be blooded. Loosen their reins, let them have their way; our sole worry is that once they spurt off, they may gallop beyond the finish line. But immoderateness per se is proof of a rich nature.

"Meanwhile the barriers will be smashed," Pécuchet cried out; hot and bothered, he filled the empty room with his negative retorts: "Anyway, you can claim all you like that these uneven lines are poetry—I refuse to see them as anything but prose, and meaningless prose at that!"

Mallarmé is equally untalented, but he is a brilliant talker. What a pity that such a gifted man should lose his mind the instant he picks up his pen. A bizarre illness that struck them as inexplicable. Maeterlinck frightens us, but only with material devices that are unworthy of the theater; art inflames us like a crime—it's horrible! Besides, his syntax is dreadful.

They then applied a witty critique to his syntax, parodying his dialogue style in the form of a conjugation:

I said that the woman had come in.
You said that the woman had come in.
He said that the woman had come in.
Why did someone say that the woman had come in?

Pécuchet wanted to submit this piece to the *Revue des Deux Mondes;* but it would be wiser, in Bouvard's opinion, to save it until it could be recited in a fashionable salon. They would instantly be classified according to their talent. They could easily send the piece to a journal later on. And when the earliest private admirers of this flash of wit read it in print, they would be retrospectively flattered to have been the first to enjoy it.

Lemaitre, for all his cleverness, struck them as scatterbrained, irreverent, sometimes pedantic and sometimes bourgeois; he retracted too often. Above all, his style was slipshod; but he should be forgiven since he had to write extempore under the pressure of regular and so frequent deadlines. As for Anatole France, he wrote well but thought poorly, unlike Bourget, who was profound but whose style was hopeless. Bouvard and Pécuchet greatly deplored the dearth of a complete talent.

"Yet it can't be very difficult," Bouvard thought, "to express one's ideas clearly. Clarity is not enough, though; you need grace (allied with strength), vivacity, nobility, and logic." Bouvard then added irony. According to Pécuchet irony was not indispensable; it was often tiring and it baffled the reader without benefiting him. In short, all writers were bad. The fault, according to Bouvard, lay with the excessive pursuit of originality; according to Pécuchet, with the decline of mores.

"Let us have the courage to hide our conclusions from the fashionable world: otherwise we would be viewed as nitpickers, we would frighten everyone, and they would all dislike us. Let us be reassuring rather than unnerving. Our originality would do us enough harm as it is. We should even conceal it. In society we can also not talk about literature."

But other things are important there.

"How do we greet people? With a deep bow or simply a nod, slowly or quickly, just as we are or bringing our heels together, walking over or standing still, pulling in the small of the back or transforming it into a pivot? Should the hands drop alongside the body, should they hold your hat, should they be gloved? Should the face remain earnest or should you smile for the length of the greeting? And how do you immediately recover your gravity once the greeting is done?"

Introductions were also difficult.

With whose name should you start? Should you gesture toward the person you are naming or should you merely nod at him or should you remain motionless with an air of indifference? Should you greet an old man and a young man in the same way, a locksmith and a prince, an actor and an academician? The affirmative answer satisfied Pécuchet's egalitarian ideas, but shocked Bouvard's common sense.

And what about correct titles?

You said "monsieur" to a baron, a viscount, or a count; however, "Good day, monsieur le marquis" sounded groveling and "Good day, marquis" too free and easy—given their age. They would resign themselves to saying "prince" and "monsieur le duc," even though they found the latter usage revolting. When it came to the highnesses, they floundered. Bouvard, gratified by the thought of his future connections, imagined a thousand sentences in which this appellation would appear in all its forms; he accompanied it with a faint and blushing smile, inclining his head slightly and hopping about. But Pécuchet declared that he would lose the thread, get more and more confused, or else laugh in the prince's face. In short, to avoid embarrassment, they would steer clear of the Faubourg Saint-Germain, that bastion of aristocracy. However, the Faubourg seeps in everywhere and looks like a compact and isolated whole purely from a distance! . . .

Besides, titles are respected even more in the world of high finance, and as for the foreign adventurers, their titles are legion. But according to Pécuchet, one should be intransigent with pseudo-noblemen and make sure not to address them with a "de" even on envelopes or when speaking to their domestics. Bouvard, more skeptical, saw this as a more recent mania that was nevertheless as respectable as that of the ancient lords. Furthermore, according to Bouvard and Pécuchet, the nobility had stopped existing when it had lost its privileges. Its members were clerical, backward, read nothing, did nothing, and were as pleasure-seeking as the bourgeoisie; Bouvard and Pécuchet found it absurd to respect them. Frequenting them was possible only because it did not exclude contempt.

Bouvard declared that in order to know where they would socialize, toward which suburbs they would venture once a year, where their habits and their vices could be found, they would first have to draw up an exact plan of Parisian society. The plan, said Bouvard, would include Faubourg Saint-Germain, financiers, foreign adventurers, Protestant society, the world of art and theater, the official world, and the learned world. The Faubourg Saint-Germain, in Pécuchet's opinion, concealed the libertinage of the Old Regime under the guise of rigidity. Every nobleman had mistresses, plus a sister who was a nun, and he conspired with the clergy. They were brave, debt-ridden; they ruined and scourged usurers and they were inevitably the champions of honor. They reigned by dint of elegance, invented preposterous fashions, were exemplary sons, gracious to commoners and harsh toward bankers. Always clutching a sword or with a woman in pillion, they dreamed of restoring the monarchy, were terribly idle, but not haughty with decent people, sent traitors packing, insulted cowards, and with a certain air of chivalry they merited our unshakable affection.

On the other hand, the eminent and sullen world of finance inspires respect but also aversion. The financier remains careworn even at the wildest ball. One of his numberless clerks keeps coming to report the latest news from the stock exchange even at four in the morning; the financier conceals his most successful coups and his most horrible disasters from his wife. You never know whether he is a mogul or a swindler: he switches to and fro without warning; and despite his immense fortune, he ruthlessly evicts a poor tenant for being in arrears with his rent and refuses to grant him an extension unless he wants to use the tenant as a spy or sleep with his daughter. Moreover, the financier is always in his carriage, dresses without taste, and habitually wears a pince-nez.

Nor did Bouvard and Pécuchet feel any keener love for Protestant society: it is cold, starchy, gives solely to its own poor, and is made up exclusively of pastors. Their temples look too much like their homes, and a home is as dreary as a temple. There is always a pastor for lunch; the servants admonish their employers with biblical verses; Protestants fear merriment too deeply not to have something to hide; and when conversing with Catholics, they reveal their undying grudge about the Revocation of the Edict of Nantes and the Massacre of Saint Bartholomew.

The art world, equally homogeneous, is quite different; every artist is a humbug, estranged from his family, never wears a top hat, and speaks a special language. He spends his life outsmarting bailiffs who try to dispossess him and finding grotesque disguises for masked balls. Nevertheless artists constantly produce masterpieces, and for most of them their overindulgence in wine and women is the sine qua non of their inspiration if not their genius; they sleep all day, go out all night, work God knows when, and, with their heads always flung back, their limp scarves fluttering in the wind, they perpetually roll cigarettes.

The theater world is barely distinct from the art world: there is no family life on any level; theater people are eccentric and inexhaustibly generous. Actors, while vain and jealous, help their fellow players endlessly, applaud their successes, adopt the children of consumptive or down-on-their-luck actresses, and are precious in society, although, being uneducated, they are often sanctimonious and always superstitious. Actors at subsidized theaters are in a class of their own; entirely worthy of our admiration, they would deserve a more honorable place at the table than a general or a prince; they nurture feelings expressed in the masterpieces they perform on our great stages. Their memory is prodigious and their bearing perfect.

As for the Jews, Bouvard and Pécuchet, though unwilling to banish them (for one must be liberal), admitted that they hated being with them; in their younger days Jews had all sold opera glasses in Germany; in Paris (with a piety that, incidentally, both men, as impartial observers, felt was all to their credit) the Jews zealously maintained special practices, an unintelligible vocabulary, and butchers of their own race. All Jews had hooked noses, exceptional intelligence, and vile souls devoted purely to self-interest; their women, on the contrary, were beautiful, a bit flabby, but capable of the loftiest sentiments. How many Catholics ought to emulate them! But why were their fortunes always incalculable and concealed? Furthermore they formed a kind of vast secret society, like the Jesuits and the Freemasons. They had—no one knew where—inexhaustible treasures in the service of some enemies or other, with a dreadful and mysterious goal.

2 Musical Tastes

Already disgusted with bicycles and paintings, Bouvard and Pécuchet now seriously took up music. But, although the everlasting champion of tradition and order, Pécuchet let himself be hailed as the utmost enthusiast of off-color songs and *Le Domino noir;* on the other hand, Bouvard, a revolutionary if ever there was one, turned out to be—it must be admitted— a resolute Wagnerian. Truth to tell, he had never laid eyes on a single score by the "Berlin brawler" (as he was cruelly nicknamed by Pécuchet, always patriotic and uninformed); after all, one cannot hear Wagner's scores in France, where the Conservatory is dying of its own routine, between Colonne, who babbles, and Lamoureux, who spells out everything; nor were those scores played in Munich, which did not maintain tradition, or in Bayreuth, which had been unendurably contaminated by snobs. It was nonsense trying to play a Wagnerian score on the piano: the theatrical illusion was necessary, as were the lowering of the orchestra and the darkness of the auditorium. Nevertheless, the prelude to *Parsifal,* ready to dumbfound visitors, was perpetually open on the music stand of Bouvard's piano, between the photographs of César Franck's penholder and Botticelli's *Primavera.*

The "Song of Spring" had been carefully torn out from the *Valkyrie.* On the first page of the roster of Wagner's operas, *Lohengrin* and *Tannhäuser* had been indignantly crossed out by a

red pencil. Of the early operas *Rienzi* alone prevailed. Disavow-
ing *Rienzi* had become banal; it was time—Bouvard keenly
sensed—to establish the opposite view. Gounod made him
laugh and Verdi shout. Less, assuredly, than Erik Satie—who
could disagree? Beethoven, however, struck Bouvard as mo-
mentous, like a Messiah. Bouvard himself, without stooping,
could salute Bach as a forerunner. Saint-Saëns lacks substance
and Massenet form, he endlessly repeated to Pécuchet, in whose
eyes, quite the contrary, Saint-Saëns had nothing but substance
and Massenet nothing but form.

"That is why one of them instructs us and the other charms
us, but without elevating us," Pécuchet insisted.

For Bouvard both composers were equally despicable.
Massenet had a few ideas, but they were coarse, and besides,
ideas had had their day. Saint-Saëns revealed some craftsman-
ship, but it was old-fashioned. Uninstructed about Gaston
Lemaire, but playing with contrasts in their lessons, they elo-
quently pitted Chausson and Cécile Chaminade against one another. Moreover, Pécuchet and, though it was repugnant to his
aesthetics, Bouvard himself gallantly yielded to Madame Chaminade the first place among composers of the day, for every
Frenchman is chivalrous and always lets women go first.

It was the democrat in Bouvard even more than the musician who proscribed the music of Charles Levadé; was it not an
obstruction of progress to linger over Madame de Girardin's
poems in the age of steam, universal suffrage, and the bicycle?
Furthermore, as an advocate for the theory of art for art's sake,
for playing without nuances and singing without modulation,
Bouvard declared that he could not stand hearing Levadé sing:
he was too much the musketeer, the jokester, with the facile elegance of an antiquated sentimentalism.

However, the topic of their liveliest debates was Reynaldo
Hahn. While his close friendship with Massenet, endlessly elic-
iting Bouvard's cruel sarcasm, pitilessly marked Hahn as the victim of Pécuchet's passionate predilections, Hahn had the knack
of exasperating Pécuchet by his reverence for Verlaine, an admiration shared, incidentally, by Bouvard. "Set Jacques Nor-

mand to music, Sully Prudhomme, the Viscount of Borrelli. There is, thank goodness, no shortage of poets in the land of the troubadours," he added patriotically. And, divided between the Teutonic sonority of Hahn's last name and the southern ending of Reynaldo, his first name, and preferring to execute him out of hatred for Wagner rather than absolving him on behalf of Verdi, Pécuchet, turning to Bouvard, rigorously concluded:

"Despite the efforts of all your fine gentlemen, our beautiful land of France is a land of clarity, and French music will be clear or it will not be," Pécuchet stated, pounding on the table for emphasis.

"A plague on your eccentricities from across the Channel and on your mists from across the Rhine—do not always look beyond the Vosges," he added, his glare bristling with hints, "unless you are defending our fatherland. I doubt whether the *Valkyrie* can be liked even in Germany. . . . But for French ears it will always be the most hellish of tortures—and the most cacophonous!—plus the most humiliating for our national pride. Moreover, doesn't this opera combine the most atrocious dissonance with the most revolting incest? Your music, sir, is full of monsters, and all one can do is keep inventing. In nature herself—the mother of simplicity, after all—you like only the horrible. Doesn't Monsieur Delafosse write melodies on bats, so that the composer's aberration will compromise his old reputation as a pianist? Why didn't he choose some nice bird? Melodies on sparrows would at least be quite Parisian; the swallow has lightness and grace, and the lark is so eminently French that Caesar, they say, placed roasted larks on the helmets of his soldiers. But bats!!! The Frenchman, ever thirsty for openness and clarity, will always detest this sinister animal. Let it pass in Monsieur Montesquiou's verses—as the fantasy of a blasé aristocrat, which we can allow him in a pinch. But in music! What's next—a *Requiem for Kangaroos?* . . ." This good joke brightened Bouvard up. "Admit that I've made you laugh," said Pécuchet (with no reprehensible smugness, for an awareness of its merit is permissible in a good mind). "Let's shake, you're disarmed!"

The Melancholy Summer
of Madame de Breyves

Ariadne, my sister, you, wounded by
   love,
You died on the shores where you had
   been abandoned.

—Racine: *Phaedra*, Act I, Scene 3

1

That evening, Françoise de Breyves wavered for a long time between Princess Élisabeth d'A.'s party, the Opera, and the Livrays' play.

At the home where she had just dined with friends, they had left the table over an hour ago. She had to make up her mind.

Her friend Geneviève, who was to drive back with her, was in favor of the princess's soirée, whereas, without quite knowing why, Madame de Breyves would have preferred either of the two other choices, or even a third: to go home to bed. Her carriage was announced. She was still undecided.

"Honestly," said Geneviève, "this isn't nice of you. I understand that Rezké will be singing, and I'd like to hear him. You act as if you'd suffer serious consequences by going to Élisabeth's soirée. First of all, I have to tell you that you haven't been to a single one of her grand soirées this year, and considering you're friends, that's not very nice of you."

Since her husband had died four years ago, leaving her a widow at twenty, Françoise had done almost nothing without Geneviève and she liked pleasing her. She did not resist her entreaties much longer, and, after bidding good night to the host and hostess and to the other guests, who were all devastated at having enjoyed so little of one of the most sought-after women in Paris, Françoise told her lackey:

"To Princess d'A."

2

The princess's soirée was very boring. At one point Madame de Breyves asked Geneviève:

"Who is that young man who escorted you to the buffet?"

"That's Monsieur de Laléande, whom, incidentally, I don't know at all. Would you like me to introduce him to you? He asked me to, but I was evasive, because he's very unimportant and boring, and since he finds you very pretty, you won't be able to get rid of him."

"Then let's not!" said Françoise. "Anyway, he's a bit homely and vulgar, despite his rather beautiful eyes."

"You're right," said Geneviève. "And besides, you'll be running into him often, so knowing him might be awkward for you."

Then she humorously added:

"Of course, if you want a more intimate relationship with him, you're passing up a wonderful opportunity."

"Yes, a wonderful opportunity," said Françoise, her mind already elsewhere.

"Still," said Geneviève, no doubt filled with remorse for being such a disloyal go-between and pointlessly depriving this young man of a pleasure, "it's one of the last soirées of the season, an introduction wouldn't carry much weight, and it might be a nice thing to do."

"Fine then, if he comes back this way."

He did not come back. He was across from them, at the opposite end of the drawing room.

"We have to leave," Geneviève soon said.

"One more minute," said Françoise.

And as a caprice, especially out of a desire to flirt with this young man, who was bound to find her very lovely, she gave him a lingering look, then averted her eyes, then gazed at him again. She tried to make her eyes seem tender; she did not know why, for no reason, for pleasure, the pleasure of charity, of a little vanity, and also gratuity, the pleasure of carving your name into a tree trunk for a passerby whom you will never see, the pleasure of throwing a bottle into the ocean. Time flowed by, it was getting late; Monsieur de Laléande headed toward the door, which remained open after he passed through, so that Madame de Breyves could spot him holding out his ticket at the far end of the cloakroom.

"It's time we left, you're right," she told Geneviève.

They rose. But as luck would have it, a friend needed to say something to Geneviève, who therefore left Françoise alone in the cloakroom. The only other person there was Monsieur de Laléande, who could not find his cane. Françoise, amused, gave him a final look. He came very near her, his elbow slightly grazing hers, and, when closest to her, with radiant eyes, and still appearing to be searching, he said:

"Come to my home, 5 Rue Royale."

She had hardly foreseen this, and Monsieur de Laléande was now so absorbed in hunting for his cane that afterwards Françoise never knew for certain whether it had not been a hallucination. Above all, she was very frightened, and since Prince d'A. chanced to come along at that moment, she called him over: she wished to make an appointment with him for an outing tomorrow and she talked volubly. During that conversation Monsieur de Laléande left. Geneviève reappeared an instant later, and the two women departed. Madame de Breyves told her friend nothing; she was still shocked and flattered, yet basically very indifferent. Two days after that, when she happened to recall the incident, she began to doubt that Monsieur de Laléande had really spoken those words. She tried but was unable to remember fully; she believed she had heard them as if in a dream and she told herself that the elbow movement had been an accidental blunder. Then she no longer thought spontaneously about Monsieur de Laléande, and when she happened to hear his name mentioned, she swiftly imagined his face and forgot all about the quasi-hallu-cination in the cloakroom.

She saw him again at the last soirée of the season (toward the end of June), but did not dare ask to meet him; and yet, though finding him almost ugly and knowing he was not intel-ligent, she would have liked to make his acquaintance. She went over to Geneviève and said:

"Why don't you present Monsieur de Laléande after all. I don't like being impolite. But don't say I suggested it. That will keep it casual."

"Later, if we see him. He's not here at the moment."

"Well, then look for him."

"He may have left."

"Oh no," Françoise blurted out, "he can't have left, it's too early. Oh my! Already midnight. Come on, dear Geneviève, it's not all that difficult. The other evening it was you who wanted it. Please, it's important to me."

Geneviève looked at her, a bit astonished, and went search-ing for Monsieur de Laléande; he was gone.

"You see I was right," said Geneviève, returning to Françoise.

"I'm bored out of my mind," said Françoise. "I've got a headache. Please, let's leave immediately."

3

Françoise no longer missed a single performance at the Opera; with vague hopes she accepted all the dinners to which she was invited. Two weeks wore by; she had not run into Monsieur de Laléande again and at night she often awoke, trying to hit on ways of finding him. Though repeating to herself that he was boring and not handsome, she was more preoccupied with him than with all the wittiest and most charming men. With the season ended, there would be no opportunity to see him again; she was determined to create an opportunity and she cast about for a possibility.

One evening she said to Geneviève:

"Didn't you tell me you knew a man named Laléande?"

"Jacques de Laléande? Yes and no. He was introduced to me, but he's never left me a card, and we're not in any communication with each other."

"Let me tell you, I'm a bit interested, very interested, for reasons that don't concern me and that I probably won't be able to tell you for another month" (by then she and he would have worked out a lie to avoid exposure, and the thought of sharing a secret with him alone gave her a sweet thrill). "I'm interested in making his acquaintance and meeting with him. Please try to find a way, since the season is over, and I won't be able to have him introduced to me."

The practices of close friendship, so purifying when they are sincere, sheltered Geneviève as well as Françoise from the stupid curiosity in which most people in high society take shameful enjoyment. Thus, devoting herself with all her heart and without, for even a moment, intending or desiring to question her friend, much less thinking of doing so, Geneviève searched and was angry only because she came up with nothing.

"It's unfortunate that Madame d'A. has left town. There's still Monsieur de Grumello, of course, but actually that won't get us anywhere—what can we say to him? Wait! I've got an idea! Monsieur de Laléande plays the cello quite badly, but that doesn't matter. Monsieur de Grumello admires him, and besides, he's so dim-witted and he'll be so happy to do you a favor. The thing is, you've always avoided him, and you don't like dropping people after making use of their services, but you won't want to be obligated to invite him next season."

However, Françoise, flushed with joy, exclaimed:

"Why, it's all the same to me, I'll invite all the adventurers in Paris if I must. Oh! Do it quickly, my dear Geneviève—how sweet you are!"

And Geneviève wrote:

Monsieur,

You know how I seek all opportunities to bring pleasure to my friend Madame de Breyves, whom you have, no doubt, already encountered. When we have talked about the cello, she has on several occasions expressed her regret at never having heard Monsieur de Laléande, who is such a good friend of yours. Would you care to have him play for her and for me? Now that the season is over, it will not be too great an imposition on you and it will be extremely generous on your part.

With all my best wishes,

Alériouvre Buivres

"Deliver this letter immediately to Monsieur de Grumello," Françoise told a servant. "Don't wait for an answer, but make sure you hand it to him personally."

The next day Geneviève sent Madame de Breyves Monsieur de Grumello's reply:

Madame,

I would have been more delighted than you can suppose to carry out your wishes and those of Madame de Breyves, whom I know slightly and for whom I feel the keenest and most respectful devotion. I am therefore dreadfully sorry to inform you that, by an unfortunate fluke, Monsieur de Laléande departed just two days ago for Biarritz, where he plans, alas, to spend several months.

Very truly yours, etc.

Grumello

Françoise, deathly white, dashed to her room to lock herself in. She barely made it. Sobs were already shattering on her lips, tears were streaming. Fully engrossed, until now, in picturing romantic ways of seeing him and getting to know him and certain she would carry them out as soon as she wished, she had been living on that yearning and that hope, without, perhaps, realizing it. But this desire had implanted itself into her by sending out a thousand imperceptible roots, which had plunged into all her most unconscious minutes of happiness or melancholy, filling them with a new sap without her knowing where it came from. And now this desire had been ripped out and tossed away as impossible. She felt lacerated, suffering horribly in her entire self, which had been suddenly uprooted; and from the depths of her sorrow through the abruptly exposed lies of her hope, she saw the reality of her love.

4

Day by day Françoise withdrew further and further from all her pleasures, and a heart haunted by a jealous grief that never left her for a moment was the only thing she could offer her most intense delights, the very ones she savored in her bonds with her mother and Geneviève or in her musical hours, her hours of reading, and her outings. Infinite was the pain caused by the impossibility of her going to Biarritz and, even had it been possible, by her absolute determination not to let a rash step compromise all the prestige she might have in the eyes of Monsieur de Laléande. A poor little victim of torture without knowing why, she was frightened at the thought that this illness could drag on for months until a remedy was found for a condition that would not let her sleep peacefully or dream freely. She was also worried about not knowing whether he might pass through Paris, soon perhaps, without her finding out. And emboldened by the fear of again letting happiness slip by so closely, she sent a domestic to question Monsieur de Laléande's concierge. The concierge knew nothing. And realizing that no sail of hope would henceforth emerge on the horizon of this sea of grief, which stretched ad infinitum and beyond which there seemed to be nothing but the end of the earth, Françoise sensed she was going to do insane things, but she did not know what, perhaps write to him; and so she became her own physician: to calm down a bit she took the liberty of trying to have him learn that she had wanted to see him; she therefore wrote Monsieur de Grumello:

Monsieur,

Madame de Buivres has told me about your generous idea. How grateful and deeply moved I am! But something worries me. Does Monsieur de Laléande consider me indiscreet? If you do not know, please ask him and get back to me once you know the full truth. I am very curious, and you will be doing me a great favor. Thank you again, Monsieur.

With my very best wishes,

Voragynes Breyves

One hour later a servant brought her this letter:

Madame,

Do not worry, Monsieur de Laléande has not learned that you wished to hear him play. I asked him on which days he could come and perform in my home but I did not tell him for whom. He replied from Biarritz that he would not come back before the month of January. And please do not thank me. My greatest pleasure would be to give you a little pleasure. . . .

Grumello

There was nothing more to do. She did nothing more, she grew sadder and sadder, and she felt remorse at being sad, at saddening her mother. She spent a few days in the country, then went to Trouville. There she heard some people talking about Monsieur de Laléande's social ambitions, and when a prince, vying for her favor, asked her, "What can I do to please you?", she almost chuckled when imagining how astonished he would be at her sincere response; and she gathered, in order to savor it, all the intoxicating bitterness there was in the irony of that contrast between all the great and difficult things that people had always done to please her and this so easy and so impossible little thing that would have restored her peace of mind, her health, her happiness, and the happiness of her loved ones.

She had a bit of solace only when among her domestics, who admired her immensely and, feeling her misery, served her without venturing to speak. Their respectful and mournful silence spoke to her about Monsieur de Laléande. She reveled in their silence and had them serve lunch very slowly in order to delay the moment when her friends would come, when she would have to stifle her emotions. She wanted to retain the bittersweet taste of all the sadness surrounding her because of him. She would have wanted to see more people dominated by him, to ease her pain by feeling that what occupied so much of her heart was taking up a little space around her; she would have liked to have energetic beasts wasting away with her affliction. For moments at a time she desperately yearned to write to him, have someone else write to him, bring shame upon herself, "nothing mattered to her."

But precisely for the sake of her love, it was better to pre-serve her social standing, which could someday give her greater authority over him, if that day ever came. And if a brief intimate relationship with him broke the spell he had cast over her (she did not want to, she could not, believe it, even imagine it for an instant; but her more astute mind per-ceived that cruel fate through the blindness of her heart), she would remain without any support in the world. And if some other love came her way, she would lack the resources that she at least now possessed, the power that, at their return to Paris, would make it so easy for her to have an intimate rela-tionship with Monsieur de Laléande.

Trying to step back from her own feelings and examine them like an object under investigation, she told herself: "I know he's mediocre and I've always thought so. That's my opinion of him; it hasn't varied. My heart may be confused now, but it can't change my mind. It's only a trifle, and this trifle is what I live for. I live for Jacques de Laléande!"

But then, having spoken his name, she could see him, this time through an involuntary and unanalyzed association, and her bliss and her sorrow were so great that she felt that his being a trifle was unimportant since he made her feel tortures and delights compared with which all others were nothing. And while she figured that all this would fade once she got to know him, she gave this mirage the full realities of her pain and her joy.

A phrase she had heard from *Die Meistersinger,* at Princess d'A.'s soirée, had the power to evoke Monsieur de Laléande with utmost precision: "*Dem Vogel, der heut sang, dem war der Schnabel hold gewachsen*" (The bird that sang today, its beak was sweet). She had unwittingly made that phrase his actual leit-motif and, hearing it one day at a concert in Trouville, she had burst into tears. From time to time, not so often as to make it pall, she would lock herself in her bedroom, to which the piano had been moved, and she would play that phrase, closing her eyes the better to see him; it was her only intoxicating joy, ending in disillusion; it was the opium she could not do without.

Sometimes pausing and listening to the flow of her distress the way one leans over to hear the sweet and incessant lament of a wellspring, she would muse about her atrocious dilemma: one alternative being her future shame, which would lead to the despair of her loved ones; the other alternative (if she did not give in) being her eternal sorrow; and she would curse herself for having so expertly dosed her love with the pleasure and the pain that she had not managed to reject immediately as an unbearable poison or to recover from subsequently. First she cursed her eyes, or perhaps before them her detestable curiosity and coquettishness, which had made her eyes blossom like flowers in order to tempt this young man, and had then exposed her to his glances, some of which were like arrows and more invincibly sweet than injections of morphine would have been.

She also cursed her imagination; it had nurtured her love so tenderly that Françoise sometimes wondered if her imagination alone had given birth to this love, which now tyrannized and tortured its birth-giver.

She also cursed her ingenuity, which, for better and for worse, had so skillfully devised so many intrigues for meeting him that their frustrating impossibility may have attached her all the more strongly to the hero of those novels; she cursed her goodness and the delicacy of her heart, which, if she surrendered, would corrupt the joy of her guilty love with remorse and shame. She cursed her will, which could rear so impetuously and leap over hurdles so dauntlessly when her desires strove toward impossible goals—her will, so weak, so pliant, so broken not only when she was forced to disobey her desires, but also when she was driven by some other emotion. Lastly she cursed her mind in its godliest forms, the supreme gift that she had received and to which people, without finding its true name, have given all sorts of names—poet's intuition, believer's ecstasy, profound feelings of nature and music—which had placed infinite summits and horizons before her love, had let them bask in the supernatural light of her love's enchantment, and had, in exchange, lent her love a bit of its own enchantment, and which had won over to this love all its most sublime and most private inner life, bonding and blending with it, consecrating to it—as a church's collection of relics and ornaments is dedicated to the Madonna—all the most precious jewels of her heart and her mind, her heart, whose sighs she heard in the evening or on the sea, and whose melancholy was now the sister of the pain inflicted on her by his total absence: she cursed that inexpressible sense of the mystery of things, which absorbs our minds in a radiance of beauty, the way the ocean engulfs the setting sun—for deepening her love, dematerializing it, broadening it, making it infinite without reducing its torture, "for" (as Baudelaire said when speaking about late afternoons in autumn) "there are sensations whose vagueness does not exclude intensity, and there is no sharper point than that of infinity."

5

And so, beginning with the rising sun, he was consumed, on the seaweed of the shore, keeping at the bottom of his heart, like an arrow in the liver, the burning wound of the great Kypris.

—THEOCRITES: THE CYCLOPS

It was in Trouville that I just recently encountered Madame de Breyves, whom I have known to be happier. Nothing can cure her. If she loved Monsieur de Laléande for his good looks or his intelligence, one could seek to find a more intelligent or better-looking young man to divert her attention. If it were his benevolence or his love for her that attached her to him, someone else could try to love her more faithfully. But Monsieur de Laléande is neither good-looking nor intelligent. He has had no chance to show her whether he is tender or brutal, neglectful or faithful. It is truly he whom she loves and not merits or charms that could be found to the same high degree in others; it is truly he whom she loves despite his imperfections, despite his mediocrity; she is thus doomed to love him despite everything. *He*—does she know what that is? Only that he induces such great thrills of despair and rapture in her that all else in her life, all other things, do not count. The most beautiful face, the most original intelligence would not have that particular and mysterious essence, so unique that no human being will ever repeat it in the infinity of worlds and the eternity of time.

Had it not been for Geneviève de Buivres, who innocently got her to attend the princess's soirée, none of this would have happened. But the chain of circumstances linked up, imprisoning her, the victim of an illness that has no remedy because it has no reason. Granted, Monsieur de Laléande, who at this very moment must be leading a mediocre life and dreaming paltry dreams on the beach of Biarritz, would be quite amazed to learn about his other life, the one in Madame de Breyves's soul, an existence so miraculously intense as to subjugate and annihilate everything else: an existence just as continuous as his own life, expressed just as effectively in actions, distinguished purely by a keener, richer, less intermittent awareness. How amazed Monsieur de Laléande would be to learn that he, rarely sought after for his physical appearance, is instantly evoked wherever Madame de Breyves happens to be, among the most gifted people, in the most exclusive salons, in the most self-contained sceneries; and how amazed he would be to learn that this very popular woman has no thought, no affection, no attention for anything but the memory of this intruder, who eclipses everything else as if he alone had the reality of a person, and all other present persons were as empty as memories and shadows.

Whether Madame de Breyves strolls with a poet or lunches at the home of an archduchess, whether she leaves Trouville for the mountains or the countryside, reads by herself or chats with her most cherished friend, rides horseback or sleeps, Monsieur de Laléande's name, his image lie upon her, delightful, truculent, unyielding, like the sky overhead. She, who always despised Biarritz, has now gone so far as to find a distressing and bewildering charm in everything regarding this city. She is nervous about who is there, who will perhaps see him but not know it, who will perhaps live with him but not enjoy it. She feels no resentment for the latter, and without daring to give them messages, she keeps endlessly interrogating them, astonished at times that people hear her talking so much around her secret yet never surmise it. A large photograph of Biarritz is one of the few decorations in her bedroom. She lends Monsieur de Laléande's features to one of the strollers whom one sees in that picture, albeit hazily. If she knew the bad music he likes and plays, those scorned ballads would probably replace Beethoven's symphonies and Wagner's operas on her piano and soon thereafter in her heart, both because of the sentimental cheapening of her taste and because of the spell cast on them by the man from whom all spells and sorrows come to her.

Now and then the image of the man she has seen only two or three times, and for moments at that, the man who has such a tiny space in the exterior events of her life and such an absorbing space in her mind and her heart, virtually monopolizing them altogether—his image blurs before the weary eyes of her memory. She no longer sees him, no longer recalls his features, his silhouette, barely remembers his eyes. Still, that image is all she has of him. She goes mad at the thought that she might lose that image, that her desire (which, granted, tortures her, but which is entirely herself now, in which she has taken refuge, fleeing everything she values, the way you value your own preservation, your life, good or bad)—that her desire could vanish, leaving nothing but a feeling of malaise, a suffering in dreams, of which she would no longer know the cause, would no longer see it even in her mind or cherish it there. But then Monsieur de Laléande's image reappears after that momentary blurring of inner vision. Her grief can resume and it is almost a joy.

How will Madame de Breyves endure going back to Paris, to which he will not return before January? What will she do until then? What will she do, what will he do after that?

I wanted to leave for Biarritz twenty times over and bring back Monsieur de Laléande. The consequences might be terrible, but I do not have to examine them; she will not stand for it. Nonetheless I am devastated to see those small temples throbbing from within, beating strongly enough to be shattered by the interminable blows of this inexplicable love. This love gives her life the rhythm of anxiety. Often she imagines him coming to Trouville, approaching her, telling her he loves her. She sees him, her eyes glow. He speaks to her in that toneless voice of dreams, a voice that prohibits us from believing yet forces us to listen. It is he. He speaks to her in those words that make us delirious even though we never hear them except in dreams when we see the very shiny and poignant, the divine and trusting smile of two destinies uniting.

Thus she is awakened by the feeling that the two worlds of reality and her desire are parallel, that it is as impossible for them to join together as it is for a body and the shadow it casts. Then, remembering that minute in the cloakroom when his elbow grazed her elbow, when he offered her his body, which she could now press against her own if she had wished, if she had known, and which may remain forever remote from her, she is skewered by cries of despair and revolt like those heard on sinking ships. If, while strolling on the beach or in the woods, she allows a pleasure of contemplation or reverie, or at least a fragrance, a singing wafted and muffled by the wind—if she allows those things to take hold of her gently and let her forget her sorrow for an instant, then she suddenly feels a great blow to her heart, a painful wound; and, above the waves or the leaves, in the hazy skyline of woods or sea, she perceives the nebulous face of her invisible and ever-present conqueror, who, his eyes shining through the clouds as on the day when he offered himself to her, flees with his quiver after shooting one more arrow at her.

Portraits of Painters and Composers

1 Portraits of Painters

ALFRED CUYP

Cuyp, the setting sun dissolving in limpid air,
Which is dimmed like water by a flight of gray doves,
Golden moisture, halo on a bull or a birch,
Blue incense of lovely days, smoking on the hillside,
Or marsh of brightness stagnating in the empty sky.
Horsemen are ready, a pink plume on each hat,
A hand on the hip; the tangy air, turning their skin rosy,
Lightly swells their fine blond curls,
And, tempted by the hot fields, the cool waves,
Without disturbing the herd of cattle
Dreaming in a fog of pale gold and repose,
They ride off to breathe those profound minutes.

PAULUS POTTER

Somber grief of skies uniformly gray,
Sadder for being blue during rare bright intervals,
And which allow the warm tears of a misunderstood sun
To filter down upon the paralyzed plains;
Potter, melancholy mood of the somber plains,
Which stretch out, endless, joyless, colorless;

The trees, the hamlet cast no shadows,
The tiny, meager gardens have no flowers.
A plowman lugs buckets home, and his puny mare
Resigned, anxious, and dreamy,
Uneasily listening to her pensive brain,
Inhales in small gulps the strong breath of the wind.

ANTOINE WATTEAU

Twilight putting makeup on faces and trees,
With its blue mantle, under its uncertain mask;
Dust of kisses around weary lips. . . .
Vagueness becomes tender, and nearness distance.

The masquerade, another melancholy distance,
Makes the gestures of love, unreal, mournful and bewitching.
A poet's caprice—or a lover's prudence,
For love needs skillful adornment—
Boats and picnics are here, silence and music.

ANTHONY VAN DYCK

Gentle pride of hearts, noble grace of things
That shine in the eyes, velvets and woods,
Lovely elevated language of bearing and poses
(The hereditary pride of women and kings!),
You triumph, van Dyck, you prince of calm gestures,
In all the lovely creatures soon to die,
In every lovely hand that still can open;
Suspecting nothing (what does it matter?),
That hand gives you the palm fronds!
The halting of horsemen, under pines, near water,
Calm like them—like them so close to sobs—
Royal children, already grave and magnificent,
Resigned in their garments, brave in their plumed hats,
With jewels that weep (like flaming waves)
The bitterness of tears that fill the souls,
Too proud to let them ascend to the eyes;
And you above them all, a precious stroller,

In a pale-blue shirt, one hand on your hip,
The other hand holding a leafy fruit picked from its branch,
I dream, uncomprehending, before your eyes and gestures:
Standing, but relaxed, in this shadowy haven,
Duke of Richmond, oh, young sage!—or charming madman?—
I keep returning to you; a sapphire at your neck
Has fires as sweet as your tranquil gaze.

2 Portraits of Composers

CHOPIN

Chopin, sea of sighs, of tears, of sobs,
Which a swarm of butterflies crosses without alighting,
And they play over the sadness or dance over the waves.
Dream, love, suffer, shout, soothe, charm, or cradle,
You always let the sweet and dizzying oblivion
Of your caprice run in between your sorrows
Like butterflies flitting from flower to flower;
Your joy is the accomplice of your grief;
The ardor of the whirlwind increases the thirst for tears.
The pale and gentle comrade of the moon,
The prince of despair or the betrayed grand lord,
You are exalted, more handsome for being pallid,
By the sunlight flooding your sickroom, tearfully smiling
At the patient and suffering at seeing him. . . .
A smile of regret and tears of Hope!

GLUCK

A temple to love, to friendship, a temple to courage,
Which a marquise had built in her English
Garden, where many a putto, with Watteau bending his bow,
Chooses glorious hearts as the targets of his rage.

But the German artist—whom she would have dreamed for
Knidos!—graver and deeper, sculpted without affectation

The lovers and the gods whom you see on this frieze:
Hercules has his funeral pyre in Armides' gardens!

The heels, when dancing, no longer strike the path,
Where the ashes of extinguished eyes and smiles
Deaden our slow steps and turn the distances blue;
The voices of the harpsichords are silent or broken.

But your mute cry, Admetes and Iphigenia,
Still terrifies us, proffered in a gesture
And, swayed by Orpheus or braved by Alcestes,
The Styx—without masts or sky—where your genius cast
    anchor.

With love, Gluck, like Alcestes, conquered death,
Inevitable for the whims of an era;
He stands, an august temple to courage,
On the ruins of the small temple to Love.

SCHUMANN
From the old garden, where friendship welcomed you,
Hear boys and nests that whistle in the hedges,
You lover, weary of so many marches and wounds,
Schumann, dreamy soldier disappointed by war.

The happy breeze imbues the shadow of the huge walnut tree
With the scent of jasmine, where the doves fly past;
The child reads the future in the flames of the hearth,
The cloud or the wind speaks to your heart about graves.

Your tears used to run at the shouts of the carnival,
Or they blended their sweetness with the bitter victory
Whose insane enthusiasm still quivers in your memory;
You can weep without end: your rival has won.

The Rhine rolls its sacred water toward Cologne.
Ah! How gaily you sang on its shores
On holidays! But, shattered by grief, you fall asleep. . . .
Tears are raining in your illuminated darkness.

Dream where the dead woman lives, where you are true
To the ingrate, your hopes blossom and the crime is dust. . . .
Then, the shredding lightning of awakening, in which thunder
Strikes you again for the very first time.

Flow, emit fragrance, march to the drumbeat or be lovely!
Schumann, oh, confidant of souls and of flowers,
Between your joyous banks holy river of sorrows,
Pensive garden, tender, fresh, and faithful.
Where the lyres, the moon, and the swallow kiss one another,
A marching army, a dreaming child, a weeping woman!

MOZART

Italian woman on the arm of a Bavarian prince,
Whose sad, frozen eyes delight in her languor!
In his frosty gardens he holds to his heart
Her shadow-ripened breasts, to drink the light.

Her tender, German soul—a sigh so profound!—
Finally tastes the ardent laziness of being loved;
To hands too weak to hold it he delivers
The radiant hope of his enchanted head.

Cherubino! Don Giovanni! Far from fading oblivion,
You stand in the scents of so many trampled flowers
That the wind dispersed without drying their tears,
From the Andalusian gardens to the graves of Tuscany!

In the German park, where grief is hazy,
The Italian woman is still queen of the night.
Her breath makes the air sweet and spiritual,
And her Magic Flute lovingly drips
The coolness of sherbets, of kisses and skies,
In the still hot shadow of a lovely day's farewell.

A Young Girl's Confession

The cravings of the senses carry us hither and yon, but once the hour is past, what do you bring back? Remorse and spiritual dissipation. You go out in joy and you often return in sadness, so that the pleasures of the evening cast a gloom on the morning. Thus, the delight of the senses flatters us at first, but in the end it wounds and it kills.

—Thomas à Kempis: *Imitation of Christ*, Book 1, Chapter 18

1

Amid the oblivion we seek in false
   delights,
The sweet and melancholy scent of lilac
   blossoms
Wafts back more virginal through our
   intoxications.

—Henri de Régnier: *Sites*, Poem 8 (1887)

At last my deliverance is approaching. Of course I was clumsy, my aim was poor, I almost missed myself. Of course it would have been better to die from the first shot; but in the end the bullet could not be extracted, and then the complications with my heart set in. It will not be very long now. But still, a whole week! It can last for a whole week more!—during which I can do nothing but struggle to recapture the horrible chain of events. If I were not so weak, if I had enough willpower to get up, to leave, I would go and die at Les Oublis, in the park where I spent all my summers until the age of fifteen. No other place is more deeply imbued with my mother, so thoroughly has it been permeated with her presence, and even more so her absence. To a person who loves, is not absence the most certain, the most effective, the most durable, the most indestructible, the most faithful of presences?

My mother would always bring me to Les Oublis at the end of April, leave two days later, visit for another two days in mid-May, then come to take me home during the last week of June. Her ever so brief visits were the sweetest thing in the world and the cruelest. During those two days she showered me with affection, while normally quite chary with it in order to inure me and calm my morbid sensitivity. On both evenings she spent at Les Oublis she would come to my bed and say good night, an old habit that she had cast off because it gave me too much pleasure and too much pain, so that, instead of falling asleep, I kept calling her back to say good night to me again, until I no longer dared to do so even though I felt the passionate need all the more, and I kept inventing new pretexts: my burning pillow, which had to be turned over, my frozen feet, which she alone could warm by rubbing them. . . .

So many lovely moments were lovelier still because I sensed that my mother was truly herself at such times and that her usual coldness must have cost her dearly. On the day she left, a day of despair, when I clung to her dress all the way to the train, begging her to take me back to Paris, I could easily glimpse the truth amid her pretense, sift out her sadness, which infected all her cheerful and exasperated reproaches for my "silly and ridiculous" sadness, which she wanted to teach me to control, but which she shared. I can still feel my agitation during one of those days of her departures (just that intact agitation not adulterated by today's painful remembrance), when I made the sweet discovery of her affection, so similar to and so superior to my own. Like all discoveries, it had been foreseen, foreshadowed, but so many facts seemed to contradict it!

My sweetest impressions are of the years when she returned to Les Oublis, summoned by my illness. Not only was she paying me an extra visit, on which I had not counted, but she was all sweetness and tenderness, pouring them out, on and on, without disguise or constraint. Even in those times when they were not yet sweetened and softened by the thought that they would someday be lacking, her sweetness and tenderness meant so much to me that the joys of convalescence always saddened me to death: the day was coming when I would be sound enough for my mother to leave, and until then, I was no longer sick enough to keep her from reviving her severity, her unlenient justice.

One day, the uncles I stayed with at Les Oublis had failed to tell me that my mother would be arriving; they had concealed the news because my second cousin had dropped by to spend a few hours with me, and they had feared I might neglect him in my joyful anguish of looking forward to my mother's visit. That ruse may have been the first of the circumstances that, independent of my will, were the accomplices of all the dispositions for evil that I bore inside myself, like all children of my age, though to no higher degree. That second cousin, who was fifteen (I was fourteen), was already quite depraved, and he taught me things that instantly gave me thrills of remorse and delight. Listening to him, letting his hands caress mine, I reveled in a joy that was poisoned at its very source; soon I mustered the strength to get away from him and I fled into the park with a wild need for my mother, who I knew was, alas, in Paris, and against my will I kept calling to her along the garden trails.

All at once, while passing an arbor, I spotted her sitting on a bench, smiling and holding out her arms to me. She lifted her veil to kiss me, I flung myself against her cheeks and burst into tears; I wept and wept, telling her all those ugly things that required the ignorance of my age to be told, and that she knew how to listen to divinely, though failing to grasp them and softening their significance with a goodness that eased the weight on my conscience. This weight kept easing and easing; my crushed and humiliated soul kept rising lighter and lighter, more and more powerful, overflowing—I was all soul.

A divine sweetness was emanating from my mother and from my recovered innocence. My nostrils soon inhaled an equally fresh and equally pure fragrance. It came from a lilac bush, on which a branch hidden by my mother's parasol was already in blossom, suffusing the air with an invisible perfume. High up in the trees the birds were singing with all their might. Higher still, among the green tops, the sky was so profoundly blue that it almost resembled the entrance to a heaven in which you could ascend forever. I kissed my mother. Never have I recaptured the sweetness of that kiss. She left the next day, and that departure was crueler than all the ones preceding it. Having once sinned, I felt forsaken not only by joy but also by the necessary strength and support.

All these separations were preparing me, in spite of myself, for what the irrevocable separation would be someday, even if, back then, I never seriously envisaged the possibility of surviving my mother. I had resolved to kill myself within a minute after her death. Later on, absence taught me far more bitter lessons: that you get accustomed to absence, that the greatest abatement of the self, the most humiliating torment is to feel that you are no longer tormented by absence. However, those lessons were to be contradicted in the aftermath.

I now think back mainly to the small garden where I breakfasted with my mother amid countless pansies. They had always seemed a bit sad, as grave as coats-of-arms, but soft and velvety, often mauve, sometimes violet, almost black, with graceful and mysterious yellow patterns, a few utterly white and of a frail innocence. I now pick them all in my memory, those pansies; their sadness has increased because they have been understood, their velvety sweetness has vanished forever.

2

How could all this fresh water of memories have spurted once again and flowed through my impure soul of today without getting soiled? What virtue does this morning scent of lilacs have that it can pass through so many foul vapors without mingling and weakening? Alas!—my soul of fourteen reawakens not only inside me but, at the same time, far away from me, outside me. I do know that it is no longer my soul and that it does not depend on me to become my soul again. Yet back then it never occurred to me that I would someday regret its loss. It was nothing but pure; I had to make it strong and able to perform the highest tasks in the future. At Les Oublis, after my mother and I, during the hot hours of the day, visited the pond with its flashes of sunlight and sparkling fish, or strolled through the fields in the morning or the evening, I confidently dreamed about that future, which was never beautiful enough for her love or my desire to please her. And if not my willpower, then at least the forces of my imagination and my emotion were stirred up inside me, tumultuously calling for the destiny in which they would be realized, and repeatedly striking the wall of my heart as if to open it and dash outside myself, into life.

If, then, I jumped with all my strength, if I kissed my mother a thousand times, running far ahead like a young dog or indefinitely lagging behind to pick cornflowers and red poppies, which I brought her, whooping loudly—if I did all those things, it was less for the pleasure of strolling and gathering flowers than for the joy of pouring out the happiness of feeling all this life within me about to gush forth, to spread out infinitely, in more immense and more enchanting vistas than the far horizon of the woods and the sky, a horizon that I yearned to reach in a single leap. Bouquets of clover, of poppies, of cornflowers—if I carried you away with blazing eyes, with quivering ecstasy, if you made me laugh and cry, it was because I entwined you with all my hopes, which now, like you, have dried, have decayed, and, without blossoming like you, have returned to dust.

What distressed my mother was my lack of will. I always acted on the impulse of the moment. So long as the impulse came from my mind or my heart, my life, though not perfect, was not truly bad. My mother and I were preoccupied chiefly with the realization of all my fine projects for work, calm, and reflection, because we felt—she more distinctly, I confusedly but intensely—that this realization would only be an image projected into my life, the image of the creation, by me and in me, of the willpower that she had conceived and nurtured. However, I always kept putting it off until tomorrow. I gave myself time, I occasionally grieved at watching time pass, but so much time still lay before me! Yet I was a bit scared, and I obscurely felt that my habit of doing without willpower was starting to weigh down on me more and more strongly as the years accumulated; and I sadly suspected that there would be no sudden change, and that I could scarcely count on an utterly effortless miracle to transform my life and create my will. Desiring a will was not enough. I would have needed precisely what I could not have without willpower: a will.

3

And the furious wind of concupiscence
Makes your flesh flap like an old flag.

—CHARLES BAUDELAIRE

During my sixteenth year I suffered a crisis that left me sickly. To divert me, my family had me debut in society. Young men got into the habit of calling on me. One of them was perverse and wicked. His manners were both gentle and brash. He was the one I fell in love with. My parents found out, but to keep me from suffering all too much, they did not force his hand. Spending all my time thinking about him when I did not see him, I finally lowered myself by imitating him as much as was possible for me. He beguiled me almost by surprise into doing wrong, then he got me accustomed to having bad thoughts which I had no will to resist—willpower being the only force capable of driving them back to the infernal darkness from which they emerged.

When love was gone, habit took its place, and there was no lack of immoral young men to exploit it. As accessories to my sins, they also justified them to my conscience. Initially I felt atrocious remorse; I made confessions that were not understood. My friends talked me out of dwelling on the matter with my father. They gradually persuaded me that all girls were doing the same and that parents were simply feigning ignorance. As for the lies I was incessantly obliged to tell, my imagination soon embellished them as silences that I had to maintain about an ineluctable necessity. At this time, I no longer really lived; I still dreamed, still thought, still felt.

To divert and expel all those evil desires, I began socializing rather intensely. The dessicating pleasure of high society accustomed me to living in perpetual company, and, together with my taste for solitude, I lost the secret of the joys that I had previously been given by nature and art. Never have I attended so many concerts as during those years. Never have I felt music less profoundly, engrossed as I was in my desire to be admired in an elegant box. I listened and I heard nothing. If I did happen to hear something, I no longer saw everything that music can unveil. My outings were likewise virtually stricken with sterility. The things that had once sufficed to make me happy all day long—a bit of sunshine yellowing the grass, the fragrance that wet leaves emit with the final drops of rain—all these things had, like myself, lost their sweetness and gaiety. Woods, skies, water seemed to turn away from me, and if, alone with them and face to face, I questioned them uneasily; they no longer murmured those vague responses that had once delighted me. The divine guests announced by the voices of water, foliage, and sky deign to visit only those hearts that are purified by living in themselves.

Because I was seeking an inverse remedy and because I did not have the courage to want the real remedy, which was so close and, alas, so far from me, inside me, I again yielded to sinful pleasures, believing that I could thereby rekindle the flame that had been extinguished by society. My efforts were useless. Held back by the pleasure of pleasing, I kept putting off, from day to day, the final decision, the choice, the truly free act, the option for solitude. I did not renounce either of those two vices in favor of the other. I combined them. What am I saying? Intent on smashing through all the barriers of thinking and feeling that would have stopped the next vice, each vice also appeared to summon it. I would go into society to calm down after committing a sin, and I sinned again the instant I was calm.

It was at that terrible moment, after my loss of innocence and before my remorse of today, at that moment, when I was less worthy than at any other moment of my life, that I was most appreciated by everybody. I had been shrugged off as a silly, pretentious girl; now, on the contrary, the ashes of my imagination were fancied by society, which reveled in them.

While I kept committing the worst crime against my mother, people viewed me as a model daughter because of my tender and respectful conduct with her. After the suicide of my thoughts, they admired my intelligence; they doted on my mind. My parched imagination, my dried-up sensitivity were enough for the people who were the thirstiest for an intellectual life—their thirst being as artificial and mendacious as the source from which they believed they were quenching it! Yet no one suspected the secret crime of my life, and everyone regarded me as an ideal girl. How many parents told my mother that if I had had a lesser standing, and if they could have dared to consider me, they would have desired no other wife for their sons! Nonetheless, in the depths of my obliterated conscience, I felt desperately ashamed of those undeserved praises; but my shame never reached the surface, and I had fallen so low that I was indecent enough to repeat them to and laugh at them with the accomplices of my crimes.

4

To anyone who has lost what he will regain
Never. . . . Never!

—Charles Baudelaire: "The Swan" (*The Flowers of Evil*)

In the winter of my twentieth year, my mother's health, which had never been vigorous, was deeply shaken. I learned that she had a weak heart, and while her condition was not serious, she had to avoid any excitement. One of my uncles told me that my mother wanted to see me get married. I was thus presented with a clear and important task. Now I could show my mother how much I loved her. I accepted the first proposal that she transmitted to me with her approval, so that my life would be changed by necessity rather than by will. My fiancé was precisely the kind of young man who, by his extreme intelligence, his gentleness and energy, could exert the finest influence on me. Furthermore he was determined that we would live with my mother. I would not be separated from her, which would have been the cruelest pain for me.

Now I had the courage to admit all my sins to my father confessor. I asked him if I owed the same avowal to my fiancé. My confessor was compassionate enough to talk me out of it, but he made me swear to turn over a new leaf and he gave me absolution. The late blossoms that joy opened in my heart, which I thought forever sterile, bore fruits. I was cured by the grace of God, the grace of youth—an age that heals so many wounds with its vitality. If, as Saint Augustine says, it is more difficult to regain chastity than to have been chaste, I got to know a difficult virtue.

No one suspected that I was infinitely worthier than before, and my mother kissed my forehead every day, having never stopped believing it was pure and not realizing it was regenerated. Moreover I was unjustly rebuked for my absent-mindedness, my silence, and my melancholy in society. But I was not angry: I drew enough pleasure from the secret that

existed between me and my satisfied conscience. The convalescence of my soul (which now smiled endlessly at me with
a face like my mother's and gazed at me with an air of tender
reproach through my drying tears) was infinitely appealing
and languorous. Yes, my soul was reborn to life. I myself
failed to understand how I could have maltreated my soul,
made it suffer, nearly killed it. And I effusively thanked God
for having saved it in time.

It was the harmony of that deep and pure joy with the
fresh serenity of the sky that I savored on the evening *when
everything was consummated.* The absence of my fiancé,
who had gone to spend a few days with his sister, the presence at dinner of the young man who had had the greatest responsibility for my past sins, did not cast even the faintest pall
on that limpid evening in May. No cloud in the sky was reflected precisely in my heart. My mother, however, as if a
mysterious solidarity existed between us despite her absolute
ignorance of my sins, was very nearly cured.

"She must be treated with care for two weeks," the doctor
had said. "After that there's no chance of a relapse."

Those words alone were for me the promise of a happy future so rapturous that I burst into tears. That evening, my
mother's gown was more elegant than customary, and for the
first time since my father's death, which, still and all, had occurred ten years ago, she had added a touch of mauve to her habitual black. Quite embarrassed to be dressed like that, as in her
younger days, she was sad and happy to violate her pain and
her grief in order to bring me pleasure and celebrate my joy. I
approached her waist with a pink carnation, which she initially
refused, but which, because it came from me, she then pinned
on with a slightly hesitant and sheepish hand.

As the company headed for the table, I drew her over to the
window and passionately kissed her face, which had delicately
recovered from its past suffering. I was wrong to say that I have
never recaptured the sweetness of that kiss at Les Oublis. The
kiss on this evening was as sweet as no other. Or rather, it was
the kiss of Les Oublis, which, evoked by the allure of a similar

minute, slipped gently from the depths of the past and settled between my mother's still vaguely pale cheeks and my lips.

We toasted my coming marriage. I never drank anything but water since wine overagitated my nerves. My uncle declared that I could make an exception at a moment like this. I can vividly picture his cheerful face as he uttered those stupid words. . . . My God! My God! I have confessed everything so calmly—will I be forced to stop here? I can no longer see anything! Now I can. . . . My uncle said that I could certainly make an exception at a moment like this. As he spoke, he looked at me and laughed; I drank quickly before glancing at my mother; I was afraid she might object.

She murmured: "One must never allow evil the tiniest nook."

But the champagne was so cool that I drank two more flutes. My head grew very heavy; I needed both to rest and to expend my nervous energy. We rose from the table. Jacques came over and, staring at me, he said: "Would you like to join me? I want to show you some of my poems."

His lovely eyes shone softly over his fresh cheeks; he slowly twisted his moustache. I realized I was doomed and I had no strength to resist. I said, shivering:

"Yes, I'd enjoy that."

It was when saying those words, perhaps even earlier, when drinking my second glass of champagne, that I committed the truly responsible act, the abominable act. After that, I merely let myself go. We locked both doors, and he embraced me, breathing on my cheeks and fondling my entire body. Then, while pleasure gripped me tighter and tighter, I felt an infinite sadness and desolation awakening at the bottom of my heart; I seemed to be causing my mother's soul to weep, the soul of my guardian angel, the soul of God. I had always shuddered in horror when reading those accounts of the tortures that villains inflict on animals, on their own wives, their children; it now confusedly struck me that in every lustful and sinful act there is as much ferocity in the bodily part that is delighting in the pleasure, and that we have as many good intentions and, in us, as many pure angels are martyred and are weeping.

Soon my uncles would be finishing their card game and coming back. We had to anticipate them; I would never stumble again, it was the last time. . . . Then I saw myself in the mirror above the fireplace. All that hazy anguish of my soul was painted not on my features, but on my entire face, from my sparkling eyes to my blazing cheeks and my parted lips, exhaled a stupid and brutal sensual pleasure. I then thought of the horror that anyone who had just watched me kissing my mother with melancholy tenderness would now see me transformed into a beast. But in the mirror, Jacques's mouth, covetous under his moustache, instantly arose against my face. Shaken in my innermost being, I leaned my head against his, when, in front of me, I saw my mother (yes, I am telling you what happened—listen to me because I can tell you), on the balcony outside the window; I saw my mother gaping at me. I do not know if she cried out, I heard nothing; but she fell back, catching her head between the two bars of the railing.

This is not the last time I am telling you this; I have told you: I almost missed, my aim was good but my shot was clumsy. However, the bullet could not be extracted, and the complications in my heart began. Still I can remain like this for one more week and I will not be able to stop mulling over the beginning and to *see* the end. I would rather my mother had seen me commit other crimes, including this one, so long as she had not seen my joyous expression in the mirror. No, she could not have seen it. . . . It was a coincidence. . . . She had suffered a stroke a minute before seeing me. . . . She had not seen my joy. . . . That is out of the question! God, who knew everything, would not have wanted it.

A Dinner in High Society

But Fundianus, who shared the happiness of that banquet with you? I'm dying to know.

—Horace: *Satires*

1

Honoré was late; he greeted his host and hostess and the people he knew, he was introduced to the rest, and they all went in to dinner. Several moments later, his neighbor, a very young man, asked him to name the others and tell him something about them. Honoré had never met him in society. He was very handsome. The mistress of the house kept darting ardent glances at him, which sufficiently indicated why she had invited him and that he would soon become part of her circle. Honoré saw him as a future power; but with no envy and out of kindness and courtesy, he set about answering him.

He looked around. Two diners across from him were not on speaking terms: with good but clumsy intentions, they had been invited and placed side by side because they were both involved in literature. But to this foremost reason for mutual hatred they added a more personal one. The older man, as a relative—doubly hypnotized—of Monsieur Paul Desjardins and

Monsieur de Vogüé, affected a scornful silence toward the younger man, who, as a favorite disciple of Monsieur Maurice Barrès, maintained a stance of irony toward his neighbor. Moreover, each man's malevolence quite involuntarily exaggerated the other's importance, as if the chief of villains were confronting the king of imbeciles.

Further away, a superb Spanish woman was eating ravenously. That evening, serious person that she was, she had unhesitatingly sacrificed a rendezvous to the probability of advancing her social career by dining in a fashionable home. And indeed, she had every prospect of success with her calculations. Madame Fremer's snobbery was, for her female friends, and that of her female friends was, for her, like mutual insurance against sinking into the bourgeoisie. But as luck would have it, on this particular evening Madame Fremer was ridding herself of a stock of people whom she had been unable to invite to her dinners, but to whom she insisted on being polite for various reasons and whom she had gathered almost higgledy-piggledy.

The event was crowned by a duchess, but the Spanish woman had already met her and could get nothing more out of her. So she exchanged irritated glances with her husband, whose guttural voice could perpetually be heard at soirées, asking at five-minute intervals that were quite filled with other kettles of fish: "Would you present me to the duke?" "Monsieur le duc, would you present me to the duchess?" "Madame la duchesse, may I present my wife?"

Fuming at having to waste his time, he was nevertheless resigned to starting a conversation with his neighbor, the host's business partner. For over a year now Fremer had been begging his wife to invite him. She had finally yielded and had tucked him away between the señora's husband and a humanist. The humanist, who read too much, ate too much. He quoted and burped, and these two complaints were equally repugnant to his neighbor, a self-made aristocrat, Madame Lenoir.

Having quickly turned the conversation to the Prince de Buivres's victories at Dahomey, she said in a deeply moved voice: "The dear boy, how delighted I am that he is honoring our family."

She was indeed a cousin of the de Buivres, who, all of them younger than she, treated her with the deference that was due her age, her allegiance to the royal family, her massive fortune, and the unfailing barrenness of her three marriages. She had transferred to all the de Buivres whatever family sentiments she might possess. She felt personally ashamed of the de Buivres whose vile deeds had earned him a court-appointed guardianship, and around her right-minded brow, on monarchist bandeaux, she naturally wore the laurels of the de Buivres who was a general. An intruder in this previously closed family, she had become its head and virtually its dowager.

She felt truly exiled in modern society and she always spoke tearfully about the "elderly noblemen of the old days." Her snobbery was all imagination and, moreover, was all the imagination she had. With names rich in history and glory exerting a singular power over her sensitive soul, she felt the same unbiased pleasure whether dining with princes or reading memoirs of the Old Regime. Always sporting the same grapevines, her coiffure was as steadfast as her principles. Her eyes sparkled with stupidity. Her smiling face was noble, her gesticulation excessive and meaningless. Putting her trust in God, she displayed the same optimistic excitement on the eve of a garden party or on the eve of a revolution, whereby her hasty gestures seemed to exorcise radicalism or inclement weather.

Her neighbor, the humanist, was speaking to her with a fatiguing elegance and a dreadful glibness; he kept quoting Homer in order to excuse his own bouts of gluttony and drunkenness in other people's eyes and to poeticize them in his own eyes. His narrow brow was wreathed with invisible roses, ancient and yet fresh. But with an equable politesse, which came easily to Madame Lenoir (since she viewed it as the exercise of her power and the respect, so rare today, for old traditions), she spoke to Monsieur Fremer's associate every five minutes. Still, the associate had nothing to complain about: at the opposite end of the table, Madame Fremer accorded him the most charming flattery. She wanted this dinner to count for several years and, determined not to dig up this spoilsport for a long time, she buried him under flowers.

As for Monsieur Fremer: working at his bank all day, dragged into society by his wife every evening or kept at home when they entertained, always ready to bite anyone's head off, always muzzled, he eventually developed, even in the most trivial circumstances, an expression that blended stifled annoyance, sullen resignation, pent-up exasperation, and profound brutishness. Tonight, however, the financier's usual expression gave way to a cordial satisfaction whenever his eyes met his associate's. Even though he could not stand him in everyday life, he felt fleeting but sincere affection for him, not because he could easily dazzle him with his wealth, but because he felt the same vague fraternity that we experience at the sight of even an odious Frenchman in a foreign country. So violently torn from his habits every evening, so unjustly deprived of the relaxation that he deserved, so cruelly uprooted, Monsieur Fremer felt a normally despised yet powerful bond, which finally linked him to someone, drawing him out of his unapproachable and desperate isolation.

Across from him, Madame Fremer mirrored her blond beauty in the charmed eyes of the guests. The twofold reputation surrounding her was a deceptive prism through which everyone tried to fathom her real traits. Ambitious, conniving, almost an adventuress, according to the financial world, which she had abandoned for a more brilliant destiny, she was nevertheless regarded as a superior being, an angel of sweetness and virtue, by the aristocracy and the royal family, both of whom she had conquered. Nor had she forgotten her old and humbler friends, and she remembered them particularly when they were sick or in mourning—poignant circumstances, in which, moreover, one cannot complain of not being invited because one does not go out anyway. That was how she indulged her fits of charity, and in conversations with kinsmen or priests at deathbeds she wept honest tears, gradually deadening one by one the pangs of conscience that her all-too-frivolous life inspired in her scrupulous heart.

But the most amiable guest was the young Duchess de D., whose alert and lucid mind, never anxious or uneasy, contrasted so strangely with the incurable melancholy of her beautiful eyes, the pessimism of her lips, the infinite and noble weariness of her hands. This powerful lover of life in all its forms—kindness, literature, theater, action, friendship— chewed her beautiful red lips like disdained flowers, though not withering them, while a disenchanted smile barely raised the corners of her mouth. Her eyes seemed to promise a spirit for- ever capsized in the diseased waters of regret. How often, in the street, at the theater, had dreamy passersby kindled their dreams on those twinkling stars! Now the duchess, while recall- ing some farce or thinking up a wardrobe, kept sadly twisting her noble, resigned, and wistful phalanges and casting about deep and desperate glances that inundated the impressionable diners in torrents of melancholy. Her exquisite conversation was casually adorned with the faded and charming elegance of an already ancient skepticism.

The company had just had a discussion, and this person, who was so absolute in life and who believed that there was only one way of dressing, repeated to each interlocutor: "But why can't one say everything, think everything? I could be right, so could you. It's so terrible and narrow-minded to have only one opinion."

Unlike her body, her mind was not clad in the latest fashion, and she readily poked fun at symbolists and believers. Indeed her mind was like those charming women who are lovely enough and vivacious enough to be attractive even when wear- ing old-fashioned garments. It may, incidentally, have been de- liberate coquetry. Certain all-too-crude ideas might have snuffed out her mind the way certain colors, which she banned from herself, would have obliterated her complexion.

Honoré had sketched these various figures rapidly for his handsome neighbor, and so good-naturedly that despite their profound differences, they all seemed alike: the brilliant Señora de Torreno, the witty Duchess de D., the beautiful Madame Lenoir. He had neglected their sole common trait, or rather the same collective madness, the same prevalent epidemic with which all of them were stricken: snobbery. Of course, depend- ing on the given character, it differed greatly with each person, so that it was a far cry from the imaginative and poetic snobbery of Madame Lenoir to the conquering snobbery of Señora de

Torreno, who was as greedy as a functionary trying to climb to the top. And yet that terrible woman was capable of rehumanizing herself. Her neighbor at the dinner had just told her that he had admired her little daughter at the Parc Monceau. She had instantly broken her indignant silence. This obscure bookkeeper had aroused her pure and grateful liking, which she might have been incapable of feeling for a prince, and now they were chatting away like old friends.

Madame Fremer presided over the conversations with a visible satisfaction brought on by her sense of the lofty mission she was performing. Accustomed to introducing great writers to duchesses, she viewed herself as a sort of omnipotent foreign minister, who displays a sovereign spirit even in ceremonial etiquette. In the same way, a spectator at the theater, while digesting his dinner, judges, and therefore looks down at, the performers, the audience, the author, the rules of dramatic art, and genius. The conversation, incidentally, was taking a rather harmonious course. The dinner had reached the point at which the men touch the knees of the women or question them about their literary preferences according to their temperament and education, according, above all, to the individual lady.

For an instant a snag seemed unavoidable. When, with the imprudence of youth, Honoré's handsome neighbor attempted to insinuate that Heredia's oeuvre might contain more substance than was generally claimed, the diners, whose habits of thinking were upset, grew surly. But since Madame Fremer promptly exclaimed, "On the contrary, those things are nothing but admirable cameos, gorgeous enamels, flawless goldsmithery," vivacity and contentment returned to all faces.

A discussion about anarchists was more serious. But Madame Fremer, as if resigned and bowing to a fateful law of nature, slowly said: "What good does it all do? There will always be rich people and poor people." And, struck by this truth and delivered from their scruples, all these people, of whom the poorest had a private annual income of at least a hundred thousand francs, drained their final flutes of champagne with hearty cheerfulness.

2 After Dinner

Honoré, sensing that the melange of wines was making his head spin, left without saying goodbye, picked up his coat downstairs, and walked along the Champs-Élysées. He was extremely joyful. The barriers of impossibility, which close off the field of reality to our dreams and desires, were shattered, and his thoughts drifted exuberantly through the unattainable, fired by their own movement.

He was drawn by the mysterious avenues that stretch between all human beings and at the ends of which an unsuspected sun of delight or desolation goes down every evening. He instantly and irresistibly liked each person he thought about, and one by one he entered the streets where he might hope to encounter them, and had his expectations come true, he would have gone up to the unknown or indifferent person without fear and with a delicious thrill. With the collapse of a stage set that had stood too nearby, life spread out far away in all the magic of its novelty and mystery, across friendly, beckoning landscapes. And the regret that this was the mirage or reality of only a single evening filled him with despair; he would never again do anything but dine and drink so well in order to see such beautiful things. He suffered only for being unable to immediately reach all the sites that were scattered here and there in the infinity of the faraway perspective. Then he was struck by the noise of his slightly threatening and exaggerated voice, which for the last quarter hour had kept repeating: "Life is sad, it's idiotic" (that last word was underlined by a sharp gesture of his right arm, and he noticed the brusque movement of his cane). He mournfully told himself that those mechanically spoken words were a rather banal translation of similar visions, which, he thought, might not perhaps be expressed.

"Alas! It's probably only the intensity of my pleasure or regret that's increased a hundredfold, but the intellectual content has remained as is. My happiness is skittish, personal, untranslatable for others, and if I were writing at this moment, my style would have the same qualities, the same defects, alas, and the same mediocrity as always." However, the physical well-being he felt kept him from pursuing those thoughts and immediately granted him the supreme consolation: oblivion.

He had reached the boulevards. People were passing to and fro, and he offered them his friendship, certain of their reciprocity. He felt like their glorious center of attention; he opened his overcoat to show them the so very becoming whiteness of his shirt and the dark-red carnation in his buttonhole. That was how he offered himself to the admiration of the passersby, to the affection he so voluptuously shared with them.

Regrets, Reveries the Color of Time

So the poet's habit of living should be set on a key so low that the common influences should delight him. His cheerfulness should be the gift of the sunlight; the air should suffice for his inspiration, and he should be tipsy with water.

—Ralph Waldo Emerson

1 The Tuileries

At the Garden of the Tuileries this morning, the sun dozed off on all the stone steps, one by one, like a blond youth whose light sleep is promptly interrupted by the passing of a shadow. Young sprouts are greening against the old palace walls. The breath of the enchanted wind mingles the fresh scent of the lilacs with the fragrance of the past. The statues, which, in our public squares, are as terrifying as lunatics, dream here in the bowers like sages under the lustrous verdure that protects their whiteness. The basins, with the blue sky basking in their depths, shine like eyes. From the terrace on the edge of the water we see a hussard riding by, as if in another era, from the old quarter of the Quai d'Orsay on the opposite bank. The morning glories spill wildly from the vases, which are crowned with geraniums. Blazing with sunshine, the heliotrope burns its perfumes. In front of the Louvre the hollyhocks soar up as slender as masts, as noble and graceful as columns, and blushing like young girls. Iridescent with sunlight and sighing with love, the water jets spurt toward the sky. At the end of the terrace a stone horseman, galloping furiously without budging, his lips glued to a joyful trumpet, embodies all the ardor of spring.

But now the sky is darkening; it is about to rain. The basins, where no azure is shining anymore, are like blank eyes or vases full of tears. The absurd water jet, whipped by the breeze, raises its now ludicrous hymn more and more swiftly toward the sky. The futile sweetness of the lilacs is infinitely sad. And over there, riding hell for leather, the immobile and furious motion of his marble feet urging on his charger in its fixed and dizzying gallop, the oblivious horseman keeps endlessly blasting his trumpet against the black sky.

2 Versailles

A canal that inspires dreams in the most inveterate chatterboxes the instant they draw near, and where I am always happy whether I feel cheerful or mournful.
—GUEZ DE BALZAC IN A LETTER TO MONSIEUR DE LAMOTHE-AIGRON

The exhausted autumn, no longer warmed by the meager sunshine, is losing its final colors one by one. The extreme ardor of its foliage, blazing so intensely as to maintain the glorious illusion of a sunset throughout the afternoons and even the mornings, is now extinguished. Only the dahlias, the French marigolds, and the yellow, violet, white, and pink chrysanthemums are still glowing on the somber and desolate face of autumn. At six in the evening, when you walk across the uniformly gray and naked Tuileries under the equally gloomy sky, where, branch for branch, the black trees sketch their profound and delicate despair, an abruptly spotted bed

of those autumn flowers brightens richly in the dusk, inflicting a voluptuous violence on our eyes, which are accustomed
to those ashen horizons.

The morning hours are gentler. The sun still shines intermit-
tently, and, leaving the terrace by the edge of the water and
going down the vast stone stairway before me, I can still see my
shadow descending the steps one by one. After so many others
(especially Mssrs. Maurice Barrès, Henri de Régnier, and Robert
de Montesquiou-Fezensac), I would hesitate to utter your name,
Versailles, your grand name, sweet and rusty, the royal cemetery of foliage, of vast marbles and waters, a truly aristocratic
and demoralizing place, where we are not even troubled by remorse that the lives of so many workers merely served to refine
and expand not so much the joys of another age as the melancholy of our own. After so many others I would hesitate to utter
your name, and yet how often have I drunk from the reddened
cup of your pink marble basins, drunk to the dregs, savoring the
delirium, the intoxicating bittersweetness of these waning autumn days. In the distance the earth, mixed with faded leaves
and rotted leaves, always seemed to be a tarnished yellow and
violet mosaic.

Passing close to the *Hameau* and pulling up my overcoat
collar against the wind, I heard the cooing of doves. I was intoxicated everywhere by the fragrance of blessed palms as on
Palm Sunday. How could I still pick a slender nosegay of spring
in these gardens ransacked by autumn? On the water the wind
crumpled the petals of a shivering rose. In this vast defoliation
of the Trianon, only the slight arch of a small white geranium
bridge raised its flowers above the icy water, their heads
scarcely bowed by the wind.

Granted, ever since I inhaled the sea breeze and the salt air
in the sunken roads of Normandy, ever since I glimpsed the
ocean shining through the branches of blossoming rhododen-
drons, I have known about everything that the closeness of
water can add to the charms of vegetation. But what more virginal purity in this sweet, white geranium, leaning with graceful
restraint over the chilly waters among their banks of dead

110

leaves. Oh, silvery old age of woods still green, oh, weeping branches, ponds and pools that a pious gesture has placed here and there, like urns offered up to the melancholy of the trees!

3 Stroll

Despite the pure sky and the already hot sunshine, the wind was still as cold, the trees were still as bare as in winter. To light a fire I had to cut down one of the branches that I thought were dead, but the sap spurted out, soaking my arm up to the elbow and exposing a tumultuous heart under the frozen bark of the tree. In between the trunks the bare winter soil was covered with anemones, cowslips, and violets, while the streams, yesterday still gloomy and empty, were now filled with a blue, vivid, tender sky basking in the watery depths. Not the pale, weary sky of lovely October evenings, a sky stretching out on the watery bottom, virtually dying there of love and melancholy, but an intense and blazing sky on the tender and cheerful azure, from which grays, blues, and pinks kept flashing by: not the shadows of pensive clouds, but the dazzling and slippery fins of a perch, an eel, or a smelt. Drunk with joy, they scooted between sky and grass, through their meadows and forests, which were all brilliantly enchanted, like ours, by the resplendent genius of spring. And the waters, gliding coolly over their heads, between their gills, and under their bellies, hurried too, singing and gaily chasing the sunbeams.

The farmyard, where you went for eggs, was no less pleasant a sight. Like an inspired and prolific poet, who never refuses to spread beauty to the humblest places, which until now did not seem to share the domain of art, the sun still warmed the bountiful energy of the dung heap, of the unevenly paved yard, and of the pear tree worn down like an old serving maid.

Now who is that regally attired personage moving gingerly among the rustic articles and farm implements, tiptoeing to

111

avoid getting soiled? It is Juno's bird, dazzling not with lifeless gems but with the very eyes of Argus: it is the peacock, whose fabled glory is astonishing in these surroundings. Just as on a festive day, strutting before the clusters of gaping admirers at the gate, several minutes before the arrival of the first few guests, the glittering mistress of the house, in a gown with an iridescent train, an azure gorgerin already attached to her royal throat, her aigrettes on her head, crosses the yard to issue a final order or wait for a prince of the blood, whom she must welcome right at the threshold.

And yet this is where the peacock spends its life, a veritable bird of paradise in a barnyard, among the chickens and turkeys, like a captive Andromache spinning her wool amid female slaves, but, unlike her, never abandoning the magnificence of royal insignia and crown jewels: a radiant Apollo, whom we always recognize even when he is guarding the herds of Admetus.

4 Family Listening to Music

For music is sweet,
It makes the soul harmonious and, like a heavenly choir,
It rouses a thousand voices that sing in the heart.
—VICTOR HUGO: *HERNANI*, ACT V, SCENE 3

For a truly dynamic family, in which each member thinks, loves, and acts, a garden is a pleasant thing. On spring, summer, and autumn evenings, they all gather there upon completing the tasks of the day; and however small the garden, however close its hedges, the latter are not so tall as not to reveal a large stretch of sky at which everyone gazes up in wordless reveries. The child dreams about his future plans, about the house he will inhabit with his best friend, never to leave him, about the secrets of earth and life. The young man dreams about the mysterious charm of the girl he loves; the young mother about her child's future; in the depths of these bright hours the once troubled wife discovers, behind her husband's cold façade, a painful and poignant regret that stirs her pity. The father, watching the smoke curling up from a roof, dwells on the peaceful scenes of his past, which are transfigured by the faraway evening light; he thinks about his coming death, about his children's lives after his death. And thus the soul of the united family rises religiously toward the sunset, while the huge fir, linden, or chestnut tree envelops the family with the blessing of exquisite fragrance or venerable shade.

But for a truly dynamic family, in which each member thinks, loves, and acts, for a family with a soul, how much sweeter it is if, in the evening, that soul can materialize in a voice, in the clear and inexhaustible voice of a girl or a young man who has received the gift of music and song. A stranger, passing the gate of a garden in which the family holds its tongue, would fear that his approach might rouse them out of a religious dream. But if the stranger, without hearing the singing, perceived the gathering of friends and relatives listening to it, then how much more would the family appear to be attending an unseen mass—that is, despite the variety of postures, how strongly the resemblance of expressions would manifest the true unity of souls, a unity momentarily realized in their sympathy for the same ideal drama, by their communion in one and the same dream.

At times, as the wind bends the grass and agitates the branches for a long time, a breath bows the heads or suddenly raises them again. Then, as if an invisible messenger were telling a thrilling tale, they all seem to be waiting anxiously, listening in rapture or terror to the same news, which, however, elicits diverse echoes in each person. The anguish of the music reaches its peak; its outbursts are shattered by deep plunges and followed by more desperate outbursts.

For the old man, the lustrous infinity, the mysterious darkness of the music are the vast spectacles of life and death; for the child, they are the urgent promises of sea and land; for the lover they are the mysterious infinity; they are the luminous darkness of love. The thinker sees his mental life unroll fully; the plunges of the _faltering_ melody are its faltering and its plunges, and its entire heart rebounds and snaps back when the melody regains its flight. The powerful murmuring of the harmonies stirs up the rich and obscure depths of his memory. The man of action pants in the <u>melee</u> of chords, in the gallop of vivaces; he triumphs majestically in the adagios.

Even the unfaithful wife feels that her sin is forgiven, is lost in infinity, her sin, which also originated in the dissatisfaction of a heart that, unappeased by the usual joys, had gone astray, but only in a quest for the mystery, and whose highest aspirations are now gratified by this music, which is as full as the voices of bells.

The musician, who, however, claims to take only technical pleasure in music, also experiences those meaningful emotions, which, however, are so thoroughly wrapped up in his concept of musical beauty as to be hidden from his sight.

And I myself, finally, listening in music to the most expansive and most universal beauty of life and death, sea and sky, I also feel what is unique and particular in your enchantment, oh darling beloved.

5

Today's paradoxes are tomorrow's prejudices, for today's grossest and most disagreeable prejudices had their moment of novelty, when fashion lent them its fragile grace. Many women today wish to rid themselves of all prejudices, and by prejudices they mean principles. That is their prejudice, and it is heavy even though it adorns them like a delicate and slightly exotic flower. They believe there is no such thing as perspective depth, so they put everything in the same plane. They enjoy a book or life itself like a beautiful day or like an orange. They talk about the "art" of a dressmaker and the "philosophy" of

"Parisian life." They would blush to classify anything, to judge anything, to say: This is good, this is bad.

In the past, when a woman behaved properly, it was the revenge of her morals, that is, her mind, over her instinctive nature. Nowadays, when a woman behaves properly, it is the revenge of her instinctive nature over her morals—that is, her theoretical immorality (look at the plays of Mssrs. Halévy and Meilhac). In an extreme loosening of all moral and social bonds, women drift to and fro between that theoretical immorality and their instinctive righteousness. All they seek is pleasure, and they find it only when they do not seek it, when they are in a state of voluntary inaction. In books this skepticism and dilettantism would shock us like an old-fashioned adornment. But women, far from being the oracles of intellectual fashions, are actually their belated parrots. Even today, dilettantism still pleases them and suits them. While it may cloud their judgment and hamstring their conduct, one cannot deny that it lends them an already withered but still appealing grace. They make us rapturously feel whatever ease and sweetness existence may have in highly refined civilizations.

In their perpetual embarcation for a spiritual Cythera— where they will celebrate not so much their dulled senses as the imagination, the heart, the mind, the eyes, the nostrils, the ears—women add some voluptuous delight to their attitudes. And I assume that the most faithful portraitists of our time will not depict them with any great tension or rigidity. Their lives emit the sweet perfume of unbound hair.

6

Ambition is more intoxicating than fame; desire makes all things blossom, possession wilts them; it is better to dream your life than to live it, even if living it means dreaming it, though both less mysteriously and less vividly, in a murky and sluggish dream, like the straggling dream in the feeble awareness of ruminant creatures. Shakespeare's plays are more beautiful when viewed in your study than when mounted on a stage. The poets who have created imperishably loving women have often known only mediocre barmaids, while the most envied voluptuaries do not understand the life that they lead or, rather, that leads them.

I knew a little ten-year-old boy who, in poor health and with a precocious imagination, had devoted a purely cerebral love to an older girl. He would sit at his window for hours, waiting for her to pass, weeping if he did not see her, weeping even more if he did see her. He would spend very rare, very brief moments with her. He could no longer sleep or eat. One day he threw himself out the window. At first, people believed that his despair at never approaching his sweetheart had driven him to suicide. But then they learned that he had just had a very long chat with her: she had been extremely kind to him. So everyone assumed he had renounced the insipid days that remained of his life after that euphoria, which he might never have a chance to relive. However, from secrets he had often confided in a friend people finally inferred that he had been disappointed whenever he saw the sovereign of his dreams; but once she was gone, his fertile imagination granted the absent girl all her former power, and he again desired to see her.

Each time, he tried to blame the accidental reason for his disappointment on the imperfection of circumstances. After that final conversation, when his already skillful imagination had carried his sweetheart to the supreme perfection of which her nature was capable, the boy, desperately comparing that imperfect perfection with the absolute perfection by which he lived, by which he died, threw himself out the window. Subsequently, having become an idiot, he lived a very long life, but his fall had cost him all memory of his soul, his mind, the voice of his sweetheart, whom he would run into without seeing her. She, despite pleas and threats, married him and died several years later without ever getting him to recognize her.

Life is like that little sweetheart. We dream it and we love it in dreaming it. We should not try to live it: otherwise, like that little boy, we will plunge into stupidity, though not at one swoop, for in life everything degenerates by imperceptible nuances. At the end of ten years we no longer recognize our dreams; we deny them, we live, like a cow, for the grass we are grazing on at the moment. And who knows if our wedding with death might not lead to our conscious immortality?

7

"Captain," said his orderly several days after the preparation of the cottage, where the retired officer was to live until his death (which his heart condition would not keep waiting for long). "Captain, now that you can no longer make love or fight, perhaps some books might distract you a little. What should I buy for you?"

"Buy me nothing; no books; they can't tell me anything as interesting as the things I've done. And since I don't have much time left, I don't want anything to distract me from my memories. Hand me the key to my large chest; its contents are what I'll be reading every day."

And he took out letters, a whitish, sometimes tinted sea of letters: some very long, some consisting of a single line, on a card, with faded flowers, objects, brief notes he had jotted down to recall the momentary surroundings where he had received them, and photographs that had spoiled despite precautions, like relics worn out by the very piety of the faithful: they kiss them too often. And all those things were very old, and there were some from women who had died and others whom he had not seen in over ten years.

Among all those things there were the slight but clear-cut traces of sensuality or affection tied to the least minutiae of the circumstances of his life, and it was like an immense fresco that, without narrating his life, depicted it, but only in its most passionate hues and in a very hazy and yet very particular manner, with a great and touching power. There were memories of

kisses on the mouth—a fresh mouth in which he had unhesitatingly left his soul and which had since turned away from him—
reminiscences that made him weep and weep. And although
quite feeble and disillusioned, he felt a good, warm thrill upon
gulping down a few of those still living memories, like a glass of
fiery wine that had ripened in the sun, which had devoured his
life; it was the kind of thrill that spring gives our convalescences
and winter's hearth our weaknesses. The feeling that his old,
worn body had nevertheless blazed with similar flames—blazed
with similar devouring flames—brought a renewal to his life.
Then, musing that the things lying down full-length upon him
were simply the enormous, moving shadows, which, elusive,
alas, would all soon intermingle in the eternal night, he began
weeping again.

And, while knowing that those were nothing but shadows,
shadows of flames, which had hurried off to burn somewhere
else, which he would never see again, he nevertheless started
worshiping them, lending them a cherished existence that contrasted with imminent and absolute oblivion. And all those
kisses and all that kissed hair and all those things made up of
tears and lips, of caresses poured out like heady wine, of despairs gathering like music or like evening for the bliss of being
infinitely permeated with mystery and destinies: the adored
woman, who had possessed him so thoroughly that nothing
had existed for him but whatever had served his adoration; she
had possessed him so thoroughly and was now slipping away,
so vague that he no longer held on to her, no longer held on to
even the perfume wafting from the fleeing folds of her cloak.
He convulsively tried to revive all those things, resurrect them,
and pin them like butterflies. And it grew more difficult each
time. And he still had caught none of the butterflies; but each
time, his fingers had rubbed off a smidgen of the glamour of
their wings; or rather, he saw them in the mirror, he vainly
banged on the mirror to touch them, but only dimmed it slightly
more each time, and he saw the butterflies only as indistinct and
less enchanting. And nothing could cleanse that tarnished mirror of his heart now that the purifying breath of youth or genius

would no longer pass over it—by what unknown law of our seasons, what mysterious equinox of our autumn. . . ?

And each time, he felt less sorrow about losing them—those kisses on those lips, and those endless hours, and those fragrances that had once made him delirious.

And he sorrowed for sorrowing less, and then even that sorrow faded. Then all sorrows drifted away, all; he did not have to banish pleasures: clutching their flowering branches and without looking back, they had long since fled on their winged heels, fled this dwelling which was no longer young enough for them. Then, like all human beings, he died.

8 Relics

I have bought everything of hers that was for sale: I had wanted to be her lover, but she refused to even chat with me for an instant. I have the small deck of cards with which she amused herself every evening, her two marmosets, three novels bearing her coat-of-arms on their boards, and her dog. Oh, you delights, dear leisures of her life: without even relishing them as I would have done, without even desiring them, you had all her freest, most secret, and most inviolable hours; you did not feel your happiness and you cannot describe it.

Cards, which she handled every evening with her closest friends, which saw her bored or laughing, which witnessed the start of her romance and which she put down so as to kiss the man who came to play with her every evening after that; novels, which she opened or closed in bed at the whim of her fancy or fatigue, which she selected according to her momentary caprice or her dreams, novels, to which she confided her dreams, which mingled with the dreams they expressed, and which helped her to dream her own dreams better—have you retained nothing about her, and will you tell me nothing?

Novels, because she too imagined the lives of your characters and of your poet; cards, because in her own way she, together with you, felt the calm and sometimes the fever of vivid intimacy—novels, have you kept nothing of her mind, which you diverted or imbued, nothing of her heart, which you unburdened or consoled?

Cards, novels, which she held so often, which lay so long on her table; you queens, kings, or jacks, who were the motionless guests at her most reckless parties; you heroes and heroines of novels, who, near her bed and under the crossed lights of her lamp and her eyes, dreamed your dream, silent yet full of voices—you could not have allowed all the perfume to evaporate, all the fragrance with which you were permeated by the air in her room, the fabrics of her frocks, the touch of her hands or her knees.

You have preserved the creases inflicted on you by her joyful or nervous hand; and perhaps you still imprison the tears of grief induced by a book or by life; and the daylight that brightened or wounded her eyes gave you that warm color. I touch you all atremble, fearful of your revelations, worried by your silence. Alas! Perhaps, like you, bewitching and fragile beings, she was the indifferent and unconscious witness to her own grace. Her most genuine beauty may have been in my desire. She lived her life, but I may have been the only one to dream it.

9 Moonlight Sonata

ONE

More than by the fatiguing trip, I was exhausted by my memory and by frightened thoughts of my father's demands, of Pia's indifference, and of my enemies' relentlessness. During the day, my mind had been diverted by Assunta's company, her singing, her gentleness toward me, whom she barely knew, her white, brown, and rosy beauty, her fragrance persisting in the blusters of the ocean wind, the feather in her hat, the pearls around her neck. But toward nine at night, feeling overwhelmed, I asked her to take the carriage back on her own and leave me to rest a bit in the fresh air. We had almost reached Honfleur; the place was well chosen: it was located against a wall, by the gateway to a double avenue lined with huge trees that shielded against the wind, and the air was mild. Assunta agreed and left. I stretched out on the grass, facing the gloomy sky; lulled by the murmuring sea, which I could hear behind me but not discern in the darkness, I shortly dozed off.

Soon I dreamed that in front of me the sunset was illuminating the distant sand and sea. Twilight was thickening, and it seemed to me that these were a sunset and a twilight like any twilight and any sunset. Then I was handed a letter; I tried to read it, but I was unable to make out anything. Only now did I realize it was very dark out despite the impression of intense and diffuse light. This sunset was extraordinarily pale, lustrous without brightness, and so much darkness gathered on the magically illuminated sand that I had to make an arduous effort merely to recognize a seashell. In this twilight, the kind special to dreams, the sun, ill and faded, appeared to be setting on a polar beach.

My distress had suddenly dissipated; my father's decisions, Pia's feelings, my enemies' cunning still weighed on me but no longer crushed me: they were like a natural and irrelevant necessity. The contradiction of that dark resplendence, the miracle of that enchanted respite for my ills, inspired no defiance in me, no dread; instead I was swept up, deluged, inundated by a growing bliss and finally awakened by its delicious intensity. I opened my eyes. Splendid and pallid, my dream spread out all around me. The wall I was resting against was brightly lit, and the shadow of its ivy was as sharp as at four in the afternoon. The leaves of a silver poplar glistened as they were turned over by a faint breeze. Whitecaps and white sails were visible on the water, the sky was clear, the moon had risen. For brief moments, wispy clouds drifted across the moon, where they were tinted with blue nuances, their pallor as deep as the jelly of a medusa or the heart of an opal. Brightness shone everywhere, but my eyes could not catch it. The darkness persisted even on the grass, which was glowing almost like a mirage. The woods and a trench were absolutely black. All at once, a slight rustle awakened slowly like a misgiving, then swelled quickly and seemed to roll over the forest. It was the shuddering of leaves crumpled by the breeze. One by one I heard them surging like waves against the vast silence of the entire night. Then the rustle itself waned and died out.

In the grassy strip running ahead of me between the two dense lines of oaks, a river of brightness appeared to flow, contained between those two embankments of gloom. The moonlight, conjuring up the gatekeeper's lodge, the foliage, a sail from the night where they had been demolished, failed to arouse them. In this dreamlike hush, the moon illuminated only the hazy phantoms of their shapes without distinguishing their contours, which made them so real for me in the daytime, which oppressed me with the certainty of their presence and the perpetuity of their trivial surroundings. The lodge without a door, the foliage without a trunk, almost without leaves, the sail without a boat, appeared to be not so much a cruelly undeniable and monotonously habitual reality as the strange, inconsistent, and luminous dreams of slumbering trees plunging into darkness. Never, indeed, had the woods slept so profoundly; I sensed that the moon had taken advantage of their slumber so that it might silently begin that grand, pale, and gentle celebration in the sky and the sea.

My sadness had vanished; I could hear my father scolding me, Pia mocking me, my enemies hatching plots, and none of that seemed real. The sole reality was in that unreal light, and I invoked it with a smile. I did not understand what inscrutable resemblance united my sorrows with the solemn mysteries celebrated in the woods, in the sky, and on the sea, but I sensed that their explanation, their consolation, their forgiveness were proffered, and that it made no difference that my mind did not share the secret since my heart understood it so well. I called my holy mother by her name, Night; my sadness had recognized her immortal sister in the moon, the moon shone on the transfigured sorrows of night, and melancholy had arisen in my heart, where the clouds had dissipated.

TWO

Then I heard footsteps. Assunta was coming toward me, her white face looming over a huge, dark coat. She murmured to me: "I was afraid you'd be cold; my brother was in bed, I've come back." I approached her; I was shivering; she pulled me inside her coat and, to keep its folds around me, she slipped her arm around my neck. We walked a few paces under the trees, in the profound darkness. Something flared up before us; I had no time to back up; I wanted to move aside, thinking we were bumping into a trunk, but the obstacle slid under our feet—we had strolled into the moon. I drew Assunta's head close to mine. She smiled; I started crying; I saw that she was crying too. Then we realized that the moon was crying and that its sadness was consistent with our own. The sweet and poignant flashes of its light went to our very hearts. Like us it was crying, and, as we do nearly always, it cried without knowing why, but with such intense feelings that its sweet and irresistible despair swept along the woods, the fields, the sky (which was again reflected in the sea), and my heart, which at last saw clearly into its heart.

10 The Source of Tears in Past Loves

When novelists or their heroes contemplate their lost loves, their ruminations, so poignant for the reader, are, alas, quite artificial. There is a gap between the immensity of our past love and the absoluteness of our present indifference, of which we are reminded by a thousand material details: a name recalled in conversation, a letter rediscovered in a drawer, an actual encounter with the person, or, even better, the act of possessing her after the fact, so to speak. In a work of art, the contrast may be so distressing, so full of restrained tears, but in life our response is cold, precisely because our present state is indifference and oblivion, our beloved and our love please us at most aesthetically, and because agitation and the ability to suffer have disappeared along with love. Thus the agonizing melancholy of this contrast is only a moral truth. This melancholy would also become a psychological reality were a writer to place it at the start of the passion he describes and not after its end.

Often, indeed, when, warned by our experience and sagacity (and despite the protests of the heart, which has the sentiment or rather the illusion that our love will last forever) that someday we will be utterly unconcerned about this woman, the very thought of whom currently sustains our life: we will be as indifferent to her as we are now to all other women. . . . We will hear her name without painful pleasure, we will see her handwriting without trembling, we will not change our route in order to catch sight of her in the street, we will run into her without anxiety, we will possess her without delirium. Then, despite the absurd and powerful presentiment that we will always love her, that certain prescience will make us weep; and love, the love that has risen over us once again like a divine, an infinitely woeful and mysterious morning, will spread a bit of its huge, strange, and profound horizons before our anguish, a bit of its bewitching desolation. . . .

11 Friendship

When you feel sorrowful, it is good to lie down in the warmth of your bed, and, quelling all effort and resistance and burying even your head under the covers, you surrender completely, moaning, like branches in the autumn wind. But there is an even finer bed, redolent with divine fragrances. It is our sweet, our deep, our inscrutable friendship. That is where I cozily rest my heart when the world turns sad and icy. Enveloping even my mind in our warm affection, perceiving nothing beyond that, and no longer wanting to defend myself, disarmed, but promptly fortified and made invincible by the miracle of our affection, I weep for my sorrow, and for my joy at having a safe place to hide my sorrow.

12 Ephemeral Efficacy of Grief

Let us be thankful to the people who bring us happiness; they are the enchanting gardeners who make our souls blossom. But let us be even more grateful to cruel or merely indifferent women, to unkind friends who have caused us grief. They have devastated our hearts, which are now littered with unrecognizable wreckage; they have uprooted tree trunks and mutilated the most delicate boughs like a ravaging wind that has nevertheless sown a few good seeds for an uncertain harvest.

By smashing all the bits of happiness that concealed our greatest misery from ourselves, by turning our hearts into bare, melancholy courtyards, they have enabled us to finally contemplate our hearts and judge them. Mournful plays are similarly good for us; we must therefore regard them as far superior to cheerful plays, which stave off our hunger instead of satisfying it: the bread that should nourish us is bitter. In a happy life, the destinies of our fellow men never appear to us in their true light: they are either masked by self-interest or transfigured by desire. But in the detachment we gain from suffering in life and from the sentiment of painful beauty on stage, other men's destinies and even our own empower our attentive souls to hear the eternal but unheard voice of duty and truth. The sad work of a true artist speaks to us in that tone of people who have suffered, who force anyone who has suffered to drop everything and listen.

Alas! What sentiment has brought it removes capriciously, and sadness, more sublime than gaiety, is not as enduring as virtue. By this morning we have forgotten last night's tragedy, which elevated us so high that we could view our lives in their entirety and their reality with sincere and clear-sighted compassion. Within a year perhaps we will get over a woman's betrayal, a friend's death. Amid this wreckage of dreams, this scattering of withered happiness, the wind has sown the good seed under a deluge of tears, but they will dry too soon for the seed to germinate.

125

13 In Praise of Bad Music

(After a performance of François de Curel's L'Invitée)

Detest bad music but do not make light of it. Since it is played, or rather sung, far more frequently, far more passionately than good music, it has gradually and far more thoroughly absorbed human dreams and tears. That should make it venerable for you. Its place, nonexistent in the history of art, is immense in the history of the emotions of societies. Not only is the respect—I am not saying love—for bad music a form of what might be called the charity of good taste, or its skepticism, it is also the awareness of the important social role played by music. How many ditties, though worthless in an artist's eyes, are among the confidants chosen by the throng of romantic and amorous adolescents. How many songs like "Gold Ring" or "Ah, slumber, slumber long and deep," whose pages are turned every evening by trembling and justly famous hands, are soaked with tears from the most beautiful eyes in the world: and the purest maestro would envy this melancholy and voluptuous homage of tears, the ingenious and inspired confidants that ennoble sorrow, exalt dreams, and, in exchange for the ardent secret that is confided in them, supply the intoxicating illusion of beauty.

Since the common folk, the middle class, the army, the aristocracy have the same mailmen—bearers of grief that strikes them or happiness that overwhelms them—they have the same invisible messengers of love, the same beloved confessors. These are the bad composers. The same annoying jingle, to which every well-born, well-bred ear instantly refuses to listen, has received the treasure of thousands of souls and guards the secret of thousands of lives: it has been their living inspiration, their consolation, which is always ready, always half-open on the music stand of the piano—and it has been their dreamy grace and their ideal. Certain arpeggios, certain reentries of motifs have made the souls of more than one lover or dreamer vibrate with the harmonies of paradise or the very voice of the beloved herself. A collection of bad love songs, tattered from overuse, has to touch us like a cemetery or a village. So what if the houses have no style, if the graves are vanishing under taste-less ornaments and inscriptions? Before an imagination sympa-thetic and respectful enough to conceal momentarily its aes-thetic disdain, that dust may release a flock of souls, their beaks holding the still <u>verdant</u> dream that gave them an inkling of the next world and let them rejoice or weep in this world.

14 Lakeside Encounter

Yesterday, before going to dine in the Bois de Boulogne, I re-ceived a letter from Her: after a week she was responding rather coldly to my desperate letter, notifying me that she feared she could not say goodbye to me before leaving. And I, yes, rather coldly replied that it was better this way, and I wished her a pleasant summer. Then I dressed and I rode across the Bois in an open carriage. I felt extremely sad, but calm. I was deter-mined to forget, I had made up my mind: it was a matter of time.

As my carriage turned into the lakeside drive, I spotted a lone woman slowly walking at the far end of the small path that circles the lake fifty meters from the drive. At first I could barely make her out. She waved casually at me, and then I recognized her despite the distance between us. It was she! I waved back for a long time. And she continued to gaze at me as if wanting me to halt and take her along. I did nothing of the kind, but I soon felt an almost ex-terior agitation pounce upon me and grip me firmly. "I guessed right!" I exclaimed. "For some unknown reason she's always feigned indifference toward me. She loves me, the dear thing."

An infinite happiness, an invincible certainty came over me; I felt dizzy and I burst into sobs. The carriage was approaching Armenonville; I dried my eyes, and the gentle greeting of her hand passed over them as if also to dry their tears, and her softly questioning eyes fixed on mine, asking if I could take her along.

When I arrived at the dinner, I was radiant. My happiness spread to each person in hearty, blissful, thankful amiability: nobody had the slightest inkling what hand unknown to them— the little hand that had waved to me—had kindled this great fire of my joy, its radiance visible to everyone; and my sense of their unawareness of that hand added the charm of secret sensual delights to my happiness. We were waiting only for Madame de T., and she soon arrived. She is the most insignificant person I know and, though somewhat attractive, the most unpleasant. But I was too happy not to forgive each individual for his faults, his ugliness, and I went over to her with an affectionate smile.

"You were less friendly just now," she said.

"Just now?" I said, astonished. "Just now? But I haven't seen you."

"What do you mean? You didn't recognize me? It's true you were far away. I was strolling along the lake, you drove by proudly in your carriage, I waved at you and I wanted to ride with you so as not to be late."

"You mean that was you?" I exclaimed and in my despair I repeated several times: "Oh, do please forgive me, please forgive me!"

"How unhappy he looks! My compliments, Charlotte," said the mistress of the house. "But you can cheer up, she's with you now."

I was crushed; my entire happiness was destroyed.

All well and good! But the most horrible part of it was that it was not as if it had not been. Even after I realized my mistake, that loving image of the woman who did not love me altered my conception of her for a long time. I attempted a reconciliation, I forgot about her less quickly, and, struggling to find solace for my distress by imagining that those were her hands as I had originally *felt,* I often closed my eyes to evoke those little hands, which had waved to me, which would have so nicely dried my eyes, so nicely cooled my brow—those little gloved hands, which she gently held out by the lake, as frail symbols of peace, love, and reconciliation, while her sad and questioning eyes seemed to ask me to take her along.

15

Like a blood-red sky that warns the passerby, "There is a fire over there," certain blazing looks often reveal passions that they serve merely to reflect. They are flames in the mirror. But sometimes even carefree and cheerful people have eyes that are vast and somber like grief, as if a filter had been stretched between the soul and the eyes so that all the live content of the soul had virtually seeped into the eyes. Warmed solely by the fervor of their egoism (that attractive fervor of egoism, to which people are drawn as strongly as they are alienated by inflammatory passion), the parched soul is henceforth nothing but an artificial palace of intrigues. However, their eyes, which endlessly burn with love, and which a dew of languor will water, set aglow, cause to float, and drown without extinguishing them—those eyes will astonish the universe with their tragic blaze. Twin spheres that are now independent of the soul, spheres of love, ardent satellites of an eternally frozen world, those spheres will continue to cast an unwonted and deceptive shimmer until the death of these false prophets, these perjurers, whose promise of love the heart will not keep.

16 The Stranger

Dominique had settled next to the extinguished fire, waiting for his guests. Every evening he would invite some aristocrat to come for supper together with men of wit; and since he was rich, well-born, and charming, he was never alone. The candles had not yet been lit, and the daylight was dying sadly in the room. All at once he heard a voice, a distant and intimate voice, saying to him: "Dominique"; and at the mere sound of it, so far and so near, "Dominique," he froze with fear. He had never heard that voice before, and yet he recognized it so clearly, his remorse recognized so clearly the voice of a victim, a noble victim that he had immolated. He tried to remember some ancient crime he had committed, but none came to mind. Yet the tone of that voice reproached him for a crime, a crime he had probably committed without realizing it, but for which he was responsible—as attested by his fear and sadness. Upon raising his eyes he saw, standing before him, grave and familiar, a stranger with a vague and gripping demeanor. Uttering a few respectful words, Dominique bowed to the stranger's obvious and melancholy authority.

"Dominique, am I the only person you won't invite to supper? You have some wrongs to right with me, ancient wrongs. Then I will teach you how to get along without other people, who will no longer come when you're old."

"I invite you to supper," Dominique replied with a warm gravity that surprised him.

"Thank you," said the stranger.

No crest was inscribed in the stone on his ring, nor had wit frosted his words with its glittering needles. However, the gratitude in his firm, brotherly gaze intoxicated Dominique with unknown happiness.

"But if you wish to keep me here, you have to dismiss your other guests."

Dominique heard them knocking at the door. The candles were unlit; the room was pitch-black.

"I can't dismiss them," Dominique replied, "*I can't be alone.*"

"With me you'll be alone, that's true," said the stranger sadly. "But you have to keep me here. You have to right ancient wrongs that you did me. I love you more than all of them do and I'll teach you how to get along without those others, who will no longer come when you're old."

"I can't," said Dominique.

And he sensed he had just sacrificed a noble happiness at the command of an imperious and vulgar habit, that no longer had even pleasures to dispense as prizes for obedience.

"Choose quickly," said the stranger, pleading and haughty.

Dominique went to open the door, and at the same time he asked the stranger, without daring to turn his head: "Just who are you?"

And the stranger, the stranger who was already disappearing, said: "Habit, to which you are again sacrificing me tonight, will be stronger tomorrow thanks to the blood of the wound that you're inflicting on me in order to nourish that habit. And more imperious for being obeyed yet again, habit will turn you away from me slightly more each day and force you to increase my suffering. Soon you will have killed me. You will never see me again. Yet you'll have owed me more than you owe the others, who will shortly abandon you. I am inside you and yet I am forever remote from you; I almost no longer exist. I am your soul, I am yourself."

The guests had entered. The company stepped into the dining room, and Dominique wanted to describe his conversation with the visitor, who had disappeared; but given the overall boredom and the obvious strain it put on the host to remember an almost faded dream, Girolamo interrupted him—to the great satisfaction of everyone, including even Dominique—and drew the following conclusion:

"One should never be alone; solitude breeds melancholy."

Then they resumed drinking; Dominique chatted gaily but without joy, though flattered by the dazzling company.

17 Dream

Your tears flowed for me, my lip drank your weeping.

—ANATOLE FRANCE

It takes no effort for me to recall what my opinion of Madame Dorothy B. was last Saturday (three days ago). As luck would have it, people talked about her that day, and I was forthright in saying that I found her to be devoid of charm and wit. I believe she is twenty-two or twenty-three. Anyway, I barely know her, and whenever I thought about her, no vivid memory ruffled my mind, so that all I had before my eyes was the letters of her name.

On Saturday I went to bed quite early. But around two A.M., the wind blasted so hard that I had to get up and close a loose shutter that had awakened me. I mused about the brief sleep I had enjoyed, and I was delighted that it had been so refreshing, with no distress, no dreams. As soon as I lay back down, I drifted off again. But after an indeterminable stretch of time, I started waking up little by little—or rather, I was roused little by little into the world of dreams, which at first was blurry, like the real world when we normally awaken, but then the world of dreams cleared up. I was in Trouville, lying on the beach, which doubled as a hammock in an unfamiliar garden, and a woman was gently studying me. It was Madame Dorothy B. I was no more surprised than I am when waking up in the morning and recognizing my bedroom. Nor was I astonished at my companion's supernatural charm and at the ecstasy of both sensual and spiritual adoration caused by her presence. We looked at each other in a profound rapport, experiencing a great miracle of glory and happiness, a miracle of which we were fully aware, to which she was a party, and for which I was infinitely grateful to her.

But she said to me: "You're crazy to thank me, wouldn't you have done the same for me?"

And the feeling (it was, incidentally, a perfect certainty) that I would have done the same for her intensified my joy into delirium as the manifest symbol of the most intimate union. She signaled mysteriously with her finger and smiled. And, as if I had been both in her and in me, I knew that the signal meant: "Do all your enemies, all your adversities, all your regrets, all your weaknesses matter anymore?"

And without my uttering a word, she heard me reply that she had easily vanquished everything, destroyed everything, voluptuously cast a spell on my suffering. And she approached me, caressed my neck, and slowly turned up the ends of my moustache. Then she said to me: "Now let's go to the others, let's enter life." I was filled with superhuman joy and I felt strong enough to make all this virtual happiness come true. She wanted to give me a flower and from between her breasts she drew a yellow and pale-pink rosebud and slipped it into my buttonhole. Suddenly I felt my intoxication swell with a new delight. The rose in my buttonhole had begun exhaling its scent of love, which wafted up to my nostrils.

I saw that my joy was causing Dorothy an agitation that I could not understand. Her eyes (I was certain of it because of my mysterious awareness of her specific individuality)—her eyes shivered with the faint spasm that occurs a second before the moment of weeping, and at that precise moment it was my eyes that filled with tears, her tears I might say. She drew nearer, turning her face up to my cheek, and I could contemplate the mysterious grace of her head, its captivating vivacity, and, with her tongue darting out between her fresh, smiling lips, she gathered all my tears on the edges of her eyes. Then she swallowed my tears with a light whisking of her lips, a noise that I experienced as an unknown kiss, more intimately troubling than if it had touched my lips directly.

I awoke with a start, recognized my room, and, the way lightning in a nearby storm is promptly followed by thunder, a dizzying reminiscence of happiness fused with, rather than preceded, the shattering certainty that this happiness was mendacious and impossible. However, despite all my reasoning, Dorothy B. was no longer the woman she had been for me only yesterday. The slight ripple left in my memory by our casual contact was nearly effaced, as if by a powerful tide that leaves unknown vestiges behind when it ebbs. I felt an immense desire, doomed in advance, to see her again; I instinctively needed to write to her and was prudently wary of doing so. When her name was mentioned in conversation, I trembled, yet it evoked the insignificant image that would have accompanied her before that night, and while I was as indifferent to her as to any commonplace socialite, she drew me more irresistibly than the most cherished mistresses or the most intoxicating destiny. I would not have lifted a finger to see her and yet I would have given my life for the other "her."

Each hour blurs a bit more of my memory of that dream, which is already quite distorted by this telling. I can make out less and less of my dream; it is like a book that you want to continue reading at your table when the declining day no longer provides enough light, when the night falls. In order to see it a bit clearly, I am obliged to stop thinking about it for a moment, the way you are obliged to squint in order to discern a few letters in the shadowy book. Faded as my dream may be, it still leaves me in deep agitation, the foam of its wake or the voluptuousness of its perfume. But my agitation will likewise dissipate, and I will be perfectly calm when I run into Madame B. And besides, why speak to her about things to which she is a stranger?

Alas! Love passed over me like that dream, with an equally mysterious power of transfiguration. And so, you who know the woman I love, you who were not in my dream, you cannot understand me; therefore do not try to give me advice.

18 Memory's Genre Paintings

We have certain reminiscences that are like the Dutch paintings in our minds, genre pictures in which the people, often of a modest station, are caught at a very simple moment of their lives, with no special events, at times with no events whatsoever, in a framework that is anything but grand and extraordinary. The charm lies in the naturalness of the figures and the simplicity of the scene, whereby the gap between picture and spectator is suffused with a soft light that bathes the scene in beauty.

My regimental life was full of these scenes, which I lived through naturally, with no keen joy or great distress, and which I recall affectionately. I remember the rustic settings, the naïveté of some of my peasant comrades, whose bodies remained more beautiful, more agile, their minds more down-to-earth, their hearts more spontaneous, their characters more natural than those of the young men with whom I associated before and after. I also remember the calmness of a life in which activity is regulated more and imagination controlled less than anywhere else, in which pleasure accompanies us all the more constantly because we never have time to flee it by dashing to find it. Today all those things unite, turning that phase of my life into a series of small paintings—interrupted, it is true, by lapses, but filled with happy truth and magic over which time has spread its sweet sadness and its poetry.

19 Ocean Wind in the Country

I will bring you a young poppy with purple petals.

—THEOCRITES: *THE CYCLOPS*

In the garden, in the grove, across the countryside, the wind devotes a wild and useless ardor to dispersing the blasts of sunshine, furiously shaking the branches in the copse, where those blasts first came crashing down, while the wind pursues them from the copse all the way to the sparkling thicket, where they are now quivering, palpitating. The trees, the drying linens, the peacock spreading its tail stand out in the transparent air as blue shadows, extraordinarily sharp, and flying with all winds, but not leaving the ground, like a poorly launched kite. Because of the jumble of wind and light, this corner of Champagne resembles a coastal landscape. When we reach the top of this path, which, burned by light and breathless with wind, rises in full sunshine toward a naked sky, will we not see the ocean, white with sun and foam? You had come as on every morning, with your hands full of flowers and with soft feathers dropped on the path in mid-flight by a ring dove, a swallow, or a jay. The feathers on my hat are trembling, the poppy in my buttonhole is losing its petals, let us hurry home.

The house groans in the wind like a ship; we hear the bellying of invisible sails, the flapping of invisible flags outside. Keep that bunch of fresh roses on your lap and let my heart weep in your clasping hands.

20 The Pearls

I came home in the morning and I went to bed, freezing and also trembling with an icy and melancholy delirium. A while ago, in your room, your friends of yesterday, your plans for tomorrow (just so many enemies, so many plots hatched against me), your thoughts at that time (so many vague and impassable distances), they all separated me from you. Now that I am far away from you, this imperfect presence, the fleeting mask of eternal absence—a mask quickly removed by kisses—would apparently suffice to show me your true face and satisfy the strivings of my love. I had to leave; I had to remain far away from you, sad and icy! But what sudden magic is causing the familiar dreams of my happiness to start rising again (a thick smoke over a bright and burning flame), rising joyously and continuously in my mind? In my hand, warmed under the bed covers, the fragrance of the rose-scented cigarettes that you got me to smoke has reawakened. With my lips pressed against my hand, I keep inhaling their perfume, which, in the warmth of memory, exhales dense billows of tenderness, happiness, and "you." Ah, my darling beloved! The instant that I can get along without you, that I swim, joyful, in my memory of you (which now fills the room), without struggling against your insurmountable body, I tell you absurdly, I tell you irresistibly: I cannot live without you. It is your presence that gives my life that fine, warm, melancholy hue, like the pearls that spend the night on your body. Like them, I live from and sadly draw my tinges from your warmth, and, like them, if you did not keep me close to you, I would die.

21 The Shores of Oblivion

"They say that Death embellishes its victims and exaggerates their virtues, but in general it is actually life that wronged them. Death, that pious and irreproachable witness, teaches us, in both truth and charity, that in each man there is usually more good than evil."

What Michelet says here about death may be even more applicable to the death that follows a great and unhappy love. If, after making us suffer so deeply, a person now means nothing to us, does it suffice to say that, according to the popular expression, he is "dead for us"? We weep for the dead, we still love them, we submit at length to the irresistible appeal of the magic that survives them and that so frequently draws us back to their graves. But the person who, on the contrary, made us experience everything, and with whose essence we were saturated, can no longer cause us even a hint of pain or joy. He is more than dead for us. After regarding him as the only precious thing in this world, after cursing him, after scorning him, we cannot possibly judge him, for his features barely take shape before our memory's eyes, which are exhausted from focusing far too long on his face. However, this judgment on the beloved person—a judgment that has varied so greatly, sometimes torturing our blind hearts with its acumen, sometimes also blinding itself so as to end this cruel discord—this judgment has to carry out a final variation.

Like those landscapes that we discover only from peaks, it is solely from the heights of forgiveness that she appears before you in her true worth—the woman who was more than dead to you after being your very life. All we knew was that she did not requite our love, but now we understand that she felt genuine friendship for us. It is not memory that embellishes her; it is love that wronged her. For the man who wants everything, and for whom everything, if he obtained it, would never suffice, receiving a little merely seems like an absurd cruelty. Now we understand that it was a generous gift from the woman, who was not discouraged by our despair, our irony, our perpetual tyranny. She was always kind. Several remarks of hers, quoted for us today, sound indulgently precise and enchanting, several remarks made by the woman whom we thought incapable of understanding us because she did not love us. We, on the contrary, spoke about her with so much unjust egotism, so much severity. Do we not, incidentally, owe her a great deal?

If that great tide of love has ebbed forever, we nevertheless can, when strolling inside ourselves, gather strange and beguiling shells, and, when holding them to one ear, we can, with a mournful pleasure and without suffering, hear the immense roaring of the past. Then, deeply moved, we think about the woman, who, to our misfortune, was loved more than she loved. No longer is she "more than dead" for us. She is a dead person whom we remember affectionately. Justice would have us revise our opinion of her. And by the all-powerful virtue of justice, she can be mentally resurrected in our hearts so as to appear for that last judgment that we render far away from her, render calmly and tearfully.

22 Physical Presence

We loved each other in the Engadine, in some remote village with a doubly sweet name: the reverie of German sonorities languished in the voluptuousness of Italian syllables. All around, three unbelievably verdant lakes reflected the fir forests. Peaks and glaciers closed off the horizon. In the evening the delicacy of the light was intensified by the variety of those perspectives. Will we ever forget the lakeside strolls in Sils-Maria, at six o'clock in the fading afternoon? The larches, so darkly serene when bordering on the dazzling snow, stretched their branches, of a sleek and radiant green, into the pale-blue, nearly mauve water.

One evening, the hour was especially favorable to us: within moments the setting sun brought out all possible nuances in the water and brought our souls all possible delights. Suddenly we gave a start: we had just seen a small, rosy butterfly, then two, then five, leaving the flowers on our shore and fluttering over the lake. Soon they looked like an impalpable rosy dust sweeping along the surface; then they reached the flowers on the opposite shore, fluttered back, and gently resumed their adventurous passage, stopping at times, as if yielding to temptation upon this preciously tinged water like a huge, fading blossom. This was too much, and our eyes filled with tears. In fluttering over the lake, these small butterflies flickered to and fro across our souls (our souls, which were tense with agitation at the sight of so many beauties and about to vibrate) and passed again and again like the voluptuous bow of a violin. Their slight flittering did not graze the water, but it did caress our eyes, our hearts, and we nearly fainted with each quiver of the tiny, rosy wings. When we spotted them returning from the opposite shore, thereby revealing that they were playing and freely strolling on the surface, a delightful harmony resounded for us; they, however, returned slowly by way of a thousand whimsical detours, which varied the original harmony as a bewitching and fanciful melody. Our souls, now sonorous, listening to the silent flight, heard a music of enchantment and freedom and all the sweet and intense harmonies of the lake, the woods, the sky, and our own lives accompanied it with a magical delicacy that made us burst into tears.

I had never spoken to you, and I had even lost sight of you that year. But how deeply we loved each other in the Engadine! I never had enough of you; I never left you at home. You came along on my strolls, ate at my table, slept in my bed, dreamed in my soul. One day (could not a sure instinct, as a mysterious messenger, have notified you about that childishness in which you were so intricately involved, which you, too, experienced, yes, truly experienced, so profound was your "physical presence" in me?), one day (neither of us had ever before seen Italy), we were amazed at what we were told about Alp Grün: "From there you can see all the way to Italy." We left for Alp Grün, imagining that in the spectacle stretching out beyond the peak, there where Italy began, the hard, physical scenery would halt brusquely, and an utterly blue valley would open up in the depths of a dream. En route it struck us that a border does not alter the soil and that even if it did, the change would be too subtle for us to perceive it all at once. Though a bit disappointed, we laughed at ourselves for being so childish.

However, upon reaching the summit, we were dazzled. Our juvenile imaginings had come true before our very eyes.

At our side, glaciers sparkled. At our feet, torrents cut through a savage, dark-green Engadine landscape. Then a slightly mysterious hill; and beyond it, mauve slopes kept half-revealing and concealing in turns a truly blue region, a radiant avenue to Italy. The names were no longer the same; they instantly harmonized with this new softness. We were shown the Lago di Poschiavo, the Pizzo di Verona, the Val Viola. Next we went to an extraordinarily savage and solitary place, where the desolation of nature and the certainty that we were utterly inaccessible, as well as invisible and invincible, would have increased the voluptuousness of our loving each other there, intensified it into a delirium. I now truly and deeply felt my sadness at not having you with me in your material form, not merely in the apparel of my regret, but in the reality of my desire. I then descended a bit lower to the still towering spot where tourists came for the view. An isolated inn has an album in which they sign their names. I wrote mine and, next to it, a combination of letters alluding to your name, because it was impossible for me not to supply material proof of the reality of your spiritual presence. By putting a trace of you in that album I felt relieved of the compulsive weight with which you were suffocating my soul. And besides, I nurtured the immense hope of someday bringing you here to read that line; then you would climb even higher with me to compensate me for all that sadness. Without my saying a word, you would grasp everything or, rather, recall everything; and, while climbing, you would depend fully on me, lean heavily against me to make me feel all the more concretely that this time you were truly here; and I, between your lips, which keep a faint scent of your Oriental cigarettes, I would find perfect oblivion. We would very loudly holler the wildest things just to glory in the pleasure of yelling without being heard far and wide; only the short grass would quiver in the light breeze of the peaks. The ascent would then cause you to slow down, puff a bit, and I would lean toward you to hear your puffing: we would be insane. We would also venture to where a white lake lies next to a black lake, as gently as a white pearl next to a black pearl. How we would have loved each other in some remote village in the Engadine! We would have allowed only mountain guides to come close, those very tall men, whose eyes reflect different things than the eyes of other men and who are virtually of a different "water." But I am no longer concerned with you. Satiety occurred before possession. Even platonic love has its saturation point. I would no longer care to bring you to this countryside, which, though not grasping it, much less knowing it, you conjured up with such touching precision. The sight of you retains only one charm for me: the magic of suddenly remembering those sweetly exotic German and Italian names: Sils-Maria, Silva Plana, Crestalta, Samaden, Celerina, Juliers, Val Viola.

23 Spiritual Sunset

Like nature, intelligence has its spectacles. Never have the sunsets, never has the moonlight, so often moving me to tears of ecstasy, produced more passionate tenderness in me than that vast and melancholy conflagration, which, during our strolls at the close of day, tinges as many waves in our souls as the brilliant rays of the vanishing sun on the sea. We then quicken our steps in the night. More electrified and exhilarated than a horseman by the increasing speed of his beloved mount, we abandon ourselves, trembling with trust and joy, to our tumultuous thoughts; and the more we possess them and direct them, the more irresistibly we feel we belong to them. With tender emotion we pass through the dark countryside, greeting the night-filled oaks as the solemn field, like the epic witnesses of the force that intoxicates us and sweeps us away. Raising our eyes to the sky, we cannot help experiencing an exaltation upon recognizing the mysterious reflection of our thoughts in the intervals between the clouds, which are still agitated by the sun's farewell: we plunge faster and faster into the countryside, and the dog that follows us, the horse that carries us, or the now silent friend, sometimes less so when no living soul is near us, the flower in our buttonhole, or the cane we twirl joyfully in our feverish hands receives an homage of looks and tears—the melancholy tribute of our delirium.

24 As in Moonlight

Night had fallen; I went to my room, nervous about remaining in the darkness and no longer seeing the sky, the fields, and the ocean radiating under the sun. But when I opened the door, I found my room illuminated as though by the setting sun. Through the window I could see the house, the fields, the sky, and the ocean, or rather I appeared to be "seeing" them again, in a dream; the gentle moon recalled them for me rather than showed them to me, engulfing their silhouettes in a wan splendor that failed to scatter the darkness, which thickened on their shapes like oblivion. And I spent hours gazing at the courtyard, watching the mute, vague, faded, and enchanted memories of the things whose cries, voices, or murmurs had brought me pleasure or brought me sorrow during the day.

Love has perished; I am fearful on the threshold of oblivion; but, appeased, slightly pale, very close to me and yet faraway and already hazy, they reveal themselves to me as if in moonlight: all my past happiness and all my healed anguish, staring at me in silence. Their hush moves me while their distance and their indecisive pallor intoxicate me with sadness and poetry. And I cannot stop looking at this inner moonlight.

25 Critique of Hope in the Light of Love

No sooner does an approaching hour become the present for us than it sheds all its charms, only to regain them, it is true, on the roads of memory, when we have left that hour far behind us, and so long as our soul is vast enough to disclose deep *perspectives*. Thus, after we passed the hill, the poetic village, to which we hastened the trot of our impatient hopes and our worn-out mares, once again exhales those veiled harmonies, whose vague promise has been kept so poorly by the vulgarity of the streets, the incongruity of the cottages huddling together and melting into the horizon, and the disappearance of the blue mist, which seemed to permeate the village. But we are like the alchemist who attributes each of his failures to some accidental and always different cause; far from suspecting an incurable imperfection in the very essence of the present, we blame any number of things for poisoning our happiness: the malignity of the particular circumstances, the burden of the envied situation, the bad character of the desired mistress, the bad state of our health on a day that should have been a day of joy, the bad weather or the bad accommodations during our travels. And, certain that we will manage to eliminate those things that destroy all pleasure, we endlessly appeal to a future we dream of; we rely on it with the sometimes reluctant but never disillusioned confidence of a realized, that is, disillusioned dream.

However, certain pensive and embittered men, who radiate in the light of hope more intensely than other people, discover all too soon, alas, that hope emanates not from the awaited hours but from our hearts, which overflow with rays unknown by nature, and which pour torrents of those rays upon hope without lighting a hearth fire. Those men no longer have the strength to desire what they know to be undesirable, the strength to chase after dreams that will wither in their hearts when they wish to pick them outside themselves. This melancholy disposition is singularly intensified and justified in love. Constantly passing back and forth over its hopes, the imagination admirably sharpens its disappointments. Unhappy love, making the experience of happiness impossible, prevents us from discovering the nothingness of happiness. But what lesson in philosophy, what advice given by old age, what blight of ambition could surpass in melancholy the joys of happy love! You love me, my little darling: how could you have been cruel enough to tell me? So this was the ardent happiness of mutual love, the mere thought of which made my head whirl and my teeth chatter!

I unpin your flowers, I lift your hair, I tear off your jewels, I reach your flesh; my kisses sweep over your body and beat it like the tide rising across the sand; but you yourself elude me, and with you happiness. I have to leave you, I go home alone and sadder. Blaming that last calamity, I return to you forever; it was my last illusion that I tore away; I am miserable forever.

I do not know how I had the courage to tell you this; I have just ruthlessly thrown away the happiness of a lifetime, or at least its consolation; for your eyes, whose happy trust still intoxicated me at times, will henceforth reflect only the sad disenchantment, which your acumen and your disappointments already warned you about. Since this secret, which one of us concealed from the other, has been loudly proclaimed by us both, no happiness is possible for us. We are not left with even the unselfish joys of hope. Hope is an act of faith. We have undeceived its credulity: hope is dead. After renouncing enjoyment, we can no longer spellbind ourselves to nurture hope. Hoping without hope, which would be wise, is impossible.

But come nearer, my dear, sweet darling. Dry your eyes so you can see; I do not know if it is the tears that blur my vision, but I think I can make out over there, behind us, large fires being kindled. Oh, my dear, sweet darling, I love you so much! Give me your hand, let us go toward those beautiful fires without getting too close. . . . I think that indulgent and powerful Memory must be wishing us well and now doing a great deal for us, my dear.

26 | Under the Trees

We have nothing to fear and a great deal to learn from that vigorous and peace-loving tribe of trees that keep producing tonic essences and soothing balms for us and that also provide gracious company in which we spend so many cool, snug, and silent hours. In those burning afternoons, when the light, by its very excess, eludes our eyes, let us descend into one of those

Norman "grounds," whose tall and thick beeches rise supplely here, and their foliage, like a narrow but resistant shore, pushes back that ocean of light, keeping only a few drops, which tingle melodiously in the dark hush under the trees. At the beach, on the plains, in the mountains, our minds may not know the joy of stretching out across the world; but here the mind experiences the happiness of being secluded from the world. And, fenced in all around by those trunks that cannot be uprooted, the mind soars like a tree. Lying on your back, with your head on dry leaves, your thoughts in a profound repose, you follow the joyful agility of your mind, which, without making the foliage tremble, ascends to the highest branches, where it settles on the edge of the gentle sky, near a singing bird. Here and there a bit of sunshine stagnates at the foot of trees, which sometimes dip into it dreamily, gilding the outermost leaves of their branches. Everything else, relaxed and inert, remains silent in a gloomy happiness. Erect and towering in the vast offering of their branches, and yet calm and refreshed, the trees, in their strange and natural posture, murmur gracefully, inviting us to participate in this so ancient and so youthful life, so different from our own, and virtually its obscure and inexhaustible reserve.

For an instant a faint breeze ruffles their glistening and somber immobility, and the trees quiver softly, balancing the light on their crowns and stirring the shade at their feet.

Petit-Abbeville, Dieppe, August 1895

27 The Chestnut Trees

More than anything, I loved pausing under the immense chestnut trees when they were yellowed by autumn. How many hours did I spend in those mysterious and greenish caverns, gazing overhead at the murmuring cascades of pale gold that poured down in coolness and darkness! I envied the robins and the squirrels for dwelling in those frail, deep pavilions of verdure in the branches, those ancient hanging gardens that each spring for two centuries now has decked out in white and fragrant blossoms. The scantly curving branches descended nobly from tree to earth, as if they were other trees planted head-down in the trunk. The pallor of the remaining leaves more sharply accentuated the boughs, which already seemed darker and more solid for being stripped bare, and which, thereby reunited with the trunk, looked like a magnificent comb holding back the sweet, blond, flowing hair.

Réveillon, October 1895

28 The Sea

The sea will always fascinate those people in whom the disgust with life and the enticement of mystery have preceded their first distress, like a foreboding of reality's inability to satisfy them. People who need rest before so much as experiencing any fatigue will be consoled and vaguely excited by the sea. Unlike the earth, the sea does not bear the traces of human works and human life. Nothing remains on the sea, nothing passes there except in flight, and how quickly the wake of a ship disappears! Hence the sea's great purity, which earthly things do not have. And this virginal water is far more delicate than the hardened earth, which can be breached only by a pick. With a clear sound a child's footstep in water leaves a deep wake, and the united tinges of the water are broken for a moment; then, every vestige is wiped away, and the sea is once more calm as it was on the earliest days of the earth. The man who is weary of earthly paths or who, before even trying them, can guess how harsh and vulgar they are will be seduced by the pale lanes of the sea, which are more dangerous and more inviting, more uncertain and more forlorn. Everything here is more mysterious, even those huge shadows that sometimes float peacefully across the sea's naked fields, devoid of houses and shade, and that are stretched by the clouds, those celestial hamlets, those tenuous boughs.

The sea has the magic of things that never fall silent at night, that permit our anxious lives to sleep, promising us that everything will not be obliterated, comforting us like the glow of a night-light that makes little children feel less alone. Unlike the earth, the sea is not separated from the sky; it always harmonizes with the colors of the sky and it is deeply stirred by its most delicate nuances. The sea radiates under the sun and seems to die with it every evening. And when the sun has vanished, the sea keeps longing for it, keeps preserving a bit of its luminous reminiscence in the face of the uniformly somber earth. It is the moment of the sun's melancholy reflections, which are so gentle that you feel your heart melting at the very sight of them. Once the night has almost fully thickened, and the sky is gloomy over the blackened earth, the sea still glimmers feebly—who knows by what mystery, by what brilliant relic of the day, a relic buried beneath the waves.

The sea refreshes our imagination because it does not make us think of human life; yet it rejoices the soul, because, like the soul, it is an infinite and impotent striving, a strength that is ceaselessly broken by falls, an eternal and exquisite lament. The sea thus enchants us like music, which, unlike language, never bears the traces of things, never tells us anything about human beings, but imitates the stirrings of the soul. Sweeping up with the waves of those movements, plunging back with them, the heart thus forgets its own failures and finds solace in an intimate harmony between its own sadness and the sea's sadness, which merges the sea's destiny with the destinies of all things.

September 1892

29 Seascape

In regard to words whose meanings I have lost: perhaps I should have them repeated by all those things that have long since had a path leading into me, a path that has been abandoned for years but that could be taken anew, and that I am certain is not blocked forever. I would have to return to Normandy, not make much of an effort, but simply head for the sea. Or rather, I would stroll along one of the woodland paths from which, now and then, one can catch glimpses of the sea, and where the breeze mingles the smells of salt, wet leaves, and milk. I would ask nothing of all those things of infancy. They are generous to the child they have known since birth; they would, on their own, reteach him the forgotten things. Everything, and above all its fragrance, would announce the sea, but I would not have seen it as yet. . . . I would hear it faintly. I would walk along a once familiar hawthorn-lined path, feeling deeply moved and also fearing that a sudden slash in the hedge might reveal my invisible yet present friend, the madwoman who laments forever, the old, melancholy queen, the sea. All at once I would see it; it would be on one of those somnolent days under a glaring sun, when the sea reflects the sky, which is as blue as the water, but paler. White sails like butterflies would be resting on the motionless surface, unwilling to budge as if fainting in the heat. Or else, quite the opposite, the sea would be choppy and yellow under the sun, like a vast field of mud, with huge swells that, from so far away, would appear inert and crowned with dazzling snow.

30 Sails in the Harbor

In the harbor, long and narrow like a watery roadway between the just slightly elevated wharves, where the evening lights shone, the passersby paused near the assembled ships and stared as if at noble strangers who have arrived on the previous day and are now ready to leave. Indifferent to the curiosity they excited in the crowd, apparently disdaining its lowness or simply ignorant of its language, the ships maintained their silent and motionless impetus at the watery inn where they had halted for a night. The solidity of each stem spoke no less about the long voyages still to come than its damage spoke about the distress already suffered on these gliding lanes, which are as old as the world and as new as the passage that plows them and that they do not survive. Fragile and resistant, they were turned with sad haughtiness toward the Ocean, over which they loom and in which they are virtually lost. The marvelous and skillful intricacies of the riggings were mirrored in the water the way a precise and prescient intelligence lunges into the uncertain destiny that sooner or later will shatter it. They had only recently withdrawn from the terrible and beautiful life into which they would plunge back tomorrow, and their sails were still limp after the bellying wind; their bowsprits veered across the water as the ships had veered yesterday in their gliding, and from prow to poop, the curving of their hulls seemed to preserve the mysterious and sinuous grace of their furrowing wakes.

The End of Jealousy

1

"Give us good things whether or not we ask for them, and keep evil away from us even if we ask for it." This prayer strikes me as beautiful and certain. If you take issue with anything about it, do not hesitate to say so.

—Plato

"My little tree, my little donkey, my mother, my brother, my country, my little God, my little stranger, my little lotus, my little seashell, my darling, my little plant, go away, let me get dressed, and I'll join you on Rue de la Baume at eight P.M. Please do not arrive after eight-fifteen because I'm very hungry."

She wanted to close her bedroom door on Honoré, but he then said, "Neck!" and she promptly held out her neck with an exaggerated docility and eagerness that made him burst out laughing:

"Even if you didn't want to," he said, "there would still be small special friendships between your neck and my lips, between your ears and my moustache, between your hands and my hands. I'm certain those friendships wouldn't stop if we fell out of love. After all, even though I'm not speaking to my cousin Paule, I can't prevent my footman from going and chatting with her chambermaid every evening. My lips move toward your neck of their own accord and without my consent."

150

They were now a step apart. Suddenly their gazes met and
locked as they tried to rivet the notion of their love in each
other's eyes. She stood like that for a second, then collapsed on
a chair, panting as if she had been running. And, pursing their
lips as if for a kiss, they said, almost simultaneously and with a
grave exaltation:

"My love!"

Shaking her head, she repeated, in a sad and peevish tone:
"Yes, my love."

She knew he could not resist that small movement of her
head; he swept her up in his arms, kissed her, and said slowly,
"Naughty girl!" and so tenderly that her eyes moistened.

The clock struck seven-thirty. He left.

Returning home, Honoré kept repeating to himself: "My
mother, my brother, my country"—he halted. "Yes, my country.
. . . My little seashell, my little tree"; and he could not help
laughing when saying those words, which he and she had so
quickly gotten accustomed to using—those little words that can
seem empty and that he and she filled with infinite meaning.
Entrusting themselves, without thinking, to the inventive and
fruitful genius of their love, they had gradually been endowed,
by this genius, with their own private language, just as a nation
is supplied with arms, games, and laws.

While dressing for dinner, he automatically kept his mind focused on the moment when he would see her again, the way an
acrobat already touches the still faraway trapeze toward which
he is flying, or the way a musical phrase seems to reach the
chord that will resolve it and that draws the phrase across the
full distance between them, draws it by the very force of the desire that heralds the force and summons it. That was how Honoré had been dashing through life for a year now, hurrying from
morning to the afternoon hour when he would see her. And his
days were actually composed not of twelve or thirteen different
hours, but of four or five half-hours, of his anticipation and his
memories of them.

Honoré had been in Princess Alériouvre's home for several
minutes when Madame Seaune arrived. She greeted the mistress

of the house and the various guests and she seemed not so much to bid Honoré good evening as to take his hand the way she might have done in the middle of a conversation. Had their affair been common knowledge, one might have assumed that they had arrived simultaneously and that she had waited at the door for several minutes to avoid entering with him. But they could have spent two whole days apart (which had never once happened during that year) and yet not have experienced the joyous surprise of finding each other again—the surprise that is at the basis of every friendly greeting; for, unable to spend five minutes without thinking about one another, they could never meet by chance because they never separated.

During dinner, whenever they conversed with one another, they showed more vivacity and gentleness than two friends, but a natural and majestic respect unknown among lovers. They thus seemed like those gods who, according to fable, lived in disguise among human beings, or like two angels whose fraternal closeness exalts their joy but does not diminish the respect inspired by the common nobility of both their origin and their mysterious blood. In experiencing the power of the roses and irises that languidly reigned over the table, the air gradually became imbued with the fragrance of the tenderness exhaled naturally by Honoré and Françoise. At certain moments, the air seemed to embalm the room with a violence that was more delicious than its usual sweetness, a violence that nature had refused to let the flowers moderate, any more than it permits heliotropes to moderate their perfume in the sun or blossoming lilacs their perfume in the rain.

Thus their affection, for not being secret, was all the more mysterious. Anyone could draw close to it as to those inscrutable and defenseless bracelets on the wrists of a woman in love—bracelets on which unknown yet visible characters spell out the name that makes her live or die, bracelets that incessantly offer the meaning of those characters to curious and disappointed eyes that cannot grasp it.

"How much longer will I love her?" Honoré mused to himself as he rose from the table. He remembered the brevity of all

152

the passions that, at their births, he had believed immortal, and the certainty that this passion would eventually come to an end cast a gloom on his tender feelings.

Then he remembered what he had heard that very morning, at mass, when the priest had been reading from the Gospel: "Jesus stretched forth his hand and told them: This is my brother, and also my mother, and all my brethren." Trembling, Honoré had, for an instant, lifted up his entire soul to God, very high, like a palm tree, and he had prayed: "Lord! Lord! Grant me Your grace and let me love her forever! Lord! This is the only favor I ask of you. Lord, You can do it, make me love her forever!"

Now, in one of those utterly physical moments, when the soul takes a backseat to the digesting stomach, the skin enjoying a recent ablution and some fine linen, the mouth smoking, the eyes reveling in bare shoulders and bright lights, he repeated his prayer more indolently, doubting a miracle that would upset the psychological law of his fickleness, which was as impossible to flout as the physical laws of weight or death.

She saw his preoccupied gaze, stood up, and approached him without his noticing; and since they were quite far from the others, she said in that drawling, whimpering tone, that infantile tone which always made him laugh—she said as if he had just spoken:

"What?"

He laughed and said:

"Don't say another word or I'll kiss you—do you hear?—I'll kiss you right in front of everybody!"

First she laughed, then, resuming her dissatisfied pouting in order to amuse him, she said:

"Yes, yes, that's very good, you weren't thinking of me at all!"

And he, seeing her laugh, replied: "How well you can lie!" And he gently added: "Naughty, naughty!"

She left him and went to chat with the others. Honoré mused: "When I feel my heart retreating from her, I will try to delay it so gently that she won't even feel it. I will always be just as tender, just as respectful. When a new love replaces my love

153

for her in my heart, I will conceal it from her as carefully as I now conceal the occasional pleasures that my body, and it alone, savors without her." (He glanced at Princess Alériouvre.) And as for Françoise, he would gradually allow her to attach her life elsewhere, with other bonds. He would not be jealous; he himself would designate the men who appeared capable of offering her a more decent or more glorious homage. The more he pictured Françoise as a different woman, whom he would not love, but all of whose spiritual charms he would relish wisely, the more noble and effortless the sharing seemed. Words of sweet and tolerant friendship, of lovely generosity in giving the worthiest people our most precious possessions—those words flowed softly to his relaxed lips.

At that instant, Françoise, noticing it was ten o'clock, said good night and left. Honoré escorted her to her carriage, kissed her imprudently in the dark, and went back inside.

Three hours later, Honoré was walking home, accompanied by Monsieur de Buivres, whose return from Tonkin had been celebrated that evening. Honoré was questioning him about Princess Alériouvre, who, widowed approximately at the same time, was far more beautiful than Françoise. While not being in love with the princess, Honoré would have delighted in possessing her if he could have been certain that Françoise would not find out and be made unhappy.

"Nobody knows anything about her," said Monsieur de Buivres, "or at least nobody knew anything when I left Paris, for I haven't seen anyone since my return."

"So all in all there were no easy possibilities tonight," Honoré concluded.

"No, not many," Monsieur de Buivres replied, and since Honoré had reached his door, the conversation was about to end there, when Monsieur de Buivres added:

"Except for Madame Seaune, to whom you must have been introduced, since you attended the dinner. If you wanted to, it would be very easy. But as for me, I wouldn't be interested!"

"Why, I've never heard anyone say what you've just said," Honoré rejoined.

"You're young," replied de Buivres. "Come to think of it, there was someone there tonight who had quite a fling with her—there's no denying it, I think. It's that little François de Gouvres. He says she's quite hot-blooded! But it seems her body isn't all that great, and he didn't want to continue. I bet she's living it up somewhere at this very moment. Have you noticed that she always leaves a social function early?"

"Well, but now that she's a widow, she lives in the same house as her brother, and she wouldn't risk having the concierge reveal that Madame comes home in the middle of the night."

"Come on, old chum! There's a lot you can do between ten P.M. and one A.M.! Oh well, who knows?! Anyhow it's almost one o'clock, I'd better let you turn in."

De Buivres rang the bell himself; a second later, the door opened; de Buivres shook hands with Honoré, who said goodbye mechanically, entered, and simultaneously felt a wild need to go back out; but the door had closed heavily behind him, and there was no light aside from the candle waiting for him and burning impatiently at the foot of the staircase. He did not dare awaken the concierge in order to reopen the door for him, and so he went up to his apartment.

2

Our acts our angels are, or good or ill,
Our fatal shadows that walk by us still.

—BEAUMONT AND FLETCHER

Life had greatly changed for Honoré since the night when Monsieur de Buivres had made certain comments (among so many others) similar to those that Honoré himself had so often heard or stated with indifference, and which now rang in his ears during the day, when he was alone, and all through the night. He had instantly questioned Françoise, who loved him too deeply and suffered too deeply from his distress to so much as dream of taking offense; she swore that she had never deceived him and that she would never deceive him.

When he was near her, when he held her little hands, to which he softly recited:

You lovely little hands that will close my eyes,

when he heard her say, "My brother, my country, my beloved," her voice lingering endlessly in his heart with the sweetness of childhood bells, he believed her. And if he did not feel as happy as before, at least it did not seem impossible that his convalescent heart should someday find happiness. But when he was far away from Françoise, and also at times when, being near her, he saw her eyes glowing with fires that he instantly imagined as having been kindled at other times (who knows?—perhaps yesterday as they would be tomorrow), kindled by someone else; when, after yielding to a purely physical desire for another woman and recalling how often he had yielded and had managed to lie to Françoise without ceasing to love her, he no longer found it absurd to assume that she was lying to him, that, in order to lie to him it was not even necessary to no longer love him—to assume that before knowing him she had thrown herself upon others with the ardor that was burning him now—and it struck him as more terrible that the ardor he inspired in her did not appear sweet, because he saw her with the imagination, which magnifies all things.

Then he tried to tell her that he had deceived her; he tried not out of vengeance or a need to make her suffer like him, but so that she would tell him the truth in return, a need above all to stop feeling the lie dwelling inside him, to expiate the misdeeds of his sensuality, since, for creating an object for his jealousy, it struck him at times that it was his own lies and his own sensuality that he was projecting onto Françoise.

It was on an evening, while strolling on the Avenue des Champs-Élysées, that he tried to tell her he had deceived her. He was appalled to see her turn pale, collapse feebly on a bench, and, worse still, when he reached toward her, she pushed his

156

hand away, not angrily but gently, in sincere and desperate de-
jection. For two days he believed he had lost her, or rather that
he had found her again. But this sad, glaring, and involuntary
proof of her love for him did not suffice for Honoré. Even had he
achieved the impossible certainty that she had never belonged to
anyone but him, the unfamiliar agony his heart had experienced
the evening Monsieur de Buivres had walked him to his door—
not a kindred agony or the memory of that agony, but that agony
itself—would not have faded, even if someone had demon-
strated to him that his agony was groundless. Similarly, upon
awakening, we still tremble at the memory of the killer whom we
have already recognized as the illusion of a dream; and similarly,
an amputee feels pain all his life in the leg he no longer has.

He would walk all day, wear himself out on horseback, on
a bicycle, in fencing—all in vain; he would meet Françoise and
escort her home—all in vain: in the evening he would gather
peace, confidence, a honey sweetness from her hands, her
forehead, her eyes, and then, calmed, and rich with the fragrant
provision, he would go back to his apartment—all in vain: no
sooner had he arrived than he started to worry; he quickly
turned in so as to fall asleep before anything could spoil his
happiness. Lying gingerly in the full balm of this fresh and recent tenderness, which was barely one hour old, his happiness
was supposed to last all night, until the next morning, intact and
glorious like an Egyptian prince; but then de Buivres's words, or
one of the innumerable images Honoré had formed since hearing those words, crept into his mind, and so much for his sleep.
This image had not yet appeared, but he felt it was there, about
to surface; and, steeling himself against it, he would relight the
candle, read, and struggle interminably to stuff the meanings of
the sentences into his brain, leaving no empty spaces, so that
the ghastly image would not find an instant, would not find
even the tiniest nook to slip into.

But all at once, the image had stolen in, and now he could
not make it leave; the gates of his attention, which he had been
holding shut with all his strength, to the point of exhaustion,
had been opened by surprise; the gates had then closed again,

and he would be spending the entire night with that horrible companion. So it was sure, it was done with: this night like all the others, he would not catch a wink of sleep. Fine, so he went to the bromide bottle, took three spoonfuls, and, certain he would now sleep, terrified at the mere notion of doing anything but sleeping, come what may, he began thinking about Françoise again, with dread, with despair, with hate. Profiting from the secrecy of their affair, he wanted to make bets on her virtue with other men, sic them upon her; he wanted to see if she would yield; he wanted to try to discover something, know everything, hide in a bedroom (he remembered doing that for fun when he was younger) and watch everything. He would not bat an eyelash since he would have asked facetiously (otherwise, what a scandal! What anger!); but above all on her account, to see if, when he asked her the next day, "You've never cheated on me?" she would reply, "Never," with that same loving air. She might perhaps confess everything and actually would have succumbed only because of his tricks. And so that would have been the salutary operation to cure his love of the illness that was killing him, the way a parasitical disease kills a tree (to be certain he only had to peer into the mirror, which was dimly lit by his nocturnal candle). But no, for the image would keep recurring, so much more powerful than the images of his imagination and with what forceful and incalculable blows to his poor head—he did not even dare picture it.

Then, all at once, he would think about her, about her sweetness, her tenderness, her purity, and he wanted to weep about the outrage that he had, for a moment, considered inflicting on her. The very idea of suggesting that to his boon companions!

Soon he would feel the overall shudder, the feebleness one experiences several minutes before sleep induced by bromide. Suddenly perceiving nothing, no dream, no sensation, between his last thought and this one, he would say to himself: "What? I haven't slept yet?" But then seeing it was broad daylight, he realized that for over six hours he had been possessed by bromidic sleep without savoring it.

He would wait for the stabbing pains in his head to weaken a bit; then he would rise and, so that Françoise would not find him too ugly, he would try in vain to liven up his worn-out eyes, restore some color to his haggard face by dousing it with cold water and taking a walk. Leaving home, he went to church, and there, sagging and exhausted, with all the final, desperate strength of his failing body, which wanted to be revitalized, rejuvenated, his sick and aging heart, which wanted to be healed, his mind, which, endlessly harassed and gasping, wanted peace, he prayed to God—God, whom, scarcely two months ago, he had asked to grant Honoré the grace of letting him love Françoise forever. He now prayed to God with the same force, always with the force of that love, which had once, certain of its death, asked to live, and which now, too frightened to live, begged for death; and Honoré implored God to grant him the grace of not loving Françoise anymore, not loving her too much longer, not loving her forever, to enable him to finally picture her in someone else's arms without suffering, for now he could not picture her except in someone else's arms. And perhaps he would stop picturing her like that if he could picture it without suffering.

Then he remembered how deeply he had feared not loving her forever, how deeply he had engraved her in his memory so that nothing would efface her, engraved her cheeks, always offered to his lips, engraved her forehead, her little hands, her solemn eyes, her adored features. And abruptly, seeing them aroused from their sweet tranquillity by desire for someone else, he wanted to stop thinking about her, only to see her all the more obstinately, see her offered cheeks, her forehead, her little hands (oh, those little hands, those too!), her solemn eyes, her detested features.

From that day forward, though initially terrified of taking such a course, he never left her side; he kept watch on her life, accompanying her on her visits, following her on her shopping expeditions, waiting for an hour at every shop door. Had he figured that this would thus actually prevent her from cheating on him, he would probably have given up for fear of incurring her hatred. But she let him continue because she enjoyed having him with her all the time, enjoyed it so much that her joy gradually took hold of him, slowly imbuing him with a confidence, a certainty that no material proof would have given him, like those hallucinating people whom one can sometimes manage to cure by having them touch the armchair, the living person who occupies the place where they think they see a phantom, and thus driving away the phantom from the real world by means of reality itself, which has no room for the phantom.

Thus, trailing Françoise and mentally filling all her days with concrete occupations, Honoré strove to suppress those gaps and shadows in which the evil spirits of jealousy and suspicion lay in ambush, pouncing on him every evening. He began to sleep again; his sufferings grew rarer, briefer, and if he then sent for her, a few moments of her presence calmed him for the entire night.

3

The soul may be trusted to the end. That which is so beautiful and attractive as these relations must be succeeded and supplanted only by what is more beautiful, and so on forever.

—RALPH WALDO EMERSON

The salon of Madame Seaune, née Princess de Galaise-Orlandes, whom we spoke about in the first part of this story under her Christian name, Françoise, remains one of the most sought-after salons in Paris. In a society in which the title of duchess would make her interchangeable with so many others, her nonaristocratic family name stands out like a beauty mark on a face; and in exchange for the title she lost when marrying Monsieur Seaune, she acquired the prestige of having voluntarily renounced the kind of glory that, for a noble imagination, exalts white peacocks, black swans, white violets, and captive queens.

Madame Seaune has entertained considerably this season and last, but her salon was closed during the three preceding years—the ones, that is, following the death of Honoré de Tenvres.

Honoré's friends, delighted to see him gradually regaining his healthy appearance and his earlier cheerfulness, now kept finding him with Madame Seaune at all hours of the day, and so they attributed his revival to this affair, which they thought had started just recently.

It was a scant two months since Honoré's complete recovery that he suffered the accident on the Avenue du Bois-de-Boulogne, where both his legs were broken by a runaway horse.

The accident took place on the first Tuesday in May; peritonitis declared itself the following Sunday. Honoré received the sacraments on Monday and was carried off at six o'clock that evening. However, from Tuesday, the day of the accident, to Monday evening, he alone believed he was doomed.

On that Tuesday, toward six P.M., after the first dressing of the injuries, he had asked his servants to leave him alone, but to bring up the calling cards of people inquiring about his health.

That very morning, at most eight hours earlier, he had been walking down the Avenue du Bois-de-Boulogne. He had, breath by breath, been inhaling and exhaling the air, a blend of breeze and sunshine; women were admiring his swiftly moving beauty, and in the depths of their eyes he had recognized a profound joy—for an instant he was lost sight of in the sheer turning of his capricious merriment, then effortlessly caught up with and quite rapidly outstripped among the steaming, galloping horses, then he savored the coolness of his hungry mouth, which was moistened by the sweet air; and the joy he recognized was the same profound joy that embellished life that morning, the life of the sun, of the shade, of the sky, of the stones, of the east wind, and of the trees, trees as majestic as men standing and as relaxed as women sleeping in their sparkling immobility.

At a certain point he had checked his watch, had doubled back, and then . . . then it had happened. Within an instant, the horse, which Honoré had not seen, had broken both his legs. In no way did that instant appear to have been inevitable. At that same instant he might have been slightly further off, or slightly nearer, or the horse might have deviated, or, had it rained, he would have gone home earlier, or, had he not checked his watch, he would not have doubled back and he would have continued walking to the cascade. Yet that thing, which might so easily not have been, so easily that for a moment he could pretend it was only a dream—that thing was real, that thing was now part of his life, and not all his willpower could alter anything. He had two broken legs and a battered abdomen. Oh, in itself the accident was not so extraordinary; he recalled that less than a week ago, during a dinner given by Dr. S., they had talked about C., who had been injured in the same manner by a runaway horse. The doctor, when asked about C.'s condition, had said: "He's in a bad way." Honoré had pressed him, had questioned him about the injuries, and the doctor had replied with a self-important, pedantic, and melancholy air: "But it's not just his injuries; it's everything together; his sons are causing him problems; his circumstances are not what they used to be; the newspaper attacks have struck him to the quick. I wish I were wrong, but he's in a rotten state." Since the doctor, having said that, felt that he himself, on the contrary, was in an excellent state, healthier, more intelligent, and more esteemed than ever; since Honoré knew that Françoise loved him more and more, that the world accepted their relationship and esteemed their happiness no less than Françoise's greatness of character; and since, finally, Dr. S.'s wife, deeply agitated by her visions of C.'s wretched end and abandonment, cited reasons of hygiene for prohibiting herself and her children from thinking about sad events or attending funerals—given all these things, each diner repeated one final time: "That poor C., he's in a bad state," downed a final flute of Champagne, and the pleasure of drinking it made them feel that their own "state" was excellent.

But this was not the same thing at all. Honoré, now feeling overwhelmed by the thought of his misfortune, as he had often been by the thought of other people's misfortunes, could no longer regain a foothold in himself. He felt the solid ground of good health caving in beneath him, the ground on which our loftiest resolutions flourish and our most gracious delights, just as oak trees and violets are rooted in the black, moist earth; and he kept stumbling about within himself. In discussing C. at that dinner, which Honoré again recalled, the doctor had said: "When I ran into C. even before the accident and after the newspaper attacks, his face was sallow, his eyes were hollow, and he looked awful!" And the doctor had passed his hand, famous for its skill and beauty, across his full, rosy face, along his fine, well-groomed beard, and each diner had pleasurably imagined his own healthy look the way a landlord stops to gaze contentedly at his young, peaceable, and wealthy tenant. Now, peering at his reflection in the mirror, Honoré was terrified by his own "sallow face," his "awful look." And instantly, he was horrified at the thought that the doctor would say the same thing about him as he had said about C., with the same indifference. Even people who would approach him full of pity would also rather quickly turn away from him as from a dangerous object; they would finally obey their protests of their good health, of their desire to be happy and to live. Then his mind turned back to Françoise, and, his shoulders sagging, his head bowing in spite of himself, as if God's commandment had been raised against him there, Honoré realized with an infinite and submissive sadness that he must give her up. With a sick man's resignation he experienced the humility of his body, which, in its childlike feebleness, was bent by this tremendous grief, and he pitied himself when, as so often at the start of his life, he had tenderly seen himself as an infant, and now he felt like crying.

He heard a knocking at the door. The concierge was bringing the cards that Honoré had asked for. Honoré knew very well that people would inquire about his condition, for he was fully aware that his accident was serious; nevertheless, he had not expected so many cards, and he was terrified to see that there were so many callers who barely knew him and who would have put themselves out only for his wedding or for his funeral. It was an overflowing mountain of cards, and the concierge carried it gingerly to keep it from tumbling off the large tray. But suddenly, when all those cards were within reach, the mountain looked very small, indeed ridiculously small, far smaller than the chair or the fireplace. And he was even more terrified that it was so small, and he felt so alone that, in order to take his mind off his loneliness, he began feverishly reading the names; one card, two cards, three cards—ah! He jumped and looked again: "Count François de Gouvres." Now Honoré would certainly have expected Monsieur de Gouvres to inquire about his condition, but he had not thought about the count for a long time, and all at once he recalled de Buivres's words: "*There was someone there tonight who had quite a fling with her—It was François de Gouvres. He says she's quite hot-blooded! But it seems her body isn't all that great, and he didn't want to continue*"; and feeling all the old suffering which in an instant resurfaced from the depths of his consciousness, he said to himself: "Now I'll be delighted if I'm doomed. Not die, remain fettered here, and spend years envisioning her with someone else whenever she's not near me, part of each day and all night long! And now there would be nothing unhealthy about envisioning her like that—it's certain. How could she still love me? An amputee!" All at once he stopped. "And if I die, what happens after me?"

She was thirty; he leaped in one swoop over the more or less long period in which she would remember him, stay faithful to him. But a moment would come. . . . "He said, '*She's quite hot-blooded.* . . .' I want to live, I want to live and I want to walk, I want to follow her everywhere, I want to be handsome, I want her to love me!"

At that moment he was frightened by the whistling in his respiration, he had a pain in his side, his chest felt as if it had shifted to his back, he no longer breathed freely, he tried to catch his breath but could not. At each second he felt himself breathing and not breathing enough. The doctor came. Honoré had only had a light attack of nervous asthma. When the doctor left, Honoré felt sadder; he would have preferred a graver illness in order to evoke pity. For he keenly sensed that, if it was not grave, something else *was* grave and that he was perishing. Now he recalled all the physical sufferings of his life, he was in grief; never had the people who loved him the most ever pitied him under the pretext that he was nervous. During the dreadful months after his walk home with de Buivres, months of dressing at seven o'clock after walking all night, Honoré's brother, who stayed awake for at most fifteen minutes after any too copious dinner, said to him:

"You listen to yourself too much, there are nights when I can't sleep either. And besides, a person thinks he doesn't sleep, but he always sleeps a little."

It was true that he listened to himself too much; in the background of his life he kept listening to death, which had never completely left him and which, without totally destroying his life, undermined it now here, now there. His asthma grew worse; he could not catch his breath; his entire chest made a painful effort to breathe. And he felt the veil that hides life from us (the death within us) being lifted, and he perceived how terrifying it is to breathe, to live.

Now he was transported to the moment when she would be consoled, and then, who would it be? And his jealousy was driven insane by the uncertainty of the event and its inevitability. He could have prevented it if alive; he could not live, and so? She would say that she would join a convent; then, when he was dead, she would change her mind. No! He preferred not to be deceived twice, preferred to know.— Who?—de Gouvres, de Alériouvre, de Buivres, de Breyves? He saw them all and, gritting his teeth, he felt the furious revolt that must be twisting his features at that moment. He calmed himself down. No, it will not be that, not a playboy. It has to be a man who truly loves her. Why don't I want it to be a playboy? I'm crazy to ask myself that, it's so obvious. Because I love her for herself, because I want her to be happy.—No, it's not that, it's that I don't want anyone to arouse her senses, to give her more pleasure than I've given her, to give her any pleasure at all. I do want someone to give her happiness, I want someone to give her love, but I don't want anyone to give her pleasure. I'm jealous of the other man's pleasure, of her pleasure. I won't be jealous of their love. She has to marry, has to make a good choice. . . . But it'll be sad all the same.

Then one of his childhood desires came back, the desire of the seven-year-old, who went to bed at eight every evening. If, instead of remaining in her room, next to Honoré's, and turning in at midnight, his mother had to go out around eleven and get dressed by then, he would beg her to dress before dinner and to go anywhere else, for he could not stand the thought of someone in the house preparing for a soirée, preparing to go out, while the boy tried to fall asleep. And in order to please him and calm him, his mother, all in evening attire and décolleté by eight o'clock, came to say good night, then went to a friend's home to wait for the ball to start. On those sad evenings when his mother attended a ball, that was the only way the boy, morose but tranquil, could fall asleep.

Now, the same plea he had made to his mother, the same plea to Françoise came to his lips. He would have liked to ask her to marry him immediately, so she would be ready and so he could at last go to sleep forever, disconsolate but calm, and not the least bit worried about what would occur after he fell asleep.

During the next few days, he tried to speak to Françoise, who, just like the doctor, did not consider Honoré doomed and who gently but firmly, indeed inflexibly, rejected his proposal.

Their habit of being truthful to one another was so deeply entrenched that each told the truth even though it might hurt the other, as if at their very depths, the depths of their nervous and sensitive being, whose vulnerabilities had to be dealt with tenderly, they had felt the presence of a God, a higher God, who was indifferent to all those precautions—suitable only for children—and who demanded and also owed the truth. And toward this God who was in the depths of Françoise and toward this God who was in the depths of Honoré, Honoré and Françoise had, respectively, always felt obligations that overrode the desire not to distress or offend one another, overrode the sincerest lies of tenderness and compassion.

166

Thus when Françoise told Honoré that he would go on living, he keenly sensed that she believed it, and he gradually persuaded himself to believe it too:

"If I have to die, I will no longer be jealous when I'm dead; but until I'm dead? As long as my body lives, yes! However, since I'm jealous only of pleasure, since it's my body that's jealous, since what I'm jealous of is not her heart, not her happiness, which I wish for her to find with the person most capable of making her happy; when my body fades away, when my soul gets the better of my flesh, when I am gradually detached from material things as on a past evening when I was very ill, when I no longer wildly desire the body and when I love the soul all the more—at that point I will no longer be jealous. Then I will truly love. I can't very well conceive of what that will be like since my body is still completely alive and rebellious, but I can imagine it vaguely when I recall those times in which, holding hands with Françoise, I found the abatement of my anguish and my jealousy in an infinite tenderness free of any desire. I'll certainly be miserable when I leave her, but it will be the kind of misery that once brought me closer to myself, that an angel came to console me for, the misery that revealed the mysterious friend in the days of unhappiness, my own soul, that calm misery thanks to which I will feel worthier when appearing before God, and not the horrible illness that pained me for such a long time without elevating my heart, like a physical pain that stabs, that degrades, and that diminishes. It is with my body, with my body's desire, that I will be delivered from that.—Yes, but until then what will become of me? Feebler, more incapable of resisting than ever, hampered on my two broken legs, when, wanting to hurry over to her and make sure she is not where I will have pictured her, I will remain here, unable to budge, ridiculed by all those who can '*have a fling with her*' as long as they like, before my very eyes, the eyes of a cripple whom they no longer fear."

The night of Sunday to Monday he dreamed he was suffocating, feeling an enormous weight on his chest. He begged for mercy, did not have the strength to displace all that weight; the feeling that all this weight had been upon him for a very long time was inexplicable; he could not endure it another second, it was smothering him. Suddenly he felt miraculously relieved of that entire burden, which was drawing further and further away after releasing him forever. And he said to himself: "I'm dead!"

And above him he saw everything that had been weighing down on him and suffocating him for such a long time, saw it all rising; at first he believed it was de Gouvres's face, then only his suspicions, then his desires, then those past days when he had started waiting in the morning, crying out for the moment when he would see Françoise, then his thoughts of Françoise. At each moment that rising burden kept assuming a different shape, like a cloud; it kept growing, growing nonstop, and now he could no longer explain how this thing, which he knew was as vast as the world, could have rested on him, on his small, feeble human body, on his poor, small, listless human heart, rested on him without crushing him. And he also realized that he *had* been crushed and that he had led the life of a crushed man. And this immense thing that had weighed on his chest with all the force of the world—he now realized it was his love.

Then he repeated to himself: "The life of a crushed man!"; and he recalled that in the instant when the horse had knocked him down, he had said to himself: "I'm going to be crushed!"; he recalled his stroll, recalled that he was supposed to have lunch with Françoise that morning; and then, through that circuitous path, he thought about his love again. And he said to himself: "Was it my love that was weighing on me? What could it be if it wasn't my love? My character, perhaps? Myself? Or was it life?" Then he thought: "No. When I die, I won't be delivered from my love, I'll be delivered from my carnal desires, my carnal longings, my jealousy." Then he said: "Oh, Lord, make that hour come to me, make it come fast, oh, Lord, so that I may know perfect love."

Sunday evening, peritonitis had declared itself; Monday morning around ten o'clock, he ran a fever; he wanted to see Françoise, called out to her, his eyes blazing: "I want your eyes to shine too, I want to give you more pleasure than I've ever given you . . . I want to give it to you . . . I want to hurt you." Then suddenly he turned livid: "I see why you don't want to, I know very well what you had someone do to you this morning, and where, and who it was, and I know he wanted to bring me there, put me behind the door so I could see the two of you, and I wouldn't be able to swoop down on you since my legs are gone, I wouldn't be able to prevent you, for the two of you would have more pleasure if you could have seen me there the whole time; he really knows everything that gives you pleasure, but I'll kill him first, and before that I'll kill you, and before that I'll kill myself. Look! I've killed myself!" And he fell back on the pillow, exhausted.

He calmed down bit by bit, still trying to determine whom she could marry after his death, but there were always the images he wanted to ward off, the face of François de Gouvres, of de Buivres, the faces that tortured him, that kept resurfacing.

At noon he received the last sacraments. The doctor had said he would not make it past the afternoon. His strength ebbed extremely swiftly; he could no longer absorb food and could barely hear. His mind remained lucid, and, saying nothing lest he hurt Françoise, who he could see was overcome with grief, he mused about what she would be once he was no more, once he knew about her no more, once she could no longer love him.

The names he had spoken mechanically that very morning, the names of men who might possess her, resumed parading through his head while his eyes followed a fly that kept approaching his finger as if to touch it, then flying away and coming back without, however, touching it; and yet, reviving his attention, which had momentarily lapsed, the name François de Gouvres kept returning, and Honoré told himself that de Gouvres might actually possess her, and at the same time Honoré thought: "Maybe the fly is going to touch the sheet? No, not yet"; then, brusquely rousing himself from his reverie: "What? Neither of those two things strikes me as more important than the other! Will de Gouvres possess Françoise, will the fly touch the sheet? Oh! Possessing Françoise is a bit more important." But his exactness in seeing the gap between those two events showed him that neither one particularly touched him more than the other. And he said to himself: "Oh, it's all the same to me! How sad it is!" Then he realized that he was saying "How sad it is!" purely out of habit and that, having changed completely, he was not the least bit sad about having changed. The shadow of a smile unclenched his lips. "This," he told himself, "is my pure love for Françoise. I'm no longer jealous; it's because I'm at death's door. But so what? It was necessary so that I might at last feel true love for Françoise."

But then, raising his eyes, he perceived Françoise amid the servants, the doctor, and two old relatives, all of whom were praying there, close to him. And it dawned on him that love, pure of all selfishness, of all sensuality, love that he wanted to have in him, so sweet, so vast, and so divine, now encompassed the old relatives, the servants, even the doctor as tenderly as Françoise, and that, already feeling for her the love for all creatures, with which his soul, kindred with their souls, was uniting him, he now felt no other love for her. And this thought could not even cause him pain, so thoroughly was all exclusive love for her, the very idea of a preference for her, now abolished.

Weeping at the foot of the bed, she murmured the most beautiful words of the past: "My country, my brother." But Honoré, having neither the will nor the strength to undeceive her, smiled and mused that his "country" was no longer in her, but in heaven and all over the earth. He repeated in his heart, "My brothers," and though looking at her more than at the others, he did so purely out of pity for the stream of tears she was shedding before his eyes, his eyes, which would soon close and had already stopped weeping. But now he did not love her any more and any differently than he loved the doctor, his old relatives, or the servants. And that was the end of his jealousy.

EARLY STORIES

NORMAN THINGS

Trouville, the capital of the canton, with a population of 6,808, can lodge 15,000 guests in the summer.

—GUIDE JOANNE

For Paul Grünebaum

For several days now we have been able to contemplate the calm of the sea in the sky, which has become pure again— contemplate it as one contemplates a soul in a gaze. No one, however, is left to enjoy the follies and serenities of the September sea, for it is fashionable to desert the beaches at the end of August and head for the country. But I envy and, if acquainted with them, I often visit people whose countryside lies by the sea, is located, for example, above Trouville. I envy the person who can spend the autumn in Normandy, however little he knows how to think and feel. The terrain, never very cold even in winter, is the greenest there is, grassy by nature, without the slightest gap, and even on the other sides of the hillocks, in the amiable arrangements called "woodlands." Often, when on a terrace, where the blond tea is steaming on the set table, you can, as Baudelaire puts it, watch "the sunshine radiating on the sea" and sails that come, "all those movements of people departing, people who still have the strength to desire and to wish." In the so sweet and peaceful midst of all that greenery, you can look at the peace of the seas, or the tempestuous sea, and the waves crowned with foam and gulls, charging like lions, their white manes rippling in the wind. However, the moon, invisible to all the waves by day, though still troubling them with its magnetic gaze, tames them, suddenly crushes their assault, and excites them again before repelling them, no doubt to charm the melancholy leisures of the gathering of stars, the mysterious princes of the maritime skies. A person who lives in Normandy sees all that; and if he goes down to the shore in the daytime, he can hear the sea sobbing to the beat of the surges of the human soul, the sea, which corresponds to music in the created world, because, showing us no material thing and not being descriptive in its way, the sea sounds like the monotonous chant of an ambitious and faltering will. In the evening, the Normandy dweller goes back to the countryside, and in his gardens he cannot distinguish between sky and sea, which blend together. Yet they appear to be separated by that brilliant line; above it that must be the sky. That must be the sky, that airy sash of pale azure, and the sea drenches only the golden fringes. But now a vessel puts a graft upon it while seeming to navigate in the midst of the sky. In the evening, the moon, if shining, whitens the very dense vapors rising from the grasslands, and, gracefully bewitched, the field looks like a lake or a snow-covered meadow. Thus, this rustic area, which is the richest in France, which, with its inexhaustible abundance of farms, cows, cream, apple trees for cider, thick grass, invites you solely to eat and sleep—at night this countryside decks itself out with mystery, and its melancholy rivals that of the vast plain of the sea.

Finally, there are several utterly desirable abodes, a few assailed by the sea and protected against it, others perched on the cliff, in the middle of the woods, or amply stretched out on grassy plateaus. I am not talking about the "Oriental" or "Persian" houses, which would be more agreeable in Teheran; I mean, above all, the Norman homes—in reality half-Norman, half-English—in which the profusion of the finials of roof timbers multiplies the points of view and complicates a silhouette, in which the windows, though broad, are so tender and intimate, in which, from the flower boxes in the wall under each window, the flowers cascade inexhaustibly upon the outside stairs and the glassed-in entrance halls. It is to one of those houses that I go home, for night is falling, and I will reread, for the hundredth time, *Confiteor* by the poet Gabriel Trarieux. . . .

MEMORY

A servant in brown livery and gold buttons opened the door quite promptly and showed me to a small drawing room that had pine paneling, walls hung with cretonne, and a view of the sea. When I entered, a young man, rather handsome indeed, stood up, greeted me coldly, then sat back down in his easy chair and continued reading his newspaper while smoking his pipe. I remained standing, a bit embarrassed, I might say even preoccupied with the reception I would be given here. Was I doing the right thing after so many years, coming to this house, where they might have forgotten me long ago?—this once hospitable house, where I had spent profoundly tender hours, the happiest of my life?

The garden surrounding the house and forming a terrace at one end, the house itself with its two red-brick turrets encrusted with diversely colored faiences, the long, rectangular vestibule, where we had spent our rainy days, and even the furnishings of the small drawing room to which I had just been led—nothing had changed.

Several moments later an old man with a white beard shuffled in; he was short and very bent. His indecisive gaze lent him a highly indifferent expression. I instantly recognized Monsieur de N. But he could not place me. I repeated my name several times: it evoked no memory in him. I felt more and more embarrassed. Our eyes locked without our really knowing what to say. I vainly struggled to give him clues: he had totally forgotten me. I was a stranger to him. Just as I was about to leave, the door flew open: "My sister Odette," said a pretty girl of ten or twelve in a soft, melodious voice, "my sister has just found out that you're here. Would you like to come and see her? It would make her so happy!" I followed the little girl, and we went down into the garden. And there, indeed, I found Odette reclining on a chaise longue and wrapped in a large plaid blanket. She had changed so greatly that I would not, as it were, have recognized her. Her features had lengthened, and her dark-ringed eyes seemed to perforate her wan face. She had once been so pretty, but this was no longer the case at all. In a somewhat constrained manner she asked me to sit at her side. We were alone. "You must be quite surprised to find me in this state," she said after several moments. "Well, since my terrible illness I've been condemned, as you can see, to remain lying without budging. I live on feelings and sufferings. I stare deep into that blue sea, whose apparently infinite grandeur is so enchanting for me. The waves, breaking on the beach, are so many sad thoughts that cross my mind, so many hopes that I have to abandon. I read, I even read a lot. The music of poetry evokes my sweetest memories and makes my entire being vibrate. How nice of you not to have forgotten me after so many years and to come and see me! It does me good! I already feel much better. I can say so—can't I?—since we were such good friends. Do you remember the tennis games we used to play here, on this very spot? I was agile back then; I was merry. Today I can no longer be agile; I can no longer be merry. When I watch the sea ebbing far out, very far, I often think of our solitary strolls at low tide. My enchanting memory of them could suffice to keep me happy, if I were not so selfish, so wicked. But, you know, I can hardly resign myself, and, from time to time, in spite of myself, I rebel against my fate. I'm bored all alone, for I've been alone since Mama died. As for Papa, he's too sick and too old to concern himself with me. My brother suffered a terrible blow from a woman who deceived him horrendously. Since then, he's been living alone; nothing can console

him or even distract him. My little sister is so young, and besides, we have to let her live happily, to the extent that she can."

As she spoke to me, her eyes livened up; her cadaverous
pallor disappeared. She resumed her sweet expression of long
ago. She was pretty again. My goodness, how beautiful she was!
I would have liked to clasp her in my arms: I would have liked
to tell her that I loved her. . . . We remained together for a long
time. Then she was moved indoors, since the evening was
growing cool. I now had to say goodbye to her. My tears choked
me. I walked through that long vestibule, that delightful garden,
where the graveled paths would never, alas, grind under my feet
again. I went down to the beach; it was deserted. Thinking
about Odette, I strolled, pensive, along the water, which was
ebbing, tranquil and indifferent. The sun had disappeared behind the horizon; but its purple rays still splattered the sky.

Pierre de Touche

PORTRAIT OF MADAME X.

Nicole combines Italian grace with the mystery of northern women. She has their blond hair, their eyes as clear as the transparency of the sky in a lake, their lofty bearing. However, she breathes a knowing softness that has virtually ripened in that Tuscan sun, which inundates the eyes of women, lengthens their arms, raises the corners of their mouths, and rhythmically scans their gait, ultimately making all their beauty divinely languorous. And not for nothing have the charms of both climates and both races fused together to make up Nicole's charm, for she is the perfect courtesan, if this simply means that in her the art of pleasing has reached a truly unique degree, that it is composed of both talents and efforts, that it is both natural and refined. Thus, the tiniest flower between her breasts or in her hand, the most ordinary compliment on her lips, the most banal act, like offering her arm to whoever escorts her to the table—all these things, when she does them, are imbued with a grace as poignant as an artistic emotion. Everything softens around her in a delightful harmony that is summed up in the folds of her gown. But Nicole is unconcerned about the artistic pleasure that she provides, and as for her eyes, which seem to promise so much bliss, she barely knows for certain on whom her gaze has fallen—barely knows for no other reason most likely than that its fall was lovely. She is concerned only about good, loves it enough to do it, loves it too much to be content with just doing it, without trying to grasp what—in doing it—she does. One cannot say that she is pedantic in her magnanimity, for it appeals to her too sincerely. Let us say rather that she is erudite about it, an enchanting erudition that places only the agreeable names of the Virtues in her mind and on her lips. This makes her charm all the sweeter, as if it were perfumed with a saintly fragrance. One can seldom admire what one loves. Hence, it is all the more exquisite to understand the seductions, the fecundity of a great heart in Nicole's soft and rich beauty, in her *lactea ubertas* [her milky abundance], in her whole alluring person.

Before the Night

"Even though I'm still quite strong, you know" (she spoke with a more intimate sweetness, the way accentuation can mellow the overly harsh things that one must say to the people one loves), "you know I could die any day now—even though I may just as easily live another few months. So I can no longer wait to reveal to you something that has been weighing on my conscience; afterwards you will understand how painful it was to tell you." Her pupils, symbolic blue flowers, discolored as if they were fading. I thought she was about to cry, but she did nothing of the kind. "I'm quite sad about intentionally destroying my hope of still being esteemed by my best friend after my death, about tarnishing and shattering his memory of me, in terms of which I often imagine my own life in order to see it as more beautiful and more harmonious. But my concern about an aesthetic arrangement" (she smiled while pronouncing that epithet with the slightly ironic exaggeration accompanying her extremely rare use of such words in conversation) "cannot repress the imperious need for truth that forces me to speak. Listen, Leslie, I have to tell you this. But first, hand me my coat. This terrace is a bit chilly, and the doctor forbade me to get up if it's not necessary." I handed her the coat. The sun was already gone, and the sea, which could be spotted through the apple trees, was mauve. As airy as pale, withered wreaths and as persistent as regrets, blue and pink cloudlets floated on the horizon. A melancholy row of poplars sank into the darkness, leaving their submissive crowns in churchlike rosiness; the final rays, without grazing their trunks, stained their branches, hanging festoons of light on these balustrades of darkness. The breeze blended the three smells of sea, wet leaves, and milk. Never had the Norman countryside more voluptuously softened the melancholy of evening, but I barely savored it—deeply agitated as I was by my friend's mysterious words.

"I loved you very much, but I've given you little, my poor friend."

Forgive me for defying the rules of this literary genre by interrupting a *confession* to which I should listen in silence," I cried out, trying to use humor to calm her down, but in reality mortally sad. "What do you mean you've given me little? And the less I've asked for, the more you've given me, indeed far more than if our senses had played any part in our affection. You were as supernatural as a Madonna and as tender as a wet nurse; I worshiped you, and you nurtured me. I loved you with an affection whose tangible prudence was not disturbed by any hope for carnal pleasure. Did you not requite my feelings with incomparable friendship, exquisite tea, naturally embellished conversation, and how many bunches of fresh roses? You alone, with your maternal and expressive hands, could cool my feverish brow, drip honey between my withered lips, put noble images into my life. Dear friend, I do not want to hear that absurd confession. Give me your hands so I may kiss them: it's cold, why don't we go inside and talk about something else."

"Leslie, you must listen to me all the same, my poor dear. It's crucial. Have you never wondered whether I, after becoming a widow at twenty, have remained one. . . ?"

"I'm certain of it, but it's none of my business. You are a creature so superior to anyone else that any weakness of yours would have a nobility and beauty that are not to be found in other people's good deeds. You've acted as you've seen fit, and I'm certain that you've never done anything that wasn't pure and delicate."

"Pure! Leslie, your trust grieves me like an anticipated re-proach. Listen . . . I don't know how to tell you this. It's far worse than if I had loved you, say, or someone else, yes, truly, anyone else."

I turned as white as a sheet, as white as she, alas, and, terri-fied that she might notice it, I tried to laugh and I repeated with-out really knowing what I was saying: "Ah! Ah! Anyone else—how strange you are."

"I said far worse, Leslie, I can't decide at this moment, how-ever luminous it may be. In the evening one sees things more calmly, but I don't see this clearly, and there are enormous shadows on my life. Still, if, in the depths of my conscience, I believe that it was not worse, why be ashamed to tell you?"

"Was it worse?" I did not understand; but, prey to a horrible agitation that was impossible to disguise, I started trembling in terror as in a nightmare. I did not dare look at the garden path, which, now filled with night and dread, opened before us, nor did I dare to close my eyes. Her voice, which, broken by deeper and deeper sadness, had faded, suddenly grew louder, and, in a clear and natural tone, she said to me:

"Do you remember when my poor friend Dorothy was caught with a soprano, whose name I've forgotten?" (I was de-lighted with this diversion, which, I hoped, would definitively lead us away from the tale of her sufferings.) "Do you recall ex-plaining to me that we could not despise her? I remember your exact words: 'How can we wax indignant about habits that Socrates (it involved men, but isn't that the same thing?), who drank the hemlock rather than commit an injustice, cheerfully approved of among his closest friends? If fruitful love, meant to perpetuate the race, noble as a familial, social, human duty, is superior to purely sensual love, then there is no hierarchy of sterile loves, and such a love is no less moral—or, rather, it is no more immoral for a woman to find pleasure with another woman than with a person of the opposite sex. The cause of such love is a nervous impairment which is too exclusively nerv-ous to have any moral content. One cannot say that, because most people see as red the objects qualified as red, those people who see them as violet are mistaken. Furthermore,' you added, 'if we refine sensuality to the point of making it aesthetic, then, just as male and female bodies can be equally beautiful, there is no reason why a truly artistic woman might not fall in love with another woman. In a truly artistic nature, physical attraction and repulsion are modified by the contemplation of beauty. Most people are repelled by a jellyfish. Michelet, who appreciated the delicacy of their hues, gathered them with delight. I was revolted by oysters, but after musing' (you went on) 'about their voyages through the sea, which their taste would now evoke for me, they have become a suggestive treat, especially when I am far from the sea. Thus, physical aptitudes, the pleasure of contact, the enjoyment of food, the pleasures of the senses are all grafted to where our taste for beauty has taken root.'

"Don't you think that these arguments could help a woman physically predisposed to this kind of love to come to terms with her vague curiosity, particularly if, for example, certain statuettes of Rodin's have triumphed—artistically—over her repugnance; don't you think that these arguments would excuse her in her own eyes, appease her conscience—and that this might be a great misfortune?"

I don't know how I managed to stifle my cry: a sudden flash of lightning illuminated the drift of her confession, and I simultaneously felt the brunt of my dreadful responsibility. But, letting myself be blindly led by one of those loftier inspirations that tear off our masks and recite our roles extempore when we fail to do justice to ourselves, when we are too inadequate to play our roles in life, I calmly said: "I can assure you that I would have no remorse whatsoever, for I truly feel no scorn, not even pity, for those women."

She said mysteriously, with an infinite sweetness of gratitude: "You are generous." She then quickly murmured with an air of boredom, the way one disdains commonplace details even while expressing them: "You know, despite everyone's secrecy, it dawned on me that you've all been anxiously trying to determine who fired the bullet, which couldn't be extracted and which brought on my illness. I've always hoped that this bullet wouldn't be discovered. Fine, now that the doctor appears certain, and you might suspect innocent people, I'll make a clean breast of it. Indeed, I prefer to tell you the truth." With the tenderness she had shown when starting to speak about her imminent death, so that her tone of voice might ease the pain that her words would cause, she added: "In one of those moments of despair that are quite natural in any truly *living* person, it was I who . . . wounded myself."

I wanted to go over and embrace her, but much as I tried to control myself, when I reached her, my throat felt strangled by an irresistible force, my eyes filled with tears, and I began sobbing. She, at first, dried my tears, laughed a bit, consoled me gently as in the past with a thousand lovely words and gestures. But from deep inside her an immense pity for herself and for me came welling up, spurting toward her eyes— and flowed down in burning tears. We wept together. The accord of a sad and vast harmony. Her pity and mine, blending into one, now had a larger object than ourselves, and we wept about it, voluntarily, unrestrainedly. I tried to drink her poor tears from her hands. But more tears kept streaming, and she let them benumb her. Her hand froze through like the pale leaves that have fallen into the basins of fountains. And never had we known so much grief and so much joy.

ANOTHER MEMORY

To M. Winter

Last year I spent some time in T., at the Grand Hôtel, which, standing at the far end of the beach, faces the sea. Because of the rancid fumes coming from the kitchens and from the waste water, the luxurious banality of the tapestries, which offered the sole variation on the grayish nudity of the walls and complemented this *exile* decoration, I was almost morbidly depressed; then one day, with a gust that threatened to become a tempest, I was walking along a corridor to my room, when I was stopped short by a rare and delectable scent. I found it impossible to analyze, but it was so richly and so complexly floral that someone must have denuded whole fields, Florentine fields, I assumed, merely to produce a few drops of that fragrance. The sensual bliss was so powerful that I lingered there for a very long time without moving on; beyond the crack of a barely open door, which was the only one through which the perfume could have wafted, I discovered a room that, despite my limited glimpse, hinted at the presence of the most exquisite personality. How could a guest, at the very heart of this nauseating hotel, have managed to sanctify such a pure chapel, perfect such a refined boudoir, erect an isolated tower of ivory and fragrance? The sound of footsteps, invisible from the hallway, and, moreover, an almost religious reverence prevented me from nudging the

186

door any further. All at once, the furious wind tore open a poorly attached corridor window, and a salty blast swept through in broad and rapid waves, diluting, without drowning, the concentrated floral perfume. Never will I forget the fine persistence of the original scent adding its tonality to the aroma of that vast wind. The draft had closed the door, and so I went downstairs. But as my utterly annoying luck would have it: when I inquired about the inhabitants of room 47 (for those chosen beings had a number just like anyone else), all that the hotel director could provide were obvious pseudonyms. Only once did I hear a grave and trembling, solemn and gentle male voice calling "Violet," and a supernaturally enchanting female voice answering "Clarence." Despite those two British names, they normally seemed, according to the hotel domestics, to speak French—and without a foreign accent. Since they took their meals in a private room, I was unable to see them. One single time, in vanishing lines so spiritually expressive, so uniquely distinct that they remain for me one of the loftiest revelations of beauty, I saw a tall woman disappearing, her face averted, her shape elusive in a long brown and pink woolen coat. Several days later, while ascending a staircase that was quite remote from the mysterious corridor, I smelled a faint, delicious fragrance, definitely the same as the first time. I headed toward that hallway and, upon reaching that door, I was numbed by the violence of fragrances, which boomed like organs, growing measurably more intense by the minute. Through the wide-open door the unfurnished room looked virtually disemboweled. Some twenty small, broken phials lay on the parquet floor, which was soiled by wet stains. "They left this morning," said the domestic, who was wiping the floor, "and they smashed the flagons so that nobody could use their perfumes, since they couldn't fit them in their trunks, which were crammed with all the stuff they bought here. What a mess!" I pounced on a flagon that had a few final drops. Unbeknown to the mysterious travelers, those drops still perfume my room.

In my humdrum life I was exalted one day by perfumes exhaled by a world that had been so bland. They were the troubling heralds of love. Suddenly love itself had come, with its roses and its flutes, sculpting, papering, closing, perfuming everything around it. Love had blended with the most immense breath of the thoughts themselves, the respiration that, without weakening love, had made it infinite. But what did I know about love itself? Did I, in any way, clarify its mystery, and did I know anything about it other than the fragrance of its sadness and the smell of its fragrances? Then, love went away, and the perfumes, from shattered flagons, were exhaled with a purer intensity. The scent of a weakened drop still impregnates my life.

THE INDIFFERENT MAN

We heal as we console ourselves; the heart cannot always weep or always love.

—LA BRUYÈRE: *CHARACTERS,* CHAPTER IV, *THE HEART*

1

Madeleine de Gouvres had just arrived in Madame Lawrence's box. General de Buivres asked:

"Who are your escorts tonight? Avranches, Lepré? . . ."

"Avranches, yes," replied Madame Lawrence. "As for Lepré, I didn't dare."

Nodding toward Madeleine, she added:

"She's very hard to please, and since it would have practically meant a new acquaintanceship for her . . ."

Madeleine protested. She had met Monsieur Lepré several times and found him charming; once she had even had him over for lunch.

"In any case," Madame Lawrence concluded, "you have nothing to regret, he is very nice, but there is nothing remarkable about him, and certainly not for the most spoiled woman in Paris. I can quite understand that the close friendships you have make you hard to please."

Lepré was very nice but very insignificant: that was the general view. Madeleine, feeling that this was not entirely her opinion, was amazed; but then, since Lepré's absence did not cause her any keen disappointment, she did not like him enough to be perturbed. In the auditorium, heads had turned in her direction; friends were already coming to greet her and compliment her. This was nothing new, and yet, with the obscure clear-sightedness of a jockey during a race or of an actor during a performance, she felt that tonight she was triumphing more fully and more easily than usual. Wearing no jewels, her yellow tulle bodice strewn with cattleyas, she had also pinned a few cattleyas to her black hair, and these blossoms suspended garlands of pale light from that dark turret. As fresh as her flowers and equally pensive, she evoked, with the Polynesian charm of her coiffure, Mahenu in Pierre Loti's play *The Island of Dreams,* for which Reynaldo Hahn had composed the music. Soon her regret that Lepré had not seen her like this blended with the happy indifference with which she mirrored her charms of this evening in the dazzled eyes that reflected them reliably and faithfully.

"How she loves flowers," cried Madame Lawrence, gazing at her friend's bodice.

She did love them, in the ordinary sense that she knew how beautiful they were and how beautiful they made a woman. She loved their beauty, their gaiety, and their sadness, too, but externally, as one of their ways of expressing their beauty. When they were no longer fresh, she would discard them like a faded gown.

All at once, during the first intermission, several moments after General de Buivres and the Duke and Duchess d'Alériouvres had said good night, leaving her alone with Madame Lawrence, Madeleine spotted Lepré in the orchestra. She saw that he was having the attendant open the box.

"Madame Lawrence," said Madeleine, "would you permit me to invite Monsieur Lepré to stay here since he is alone in the orchestra?"

"All the more gladly since I'm going to be obliged to leave in an instant, my dear; you know you gave me permission.

Robert is a bit under the weather. Would you like me to ask Monsieur Lepré?"

"No, I'd rather do it myself."

Throughout intermission, Madeleine let Lepré chat with Madame Lawrence. Leaning on the balustrade and gazing into the auditorium, she pretended to ignore them, certain that she would soon enjoy his presence all the more when she was alone with him.

Madame Lawrence went off to put on her coat.

"I would like to invite you to stay with me during the next act," said Madeleine with an indifferent amiability.

"That's very kind of you, Madame, but I can't; I am obliged to leave."

"Why, I'll be all alone," said Madeleine in an urgent tone; then suddenly, wanting almost unconsciously to apply the maxims of coquetry in the famous line from Carmen, "If I don't love you, you'll love me," she went on:

"Oh, you're quite right, and if you have an appointment, don't keep them waiting. Good night, Monsieur."

With a friendly smile she tried to compensate for what struck her as the implicit harshness of her permission. However, that harshness was impelled by her violent desire to keep him here, by the bitterness of her disappointment. Aimed at anyone else, her advice to leave would have been pleasant.

Madame Lawrence came back.

"Well, he's leaving; I'll stay with you so you won't be alone. Did you have a tender farewell?"

"Farewell?"

"I believe that at the end of this week he's starting his long tour of Italy, Greece, and Asia Minor."

A child who has been breathing since birth without ever noticing it does not know how essential the unheeded air that gently swells his chest is to his life. Does he happen to be suffocating in a convulsion, a bout of fever? Desperately straining his entire being, he struggles almost for his life, for his lost tranquillity, which he will regain only with the air from which he did not realize his tranquillity was inseparable.

Similarly, the instant Madeleine learned of Lepré's departure, of which she had been unaware, she understood only
what had entered into his leaving as she felt everything that was
being torn away from her. And with a painful and gentle de-
spondency, she gazed at Madame Lawrence without resenting
her any more than a poor, suffocating patient resents his asthma
while, through eyes filled with tears, he smiles at the people
who pity him but cannot help him. All at once Madeleine rose:

"Come, my dear, I don't want you to get home late on my
account."

While slipping into her coat, she spotted Lepré, and in the
anguish of letting him leave without her seeing him again, she
hurried down the stairs.

"I'm devastated—especially since Monsieur Lepré is going
abroad—to think he could assume he might offend me."

"Why, he's never said that," replied Madame Lawrence.

"He must have: since you assume it, he must assume it as
well."

"Quite the contrary."

"I tell you it's true," Madeleine rejoined harshly. And as they
caught up with Lepré, she said:

"Monsieur Lepré, I expect you for dinner on Thursday, at
eight P.M."

"I'm not free on Thursday, Madame."

"Then how about Friday?"

"I'm not free on Friday either."

"Saturday?"

"Saturday would be fine."

"But darling, you're forgetting that you're to dine with
Princess d'Avranches on Saturday."

"Too bad, I'll cancel."

"Oh! Madame, I wouldn't want that," said Lepré.

"I want it," cried Madeleine, beside herself. "I'm not going to
Fanny's no matter what, I never had any intention of going."

Once home again, Madeleine, slowly undressing, reviewed
the events of the evening. Upon reaching the moment when
Lepré had refused to stay with her for the last act, she turned

crimson with humiliation. The most elementary coquetry as well as the most stringent dignity commanded her to show him an extreme coldness after that. Instead, that threefold invitation on the stairway! Indignant, she raised her head proudly and appeared so beautiful to herself in the depth of the mirror that she no longer doubted that he would love her. Unsettled and disconsolate only because of his imminent departure, she pictured his affection, which he—she did not know why—wanted to conceal from her. He was going to confess it to her, perhaps in a letter, quite soon, and he would probably put off his departure, he would sail with her. . . . What? . . . She must not think about that. But she could see his handsome, loving face approaching her face, asking her to forgive him. "You naughty boy!" she said. But then, perhaps he did not love her as yet; he would leave without having time to fall in love with her. . . . Disconsolate, she lowered her head, and her eyes fell upon her bodice, upon the even more languishing eyes of the wilted blossoms, which seemed ready to weep under their withered eyelids. The thought of the brevity of her unconscious dream about him, of the brevity of their happiness if ever it materialized, was associated for her with the sadness of those flowers, which, before dying, languished on the heart that they had felt beating with her first love, her first humiliation, and her first sorrow.

The next day she wanted no other flowers in her bedroom, which was normally filled and radiant with the glory of fresh roses.

When Madame Lawrence came by, she halted before the vases where the cattleyas were finally dying and, for eyes without love, were stripped of beauty.

"What, darling, you who love flowers so much?"

Madeleine was going to say, "It seems to me that I have only begun loving them today"; she stopped, annoyed at having to explain herself and sensing that there are realities that people cannot be made to grasp if they do not already have them inside themselves.

She contented herself with smiling amiably at the reproach. The feeling that no one, perhaps not even Lepré himself, was aware of her new life gave her a rare and disconsolate pleasure of pride. The servant brought the mail; finding no letter from Lepré, she was overwhelmed with disappointment. Upon measuring the gap between the absurdity of her disappointment, when there had not been the slightest chance of hope, and the very real and very cruel intensity of that disappointment, she understood that she had stopped living solely a life of events and facts. The veil of lies had started unrolling before her eyes for a duration that was impossible to predict. She would now see things only through that veil, and, more than all other things, those she would have wanted to know and experience the most concretely and in the most similar way as Lepré, those that had to do with him.

Still, she had one remaining hope—that he had lied to her, that his indifference was feigned: she knew by unanimous consensus that she was one of the most beautiful women in Paris, that her reputation for wit, intelligence, elegance, her high social standing added prestige to her beauty. Lepré, on the other hand, was considered intelligent, artistic, very gentle, a very good son, but he was barely sought after and had never been successful with women; the attention she gave him was bound to strike him as something improbable and unhoped for. She was astonished and hopeful. . . .

2

Although Madeline would, in an instant, have subordinated all the interests and affections of her life to Lepré, she nevertheless still believed—and her judgment was fortified by the universal judgment—that, without being disagreeable, he was inferior to the remarkable men who, in the four years since the death of the Marquis de Gouvres, had been dropping by several times a day to console the widow and were thus the most precious ornament of her life.

She very keenly sensed that her inexplicable inclination, which made him a unique person for her, did not make him the equal of those other men. The reasons for her love were inside her, and if they were a bit inside him too, they were not in his intellectual superiority or even in his physical superiority. It was precisely because she loved him that no face, no smile, no conduct was as agreeable to her as his, and it was not because his face, his smile, his conduct were more agreeable that she loved him. She was acquainted with more handsome, more charming men, and she knew it.

Thus, when Lepré entered Madeleine's drawing room on Saturday at a quarter past eight, he faced, without suspecting anything, his most passionate friend, his most clear-sighted adversary. While her beauty was armed to vanquish him, her mind was no less armed to judge him; she was ready to pick, like a bitter flower, the pleasure of finding him mediocre and ridiculously disproportionate to her love for him. She was not acting out of prudence! She quite keenly sensed that she would continually be caught again in the magic net, and that once Lepré left, her prolific imagination would repair the meshes that her too incisive mind would have torn in his presence.

And in fact, when he walked in, she was suddenly calmed; by shaking his hand, she appeared to drain him of all power. He was no longer the sole and absolute despot of her dreams; he was just a pleasant visitor. They chatted; now all her assumptions vanished. In his fine goodness, in the bold precision of his mind, she found reasons that, while not absolutely justifying her love, explained it, at least slightly, and, by showing her that something corresponded to it in reality, made its roots plunge deeper in that reality, draw more life from it. She also noticed that he was more attractive than she had thought, with a noble and delicate Louis XIII face.

All her artistic memories of the portraits of that period were henceforth tied to the thought of her love, gave it a new existence by letting it enter the system of her artistic sensibilities. She ordered a photograph from Amsterdam, the picture of a young man who resembled Lepré.

She ran into him a few days later. His mother was seriously ill; his trip was put off. She told him that she now had a picture on her table, a portrait that reminded her of him. He appeared moved but cold. She was deeply pained, but consoled herself with the thought that he at least understood her attention though he did not enjoy it. Loving a boor who did not realize it would have been even crueler. So, mentally reproaching him for his indifference, she wanted to see the men who were enamored of her, with whom she had been indifferent and coquettish; she wanted to see them again in order to show them the ingenious and tender compassion that she would have at least wanted to obtain from him. But when she encountered them, they all had the horrible defect of not being Lepré, and the sight of them merely irritated her. She wrote to him; four days wore by without a response; then she received a letter that any other woman would have found friendly but that drove Madeleine to despair. He wrote:

"My mother has improved; I am leaving in three weeks; until then, my life is quite full, but I will try to call on you once to pay my respects."

Was it jealousy of everything that "filled his life," preventing her from penetrating it, was it sorrow that he was going abroad and that he would come by only once, or even the greater sorrow that he did not feel the need to come and visit her ten times a day before his departure: she could no longer stay at home; she hastily donned a hat, went out, and, hurrying, on foot, along the streets that led to him, she nurtured the absurd hope that, by some miracle she was counting on, he would appear to her at the corner of a square, radiant with tenderness, and that a single glance of his would explain everything to her. All at once she spotted him walking, chatting gaily with friends. But now she was embarrassed; she believed he would guess that she was looking for him, and so she brusquely stepped into a shop. During the next few days she no longer looked for him; she avoided places where she might run into him—she maintained this final coquetry toward him, this final dignity for herself.

One morning, she was sitting alone in the Tuileries, on the waterside terrace. She let her sorrow float, spread out, relax more freely on the broader horizon, she let it pick flowers, spring forth with the hollyhocks, the fountains, and the columns, gallop behind the dragoons leaving the Quartier d'Orsay, she let her sorrow drift on the Seine and soar with the swallows across the pale sky. It was the fifth day since the friendly letter that had devastated her. All at once she saw Lepré's fat, white poodle, which he allowed to go out alone every morning. She had joked about it, had said to him that one day somebody would kidnap it. The animal recognized her and came over. After five days of repressing her emotions, she was utterly overwhelmed with a wild need to see Lepré. Seizing the animal in her arms and shaking with sobs, she hugged it for a long time, with all her strength; then, unpinning the nosegay of violets from her bodice and attaching it to the dog's collar, she let the animal go.

But, calmed by that crisis, also mollified, and feeling better, she noticed her resentment vanishing bit by bit, a little cheer and hope coming back to her with her physical well-being, and she perceived that she valued life and happiness again. Lepré would be leaving in seventeen days; she wrote him, inviting him to dinner the next day, apologizing for not responding earlier, and she spent a rather pleasant afternoon. That evening, she would be attending a dinner; the guests probably included many artists and athletes who knew Lepré. She wanted to know if he had a mistress, any kind of attachment that prevented him from getting close to Madeleine, that explained his extraordinary behavior. She would suffer greatly upon finding out, but at least she would know, and perhaps she might hope that in time her beauty would carry the day. She went out, determined to inquire immediately, but then, stricken with fear, she lost her nerve. In the last moment, upon arriving, she was impelled less by the desire to know the truth than by the need to speak to others about him, that sad charm of vainly conjuring him up wherever she was without him. After dinner she said to two men who were near her, and whose conversation was quite free:

"Tell me, do you know Lepré well?"

"We've been running into him every day forever, but we're not very close."

"Is he a charming man?"

"He's a charming man."

"Well, perhaps you can tell me. . . . Don't feel obligated to be too benevolent—you see, I have a very important reason for asking. A girl I love with all my heart likes him a bit. Is he a man whom a woman could marry with an easy mind?"

Her two interlocutors paused for a moment, embarrassed:

"No, that's out of the question."

Madeleine, very courageously, went on, all the more quickly to get it over with:

"Does he have any long-term attachment?"

"No, but still, it's impossible."

"Tell me why, seriously, I beg you."

"No."

"But still, it would be better to tell her after all. Otherwise she might imagine worse things or silly things."

"Very well! This is it, and I don't think we're hurting Lepré in any way by revealing it. First of all, you are not to repeat it; besides, the whole of Paris knows about it anyway; and as for marrying, he's far too honest and sensitive to even consider it. Lepré is a charming fellow, but he has one vice. He loves the vile women that are found in the gutter, he's crazy about them; he occasionally spends whole nights in the industrial suburbs or on the outer boulevards, running the risk of getting killed eventually; and not only is he crazy about them, but he loves only them. The most ravishing socialite, the most ideal girl leave him absolutely indifferent. He can't even pay them any attention. His pleasures, his preoccupations, his life are somewhere else. People who didn't know him well used to say that with his exquisite nature a great love would rescue him. But for that he would have to be capable of experiencing it, and he's incapable of doing so. His father was already like that, and if it doesn't happen to Lepré's sons, then only because he won't have any."

At eight the next evening, Madeline was informed that Monsieur Lepré was in the drawing room. She went in; the windows were open, the lamps were not yet lit, and he was waiting on the balcony. Not far from there, several houses surrounded by gardens rested in the gentle evening light, distant, Oriental, and pious, as if this had been Jerusalem. The rare, caressing light gave each object a brand-new and almost poignant value. A luminous wheelbarrow in the middle of the dark street was as touching as, there, a bit further, the somber and already nocturnal trunk of a chestnut tree under its foliage, which was still basking in the final rays. At the end of the avenue the sunset was gloriously bowing like an arch of triumph decked out with celestial flags of gold and green. In the neighboring window, heads were absorbed in reading with familiar solemnity. Walking over to Lepré, Madeleine felt the appeased sweetness of all these things mellow her heart, half open it, make it languish, and she held back her tears.

He, however, more handsome tonight and more charming, displayed sensitive kindness such as he had never exhibited to her before. Then they had an earnest conversation, and now she first discovered how sublime his intelligence was. If he was not popular socially, it was precisely because the truths he was seeking lay beyond the visual horizon of intelligent people and because the truths of high minds are ridiculous errors down here. His goodness, incidentally, sometimes lent them an enchanting poetry the way the sun gracefully colors the high summits. And he was so genial with her, he acted so grateful for her goodness that, feeling she had never loved him this much and abandoning all hope of his requiting her love, she suddenly and joyously envisaged the prospect of a purely friendly intimacy that would enable her to see him every day; she inventively and joyfully revealed the plan to him. He, however, said that he was very busy and could hardly spare more than one day every two weeks. She had told him enough to make him understand she loved him—had he wanted to understand. And had he, timid as he was, felt a particle of love for her, he would have come up with even negligible words of friendship. Her sickly gaze was focused so intently on him that she would have promptly made out those words and greedily feasted on them. She wanted to stop Lepré, who kept talking about his demanding agenda, his crowded life, but suddenly her gaze plunged so deep into her adversary's heart that it could have plunged into the infinite horizon of the sky that stretched out before her, and she felt the futility of words. She held her tongue, then she said:

"Yes, I understand, you're very busy."

And at the end of the evening, when they were parting, he said:

"May I call on you to say goodbye?"

And she gently replied: "No, my friend, I'm somewhat busy; I think we should leave things as they are."

She waited for a word; he did not utter it, and she said:

"Goodbye."

Then she waited for a letter, in vain. So she wrote him that it was preferable for her to be frank, that she may have led him to believe she liked him, that this was not the case, that she would rather not see him as often as she had requested with imprudent friendliness.

He replied that he had never really believed in anything more than her friendship, for which she was famous, and which he had never meant to abuse to the point of coming so often and bothering her.

Then she wrote him that she loved him, that she would never love anyone but him. He replied that she must be joking.

She stopped writing to him, but not, at first, thinking about him. Then that also stopped. Two years later, weighed down by her widowhood, she married the Duke de Mortagne, who was handsome and witty and who, until Madeleine's death—for over forty years, that is—filled her life with a glory and affection that she never failed to appreciate.

About the Translator

Joachim Neugroschel works in French, German, Russian, Yiddish, and Italian. The winner of three PEN Translation Awards and the French-American Translation Prize, he has translated over 180 books, including works by such authors as Franz Kafka, Elias Canetti, Martin Buber, Thomas Mann, Paul Celan, Jean Arp, Herman Hesse, Leopold von Sucher-Masoch, and Albert Schweitzer. He lives in New York.

OTHER COOPER SQUARE PRESS
TITLES OF INTEREST

HEMINGWAY
Life into Art
Jeffrey Meyers
192 pp.
0-8154-1079-4
$27.95 cloth

THE GROTTO BERG
Two Novellas
Charles Neider
Introduction by Clive Sinclair
184 pp.
0-8154-1123-5
$22.95 cloth

EDGAR ALLAN POE
His Life and Legacy
Jeffrey Meyers
376 pp., 12 b/w photos
0-8154-1038-7
$18.95

SCOTT FITZGERALD
A Biography
Jeffrey Meyers
432 pp., 25 b/w photos
0-8154-1036-0
$18.95

TOLSTOY
Tales of Courage
and Conflict
Edited by Charles Neider
576 pp.
0-8154-1010-7
$19.95

ESSAYS OF THE MASTERS
Edited by Charles Neider
480 pp.
0-8154-1097-2
$18.95

LIFE AS I FIND IT
A Treasury of Mark Twain
Rarities
Edited by Charles Neider
with a new foreword
343 pp., 1 b/w photo
0-8154-1027-1
$17.95

THE TRAVELS
OF MARK TWAIN
Edited by Charles Neider
448 pp., 6 b/w line drawings
0-8154-1039-5
$19.95

THE SELECTED LETTERS
OF MARK TWAIN
Edited by Charles Neider
352 pp., 1 b/w photo
0-8154-1011-5
$16.95

MARK TWAIN:
PLYMOUTH ROCK
AND THE PILGRIMS
and Other Speeches
Edited by Charles Neider
368 pp., 1 b/w photo
0-8154-1104-9
$17.95

THE FAIRY TALE
OF MY LIFE
An Autobiography
Hans Christian Andersen
New introduction by
Naomi Lewis
610 pp., 20 b/w illustrations
0-8154-1105-7
$22.95

GRANITE AND RAINBOW
The Hidden Life of
Virginia Woolf
Mitchell Leaska
536 pp., 23 b/w photos
0-8154-1047-6
$18.95

SHAKESPEARE
The Man and His
Achievement
Robert Speaight
416 pp., 24 b/w illustrations
0-8154-1063-8
$19.95

THE LANTERN-BEARERS
AND OTHER ESSAYS
Robert Louis Stevenson
Edited by Jeremy Treglown
320 pp., 27 b/w maps
0-8154-1012-3
$16.95

**THE LIFE AND DEATH
OF YUKIO MISHIMA**
Henry Scott Stokes
318 pp., 39 b/w illustrations
0-8154-1074-3
$18.95

Available at bookstores; or call 1-800-462-6420

 Cooper Square Press

200 Park Avenue South, Suite 1109
New York, New York 10003
www.coopersquarepress.com